Dedicated to Farley and Diane Dunn

without whom this book would not have existed.

Shadow
of the
Hawk

We respect the tribes and culture of Native Americans.

This story occurs in a timeframe when Native Americans were referred to as Indians. To maintain the authenticity of the time, in this novel, Native Americans are referred to as Indians, warriors, and braves.

The Kerrigans

Shadow
of the
Hawk

DeLora Conley-Walls

THREE SKILLET

SHADOW OF THE HAWK, Conley-Walls, DeLora
First Edition

The Kerrigans, Book 1

 THREE SKILLET
www.ThreeSkilletPublishing.com

Cover by Farley L Dunn

All characters are fictitious, and any resemblance to actual persons living or dead is purely coincidental.

ISBN: 978-1-943189-59-5

— 1 —

DARKNESS WRAPPED LONG, concealing fingers around the world as the silence of the upcoming night swallowed the busy activities of the day. The ranch's vast stables finally belonged to the young Cheyenne warrior. Only the steadily rising wind kept him company. Now the young warrior could take his chance on stealing the horse he must have.

The barn wouldn't be easy to access, but the desperate brave had been hiding in the deep shadows, holding his breath and breathing through his nose ever so shallowly, while the stableman made his rounds. There would be no reason for the man to return to this corner of the barn. Still, the warrior waited, his chest barely moving, as his heart beat with a pulse that was inaudible to all but him.

With no noise in his step or actions, the warrior knew he must disappear, just like in the hunt. When pursuing an antelope or deer, only the warrior could know the pursuer was there. The animal must sense only the feeling of safety. Then, the warrior could attack. Only, this time, it wasn't an animal's life at stake.

It was his own.

The young warrior was glad he had washed in the river at midday to smell more like the white man. The cold water had burned his skin, but he'd rubbed his arms and legs vigorously with a flat rock to scour away the scent of the wilderness, letting the clear, rushing water carry it away. His sturdy, leather clothing was folded and stashed under a large rock should he need it again, marked by a branch he'd notched with his knife. He was wearing a white man's clothes that had been left behind from many years ago. He had been a little over nine at the time. He was more than twice that age now, and the clothes fit well. The pants were neither too long nor too short. His knife sheath hung snugly at his side. His tanned, muscular arms just reached the end of his shirtsleeves. Even the leather jacket fit him well.

Nevertheless, he felt strange in them. He'd fumbled with the strange buttons, and the pockets for carrying things seemed unnecessary. And the fabric, so stiff. They weren't soft like the buckskin now lying under his rock. He had known he could adapt to the strangeness of the white man's clothing, just like the butterfly that sheds its cocoon to wear a new skin, but the boots were a different thing. For silence as he walked in the white man's world, he continued to wear his knee-high moccasins. Beautifully beaded by his mother with a traditional design, they would keep his feet warm and his steps silent.

He hadn't cut his long, thick wavy hair, but that would come soon, and then he could pass for a white man. He had been teased often enough about being a "half-breed" when he first came into the Cheyenne camp. Now, for once in his life, his light skin color would be to his advantage. He would walk among the white man to fulfill his destiny. They wouldn't know him for who he really was, Shadow Hawk, a Warrior, a Wolf Soldier of the Southern Cheyenne Tribe. Until then, his thick mane was bound and hung in a dark bundle just below his broad shoulders. His knife was at the ready when he must remove the strands from his head.

The medicine man had told him he would find his answers among the white people. He knew Shadow Hawk had many questions. The wise Old One was right. He only confirmed what Shadow Hawk had known all along. He must go into the white man's world to find the one who had disgraced his family. It might take many years, but he had the small leather pouch of gold from years ago to help him buy the time he needed. He would find that man, and when he did, he would kill him and then return to his mother's people, forever an Indian.

EVEN THOUGH SHADOW HAWK fit into the white man's clothes, the young warrior wasn't yet considered an adult, for he hadn't taken a wife. His mother was alone, and no other warrior in the tribe would have her. She had needed him, so he had remained in her tent out of a deep sense of obligation and protectiveness. Also, the bitterness of his childhood and the fear of rejection he felt within the tribe kept him from approaching the unmarried maidens.

At those oddly-spaced occasions or ceremonial events when a young woman of the tribe did try to speak with him, he would shy away out of fear of ridicule. He had never shared the many times he'd been taunted by the young people of the tribe, even with his mother. He had focused on one thing, avenging his mother's dishonor, and his own retribution for the injustices of the white man's betrayal.

There were also the dreams of a girl that kept him from the young maidens of his tribe. He wouldn't admit to them, for he would be embarrassed to reveal his dreams weren't of an Indian girl, but of one with the skin of the white man. He tossed on his buckskins at night, and the older he grew, the more the dreams possessed him, until he couldn't drive them from his head, and only the mornings brought relief. Yet, even in the daylight, the memories of the dreams tugged at him as if they were burrs underneath a softened strip of tanned hide. Some nights, darker visions haunted him, ones of a father who had abandoned both Shadow Hawk and his mother. He had said he loved his wife and son, that he was proud of Shadow Hawk, but his promises were the hiss of a snake, spoken with a forked tongue, a white man's words that carried no substance, Shadow Hawk now knew. The Cheyenne told Shadow Hawk never to trust the white man, and his father's behavior was just cause not to.

After waiting almost eight days alone, with no sign of his return, Shadow Hawk's mother, Laughing River, stood among the tall trees along the riverbank and told him to prepare to return with her to her tribe. As the wind whipped through the topmost branches, and an eagle circled overhead, Shadow Hawk had begged his mother to stay and wait one more day for his father. The tall grasses along the shore were buffeted by the freshening breeze, and the sun cast ever-lengthening shadows as he waited for her answer, needing her to feel his hope. Instead, she drew a deep breath and replied quietly, saying if he were coming back, he would have arrived by now, that he was not returning. She led him inside, and the light of hope dimmed in Shadow Hawk, as Laughing River began to sort their few belongings. Packing only the essentials and things needed for trade, they left and never returned to the comfortable trapper's cabin they had called home, leaving behind the only life young Shadow Hawk had ever known.

ALTHOUGH ABANDONED AND forced to return to her people without a husband and accompanied by her half-white child, Laughing River walked with her back straight and her head held high. Shadow Hawk steeled himself to be laughed at and told to go away, but warm words and a welcome fire greeted them, as Laughing River and Shadow Hawk were welcomed by the tribe. That night, Laughing River shared with her son that the Cheyenne tribe's custom was to always receive a member back without questions. Later, young Shadow Hawk decided it was also because of the three horses and the many hides and furs they brought with them. It was only years later that his mother revealed to him the three large saddlebags of gold hidden among her things. She had buried them in a shallow trench under the tent, taking care to retrieve them each time the tribe was on the move. Shadow Hawk knew then his father had left her prepared for any emergency, even though he had left, never to return. He didn't understand how it could be so.

Upon returning to his mother's people as a child, Shadow Hawk had endured brutal teasing, which only made him more determined to show the other Indian children that he could do everything they could do, and even better. How embarrassed he'd felt when he couldn't understand what the other children were saying to him! His father had spoken English with his mother, except when they wanted to keep a secret from him, and Shadow Hawk had learned little Cheyenne. He worked hard to prove himself, and much to his tribe's dismay, despite what he endured, he became known as one of its strongest braves, as well as one of the best trackers and hunters in the Southern Cheyenne band. He received many eagle feathers for his accomplishments and bravery and earned the honor to wear a war bonnet.

Despite all his abilities, he felt hollow and empty inside. The shame of abandonment always brought up cruel and hurtful memories of his youth. His father's desertion and humiliation had left a mark on his pride no victory in the hunt or any feats of strength were able to erase.

Upon returning to her tribe, Laughing River, called Lari by Shadow Hawk's father, never remarried. At first Shadow Hawk thought it was because of her humiliation. It wasn't until he was almost grown that he realized the devotion his mother still felt for his father. Her love for the man who had abandoned them made him angry, for they had been betrayed. Though she seldom spoke of his father, Shadow Hawk heard her softly whisper a prayer for him many nights before she went to sleep.

LAUGHING RIVER COULDN'T understand why Shadow Hawk felt the way he did about his father. He had been a good man and an excellent provider for them both. In her heart she knew he would have returned if he were able. The only thing that would have kept her man from returning was if he were dead.

Jeremiah had told her before he took the final load of furs that his life was in danger. Someone had been snooping around, watching him. The word had come back to him from the fort that some folks thought he'd found gold.

The idea of gold made some people desperate.

He took no chances. He left the gold behind with Laughing River, just in case the worst came to pass. He held Lari close to him and whispered in her ear that he'd be back in a week if everything went well. He also told her to leave immediately after the seventh day if she was convinced he wasn't returning. The people that might come after him would also come to the cabin looking for the gold. He didn't want Lari or his son to be in peril.

Jeremiah's worst fears became fact. After he didn't return at the end of a full week, Laughing River dreaded what she must do. She had no choice but to flee to the nearby summer camp of her people, a three-day ride.

WHEN SHADOW HAWK was old enough to understand, she tried to talk to him, but he would rush from the lodge in anger, only to return with a silent sulk still surrounding him. He refused to listen to anything about his father. He knew his mother had to feel shame, because he felt it inside of him, constantly boiling just below the surface in everything he did, ready to explode at any time.

Once more, two days ago, she had tried to explain why his father hadn't returned. Laughing River always defended his father, which made Shadow Hawk even angrier. How could she still love someone who had betrayed her? On this occasion, he stormed out with a purpose into the darkening skies of a gathering, winter storm. He needed nothing from his father or his mother. Now was the time to let his anger take its vengeance. He would repay his father for leaving them all those years ago. He would take nothing that would not fit in his buffalo hide satchel. He would prove his manhood.

Shadow Hawk hadn't considered the consequences of either leaving on foot or not taking any provisions with him. He hadn't thought at all, blinded by the tortured reminder of his abandonment and the words of the medicine man. He left with only the white man's clothes in a small pack. He knew he wouldn't return until he had found peace from the tormented anguish of his father's abandonment and his feelings of desertion.

But that had been two days ago, and now he was beginning to realize he had indeed been foolish to leave as irate as he was. Acting or reacting to anger had constantly been his downfall. His lack of foresight had him stuck in a predicament of his own making. He had no one to blame but himself, and he had no one to help him. His had been a foolish decision from the beginning.

Despite that, his heart remained set on revenge. With only himself to depend on, he must figure out life for himself. He also knew one other thing. His past emotions no longer mattered. Whether he had once been loved or even whether he had returned that love as a boy was of no consequence. Even the hate he had felt since made no difference. He knew his fate, that of the medicine man's words. Fulfilling that destiny now involved getting out of this barn with a horse.

After the stableman had secured the barn for the night, Shadow Hawk waited for what seemed like an eternity. His stomach growled with hunger. He hadn't eaten since he left the Southern Cheyenne spring camp. That was another thoughtless gesture on his part, not bringing any provisions with him. However, food would have to wait. He must escape first. With his senses finely tuned, he was ready to steal a horse. The Indian scout felt a small twinge of guilt, but only for a minute. His father had known the people that owned this ranch, and as a boy, he had been here a few times to visit the family. That was how the young brave knew they had plenty of good horses.

Shadow Hawk remembered when his father had brought him here the last time. Shadow Hawk had been about seven or eight years old. They had traded with the family and shared conversation. His father and one of the men had gone alone into the mountains early that day. Shadow Hawk had stayed at the ranch and followed the cowboys around. He had been fascinated at the way they handled the horses and the cows. Several of them had called to him and let him walk up and ride their gallant and beautiful horses with them.

There had been several children there, also, including one small girl who was about his age. She seemed shy, although she was very pretty in the white man's way. He remembered her hair the color of the fire of autumn, and her eyes the turquoise color of the river, when he thought of her for many days after that. He would hate to admit it, but he still thought of her autumn leaves and turquoise-colored river when he was alone at night. Sometimes still, he would wake, and as he turned to find a comfortable position, he would imagine it was once again that day back on the ranch, and she was running through the tall, grassy pastures.

It was much later in the afternoon when Shadow Hawk's father and the ranch owner returned with very somber faces. His father didn't speak much the rest of the evening. Their ride home the next day had been exceptionally quiet also, the reason he remembered it so clearly. It had been unusual for his father not to talk and point out things on the trail or share funny stories with him on any type of outing; and on this return trip, he was as quiet as a deer's footsteps as it traversed the forest paths.

Now, all these years later, the young warrior felt a twinge of guilt at what he intended to do. This family had trusted his father. That was a long time ago, however, and a great number of things had changed. The past couldn't help him now. Only what he took in the quiet of the night could be of benefit to him.

Slowly, Shadow Hawk got up from the dim corner and made his way toward the animals, talking softly to them. The horses only understood commands in English, so he had to concentrate and remember his childhood tongue. After passing up a stallion and two other horses, he observed a young mare. She was the color of his soft doeskin moccasins. She also looked to be part paint pony, the preferred horse of his tribe. Carefully he approached her, speaking softly in his rusty English.

"Come to Shadow. Shadow not hurt you. Shadow need you."

His English wasn't perfect, but the horse seemed to understand, and she moved toward him. He slipped the bridle into her mouth and grabbed an old saddle blanket from the corner. Carefully, he led the horse to the double doors of the barn. He put his hand through the narrow crack in the door to feel the heavy plank in its cradle on the outside. He had to move it very slowly and cautiously, if he wanted to escape undetected.

The minutes crept by as he quietly tried to inch the plank along, holding it firmly against the door to keep any sound from escaping. But even with his warrior's strength, he couldn't dislodge the heavy wooden crossbar. A light sweat formed on his brow despite the cold damp night air. If he were caught, he would be killed for sure. The white man felt the same as his own people about horses and horse thieves.

He could do no more with the heavy plank still in place. He had no choice but to escape through the only other available exit, the hayloft, to move the beam from the other side. He crept to one of the log columns supporting the four-story barn. He couldn't use the ladder; it would be much too clumsy and would make too much noise.

He made the fateful decision to climb.

He judged his path with a keen eye and placed his hands on the rough wood, thrusting his body upward as he shifted from handhold to handhold. With barely a pause, he effortlessly scaled the twenty-five-foot pole and grabbed onto the edge of the second story floor to throw himself onto the loft. Swinging his weight out and grasping for the uneven wood of the loft floor, his right hand was jabbed by a long splinter, deeply imbedding itself from his finger into his palm. He almost fell; the piercing agony made him want to cry out, but he knew he couldn't. A low groan escaped his throat, and he quieted it as soon as it formed. With a grimace of pain, he slowly pulled himself onto the loft.

He lay there for a minute in extreme anguish, trying to overcome the pain. Now he would have to carefully crawl to the hay window and jump to the ground below. He couldn't think about the burning in his hand and finger. He had to escape the barn with a horse, if he was ever to fulfill his destiny.

Crawling to the small hay window, he opened it cautiously and peered into the darkness. All was quiet on the ranch. Only the howling wind could be heard. With the quarter moon high in the sky and surrounded by clouds, he knew it was time to leap the twenty-five feet to the ground below. Even though the pain in his hand kept him distracted, there was no wavering in his intent. This horse would be his. He knew more pain would be, also, and he paused, grimacing.

Still, the man in him refused to delay what he had to do. He held his breath and leaped into the frosty night air. The cold wind buffeted his body and whipped his clothes against his chest and legs. The ground came at him faster than he expected, and he landed with a soft thud on the ground. He let out a huffing sound as the air was forced from his lungs. He immediately knew he'd landed on his right knee, and he doubled over in an agony so intense it was un-endurable . . . that was if he had truly been born a white man.

He rubbed the leg and felt carefully for broken bones. It seemed to be no more than jammed and stiff. He gingerly tried to balance himself, when agony seared him like a heated knife. His knee was another predicament he had gotten himself into.

Dragging himself through the cold and facing winds that had become more than just a simple, in-convenient night breeze, Shadow Hawk opened the barn door and gently whispered to the horse. The beautiful little mare followed him willingly. Once the horse was outside, he struggled to replace the thick plank on the barn door, so as not to arouse suspicion in the early morning ranch hands.

Limping, he pulled the horse behind him, heading toward the mountains. He couldn't afford to try mounting her yet. She might spook and run, or make noises that would awaken the ranch workers, preventing him from completing his escape.

Shadow Hawk continued to walk cautiously, limping slightly, his moccasins making only the lightest of footsteps, all the time wincing with pain. He wouldn't need to cover their tracks, and he was thankful for that. The strong wind would take care of hiding his footprints. The young brave focused on his knee and hand that throbbed with excruciating agony, shivering in the brisk breeze. He needed a place to rest his leg and pull the splinter from his hand. He also needed to make it deep into the mountains before the stars faded and daylight appeared. Surrounded by the cold night, the familiar mountains seemed a long way off.

With determination in his heart, he pushed on through the darkness, enduring the grueling pain that turned the minutes into hours. He passed the stockade fence and the cattle pens, working his way around the manmade obstacles. After a time, he could sense the far meadow, and beyond, he knew he would find the mountains.

Shadow Hawk wrapped an arm around the horse's neck only a few feet into the meadow, whispering his words only when no sound would be carried on the wind.

"You are good to Shadow. Shadow like you."

The beast let the young brave mount without incident, and he rode through the rest of the grassy pasture. During the unendurable night, the young scout continually climbed upwards toward the mountains, always whispering to the horse and gently nudging her on.

By early sunrise, as the night sky began to fade, the Indian was exhausted and had to find a place to rest. A gentle snow had begun to fall with the first soft glow of morning light. The young Cheyenne brave was aware of the excruciating cold and damp. He knew he had to have shelter soon, if he was to survive. In this weather, the heartiest of men could die with continued exposure to the elements. His hand was stiff and throbbed with pain, and his knee rippled with unendurable agony at each step of the horse.

He continued to climb into crags of the Rocky Mountains, making slow progress and growing wearier and more chilled as the hours passed. Pushing himself until the daylight started to grow long, he knew the sun would dip behind the mountains shortly. He had needed shelter long before, and now he couldn't go farther without stopping to rest. He also knew that stopping unprotected in the cold meant certain death.

The area grew steep, and pockets of snow littered the path. This could be a dangerous journey, Shadow Hawk knew. He reached his good hand to the mare's face and, rubbing her jaw, he whispered to her, "Be strong, my girl. Together we will make this journey. You are young as I am. When we are young, we have the strength of many men."

The young mare stepped carefully. Painstakingly, with his head bent into the stiff breeze, Shadow Hawk persuaded the horse to continue up the nearly vertical slope. Snow-covered pines and aspen whipped in the strong wind. Their branches roughly scraped against the man and the horse, and Shadow Hawk knew the animal must also sting with pain. Yet, to give up was never an option, and together they continued the ascent, with Shadow Hawk gently encouraging the mare.

A large boulder appeared to block the narrow animal trail they were following. Shadow Hawk softly whispered to the horse to be careful. When she balked at the narrow track and the steep precipice at the edge, he rubbed her neck and let himself to the ground, holding to her as he balanced on his one good leg.

Placing his face next to hers, the brave stepped carefully, limping when he must, as he worked the mare around the boulder. He knew if he could distract her attention, she could be inched along the huge, snow-dusted precipice. Once clear, Shadow Hawk pulled himself awkwardly onto his new steed, and the young brave pressed his knees into her sides to encourage her a little farther. The sure-footed beast whinnied and began to step forward up the incline.

In the dappled sunlight a hundred feet in front of him, Shadow Hawk spied what appeared to be a shallow cave, hidden mainly by spruce and pine. He pushed the mare closer to the welcome opening in the rock. It was, he saw with relief, only a short distance away. He could stop there, and if everything was safe, he could both breathe a sigh of relief and get some much-needed sleep. He needed to recuperate from his injuries from the night before.

"After I find food," he whispered to his new steed, "then maybe I will be able to decide how to fulfill my destiny." Just reminding himself of his plans kept his heart encouraged, and hungry and hurting, he needed as much encouragement as he could get. Weary and fatigued, he started to dismount, only to have the horse cry out and shy away from him. He stumbled but held to the reins, and once the animal was steadied, he examined her carefully. The horse didn't have any noticeable cuts on her hide or stones in her hooves.

All Cheyenne understood that animals could sense danger before humans did. This mare must realize something he was unaware of. Shadow Hawk knew to take the horse's actions seriously. She must hear or smell something that his human senses hadn't yet discovered. Maybe another animal was nearby, already occupying this domain. Shadow Hawk tied the horse to a limb away from the cave and warily moved closer to investigate. He had only taken a few limping steps up the dangerous slope when his heart stopped, and a chill went up his spine. He sucked in his breath and held it for a long, painful time. He could smell now what he hadn't been able to hear before. The realization of all that was around him came into focus in his thoughts.

Bear.

The noise and smell of the horse must have finished arousing it from its deep winter slumber. Shadow Hawk had smelled bears and hunted them many times, both with his father and with the Cheyenne. This was the first time he had ever been alone with one. The thought didn't encourage him, either. He was in the presence of a bear, hurt and definitely alone.

What were his choices? Should he leave and take the risk of being tracked by the beast, or should he take a chance at trying to kill the sleepy giant? If he left, would he find another shelter? Could he survive much longer without protection, warmth, or food?

The choice seemed evident. He would have to kill the animal, if he was to survive. As it emerged, Shadow Hawk could see that the bear, small and therefore young, was a black. He hated to fight against such a creature. However, it was giving him little time for thought, for it was up and lumbering toward him.

Adrenaline began to surge through Shadow Hawk's body, and he could feel a strength that belied his injuries. He pulled his long hunting knife from its sheath and began to yell at the bear, trying his best not to show any fear. The bear took a swipe at him. Having just awakened, the groggy animal roared a frustrated howl when its claws went wide.

Shadow Hawk tried to back up, and his foot caught a stone, forcing his knee to give way. He stumbled, nearly dropping his knife. It took only seconds for him to recover, but the bear was on him in an instant. Its growls and hot breath pressed toward him. One of the bear's thick paws scraped Shadow Hawk's back, shredding the jacket and shirt and flooding his flesh with pain. The warmth of his blood flowed from the deep crevices torn in his body like a blanket of heat roasted beside a fire.

Shadow Hawk called on the power of the Indian medicine man, and pulling on the inner strength of his oldest ancestors, he used all his might to roll over and plunge his knife deep into the chest of the attacking monster, holding on tightly to the back of the thickly furred body. Twisting to avoid the savage teeth, he remembered the words his father had spoken.

"Son, the closer you cling on the bear, the less power it has."

The admonition flashed quickly through the young brave's mind, and instinctively he hung onto the fur as tightly as possible. Again and again Shadow Hawk tore the knife from the bear's body and plunged his weapon deep into the bear's quivering flesh, ripping apart muscle, and taking care to avoid the animal's ferocious head, in order to keep from being viciously ripped apart.

"Brother Bear, you do not know me, but I need this cave. You must let me have it," Shadow Hawk shouted in Cheyenne, as the bear wobbled and stumbled out of the cave's entrance. He had succeeded. Watching cautiously, he breathed a sigh of relief when the bear finally sank to the ground and tumbled down the escarpment, dripping a trail of blood onto the white snow below, never to rise again. He was thankful it wasn't an adult bear, or the outcome might have been quite different.

The horse was skittish from the smell of the bear and blood. It pulled at the tree branch as Shadow Hawk approached.

"Shadow here. Don't be afraid. Come in cave. Get warm. Shadow needs rest," the Indian brave softly crooned. His short, choppy sentences seemed to sooth the mare, and she settled under his grip.

He knew he would survive. Later, he could climb down the slope and carve meat from the bear. The hide could be skinned, prepared, and made useful for many things. He smiled, considering that perhaps his father's white God had come to his aid in the form of a bear. If so, his father's God had given himself to Shadow Hawk for a gift. His smile falling away, the youth conceded it was more likely that Brother Bear had been in just the right place at just the right time to offer himself to a brave of the Cheyenne people. In any case, the bear would provide food, and the hide could be used for trade.

The mare relaxed as the weakened young Indian held his arm under her neck and gently led the animal toward the cave. She shied where Shadow Hawk had fought and mortally wounded the bear, but the brave was able to talk the soft words of encouragement to her, and she seemed more secure as they moved past the place.

Approaching the cave, Shadow Hawk could see it was a sharp indention in the mountain wall where a slide must have happened many years before, digging out this small fissure. With the tall trees around it, the cave remained camouflaged from the outside. It went back into the mountain quite some way, though it was narrow, perhaps only ten to twelve feet in width.

Shadow Hawk gathered a few dry twigs and made a small fire. He put the horse toward the front of the cave. He knew its nature was such to allow it to alarm him if any other beasts approached.

Even though weakened, the young brave managed to push a rock on the reins to keep the mount from wandering off. He was drained of all his strength, and his back was hurting from the bear's claw. He knew he had to sit down, as the heat from the fire started to warm him. Without rest, his injuries would soon cause him to collapse. He laid the saddle blanket near the fire, so he wouldn't be on the cold, damp cavern floor. Then he cleaned and heated his knife.

"If there's a God, I need Him now," he murmured softly in his people's language, as he watched the metal warm and then begin to glow. He glanced at the horse that had carried him all this way, and he watched the moisture form clouds in the air around her nostrils, as her breath exited her body. He knew what he had to do, and he knew it wouldn't be pleasant.

"Maybe a little prayer to You wouldn't hurt,"

Shadow Hawk whispered, as he glanced up to where his father had always said his white man's God lived. Shadow Hawk couldn't understand how a god could live in the air with no food to eat or water to drink, but his father had said it was so. He had even believed it at one time, too. He had been a boy, though, and once back with the Cheyenne, he had learned of the true gods of his people. Still, Shadow Hawk knew it never hurt to step on all the rocks when the ground in the forest grew soft. He whispered a simple prayer asking for help from the white man's God that lived in the sky before he dropped his eyes back to the task at hand.

Shadow Hawk was thankful he was warming up and would have shelter, as night was approaching again. This was rough country, and with the injuries his body had sustained at the ranch, he soon wouldn't be able to move well at all. If his injuries from today didn't get better quickly, he might have to return to the ranch where he had stolen the horse. It might be the only way he could survive.

With a deeply drawn breath, Shadow Hawk began the painful task of cutting the splinter from his hand. He placed the knife against his skin just at the splinter's edge and pressed down. There was a sharp sting, and then he saw thick yellow pus and pale pink blood burst forth.

With his eyes starting to blur, and his breathing rapidly becoming shallower, the young brave realized the cave around him had begun to swim. The crackle of the fire became distant, and he faintly heard the horse whinny. He caught the ting of metal on stone echoing in the stone chamber, as his knife fell from his hand. Then, he closed his eyes for a moment, and that was the last thing he remembered.

— 2 —

THE WIND BLEW fiercely as Laurie Kerrigan stepped out of her family's massive log home. She pulled her long, wool-lined, elk-skin robe closer to her and began to walk into the torrent of frigid air. Even for the future territory of Colorado, it was an unusually cold April day. A pine tree crackled in the strong breeze, but Laurie wasn't worried about the stability of the structure behind her. Her grandfather, Sean Murchadh Kerrigan, had built the house to endure, and that it had done for over thirty years. The two-story landmark, carefully and solidly built, had weathered with time, giving it an aged look of wisdom and superiority when contrasted to the fresh green woodlands behind. More than once it had served as a fortification against an Indian siege. Scars were imbedded deep into its log walls, and dark stains etched across the wood's surface were a reminder of the blood that had been shed.

Still, the house and land remained, and in the face of all odds had endured as a testament of the human spirit. It seemed to belong there on the sloping precipice of the mountain, with valleys and grass-covered meadows stretched out below on either side like a thick, deep carpet. In this vast wilderness that reflected the grandeur of God's mighty handiwork, the rough-hewn, expansive building had taken on the attributes of a fortress designed to withstand weather, physical attacks, and the ravages of time.

Laurie supposed it reflected her grandfather's tribulations in his native Scotland. With government corruption in his homeland, her grandfather's Christian ideals hadn't made him a popular man. During a political upheaval, he had been forced to flee the land of his birth, and he chose to settle in the wild, untamed mountains of this land that seemed to know no end. Yet, as remote and rugged as these surroundings were, Laurie could think of nowhere else she would want to live. The beauty of the mountains was a part of her, and the dense forests of pine, moody and dark, spoke to her inner soul.

Today, her delicate brow was creased with lines of worry. Her smoky turquoise eyes had a preoccupied look in them as she absently pushed her long, unruly mahogany hair back under the hood of her robe. Her heavy robe couldn't disguise her womanhood, yet her face was a reflection of youth and innocence, with ivory skin, soft blushing cheeks, and a light sprinkling of freckles across her nose.

Long, dark, thick lashes framed her liquid, deep blue-green eyes. They reminded her grandfather of the color of the sea off Scotland's shores, or so he had often teased her. Her mouth bore full, dark ruby lips, and when she smiled, her teeth sparkled with perfection. Her creamy complexion set off her striking features, contrasted by her thick, rich auburn hair.

In the mountains surrounding her grandfather's home, few could remember a countenance that had ever been as captivating as Laurie's. It wasn't uncommon for a guest to turn and stare at her, recognizing that they might never again see such an entrancing young woman.

Laurie seemed oblivious to it all, smiling at strangers and laughing with friends. She wasn't unlike her Scottish ancestors, even if she had never lived with them at her side. Her people in the old country prided themselves as strong, independent, and proud. If she had been with them, they would have seen her as no different, and she would have fit in as one of their own.

What moved her today was determination, and it was determination motivated by love. As she walked, Laurie began to worry about the misfortune that prompted her to be out on a day like this. Her beloved horse, Little Shadow, was missing.

Laurie had received her as a colt only three years

before on her fourteenth birthday. The horse had been a present from her father, Aidan Kerrigan. At the colt's gifting, multiple remarks had been overheard about how the young colt looked like her mother, just a shadow of her in her appearance, and the young animal's name had been decided. Even so, many of the ranch hands, as well as her father, often called the beast by another name, one that seemed more in line with what they saw every day. Laurie's Shadow was the name they used, because the two were almost inseparable.

As was her daily routine, yesterday Laurie had gone to saddle her mare for an early morning ride. But when she arrived at the barn, Shadow wasn't in her stall. Her saddle was there, but the bridle was missing. She had gone to Papa, but he had put her off, telling his daughter that the horse was surely wandering the pasture. Even though Laurie pleaded, he refused to send out a party to search for her. She knew she would have to look on her own, and she would need to discount her papa's suggestion first.

"It would be unusual for Shadow to already be out and pastured," murmured Laurie, as she pushed through the wind on her way toward the corral. When she got there, she looked across the dew-covered grass, knowing that a hungry horse would have disturbed the morning's sheen, but again she didn't see a sign of the beautiful creature. Becoming more perplexed, she immediately went to Daniel Gates, the stableman, and asked of the horse's whereabouts. He would know if anyone did. His short, stocky stature commanded the respect of the toughest of ranch hands. He knew what was going on around the ranch better than Papa sometimes did.

WHEN ASKED, DANIEL stopped and dropped the harness in his hand onto a rough hook on the barn wall. Resting his arms on an empty saddle jack, he cocked one eyebrow at Laurie and chewed the straw in his mouth before replying. He knew how much this ranch depended on him, and he knew how to apportion his time. He couldn't waste it on keeping up after a horse that someone else was already tending to, not and keep this ranch running properly.

"Nobody pays your hoss much mind since you do all the tendin' to 'er, Laurie girl. She's a spoilt beast, that's for dang sure. Your pa's orders say she stays in the barn 'til you come an' fetch 'er." Daniel dropped his head to spit the chewed straw to the barn floor at his feet.

Glancing up, his eyes narrowed. One quick look at Laurie's distraught face told him she hadn't been up to fetch her favorite horse, Little Shadow. Something was amiss, and it had him puzzled. Daniel pondered for a moment, then a hardened looked came across his usually agreeable face.

"Well, maybe that feller of yours took 'er as a joke. His funnin' has always been a little peculiar to me, anyhow."

Daniel straightened his body, and he slipped his

hands into his pockets. He tried to stand as if unconcerned, hoping to ease the growing look of panic in the girl's sweet face. Daniel's distaste for Laurie's suitor was obvious to nearly everybody on the ranch. Even so, for the girl's sake, he tried to keep it veiled, however thinly it was.

Daniel's thoughts slipped back to almost a year ago, and how Arthur Stuart had mocked the family's Scottish ancestry by wearing a woman's skirt to imitate a kilt. Laurie's grandfather had felt highly insulted by the scene, but Arthur assured Laurie that he only meant it as an amusing and lighthearted riff on the family's history across the seas. It was only after the old man's death six months ago that he had truly apologized, and then, in Daniel's mind, it had been too little, too late. That slicked-tongue dude had only expressed his regret to avoid losing Laurie's affections, and the old man knew that for certain. He could take it to the bank, or more wisely, stuff it in his mattress. For in truth, he felt it might be safer there.

"WHY WOULD ARTHUR want Shadow?" Laurie questioned.

Laurie strongly suspected Arthur disliked her "half-breed" horse, as he called her, and doubted seriously if he would ever go near the beast, unless Laurie herself was present. Old Daniel didn't know of her suspicions, though. Laurie had never spoken of them to anyone.

Tendrils of the early morning chill snuck into the

barn, writhing thin fingers of cold into the warm, earthy space, and then a sudden gust of wind blew Daniel's hat off. He reached down and picked it up, holding it in his hand. Not donning it was his way of showing his respect towards the young woman. Then he looked Laurie straight in the eyes.

"That feller'll do most anythin' to get yer attention," he replied gruffly. He continued, muttering, "I don't mean to be speakin' out of turn, but I keep my eyes peeled, and I cain't help noticing a yearnin' glint in the man's eyes as he tries to gaze unnoticed at ya'. I seen it, though. Every time. My eyes are quick, and there's not much that yer feller does outside my notice."

"A yearning glint?" Laurie chuckled. "Come now, Daniel. Then, why didn't Arthur speak to me or stop by the house to call? Why would he come straight to the barn?"

Laurie didn't like this. It was too unlike Arthur, and that man always stayed true to form. She looked to the stableman for answers. Daniel rubbed his stubbled jaw and appeared thoughtful before slowly commenting.

"I think maybe ya' are right, Miss Laurie. I don't think 'e would take your Shadow. That man wouldn't want to muss up 'is high felutin' duds comin' down here to the barn, what with the muck and all. He's a little too good fer that. Nope, I reckon ya' are right as rain on this one. 'E fer sure didn't take your Shadow," he chuckled.

Laurie chose to ignore the obvious gibes aimed at Arthur. For the moment her mind was intent on finding the location of her horse.

"Daniel, when exactly did you see her last?" The question was very pointed, and she didn't want him to feel put off by her pressure. She added a note of trust as she continued, "You've been one of my father's most trusted hands. You know that, and you would never let intentional harm come to one of my father's animals. Or one of mine, either. You must help me, Daniel."

The man looked up at her, and his face softened. "Well, Miss Laurie, she was in 'ere evenin' before last when I checked on the stock an' barred the door." He looked at the floor as if thinking, then he cleared his throat and tapped his hat against his leg. "The door was still barred when I got here yesterday mornin'. The only thing out of place was up in the 'ayloft. That strong wind we had the night before must've jarred the door up there loose, an' it blew open. I thought it was latched tight, but I 'adn't been up the ladder to check on it in a while. With my ol' knees like they are, I don't git around like I used to. But there's nothin' out of the ordinary goin' on around 'ere."

He scratched his head before replacing his hat. With a twist of his lips and an unconscious movement of his hand that Laurie would have missed if she hadn't been watching, Daniel reached to his pocket, and a second piece of straw was instantly in his mouth. She smiled as the grassy tuber began to jostle with the meanderings she could see going on in his brain.

She felt confidence in the words Daniel had spoken to her. He and his wife were both kind Christian people who had worked for her family for nearly ten years. Her entire household knew Daniel Gates to be a trustworthy and honest man. She also knew Daniel would have rather endured something happening to his own horse than have something happen to hers. The old man was fond of Laurie's young mare despite everything he said about her. She had caught him giving her an apple now and then, or an extra handful of oats on several occasions. As for the other ranch hands, Laurie thought they were a decent lot, and she couldn't think of one of them that would be low enough to steal a horse from a woman. Besides, they all knew what would happen to them if they were caught stealing anything from the ranch. Jobs were not all that easy to find in this remote wilderness. Anyone who had a job wanted to keep it.

All of that said and done, how could Shadow be missing? Who could explain that? Horses didn't just disappear, and especially not hers.

— 3 —

LAURIE KNEW HER papa wouldn't let her look for her horse alone, especially not when a possible snowstorm was blowing in. She had tried to talk him into letting her search the previous day, but he had other jobs for her to do and had put off hunting for the horse, telling her Little Shadow might find her way home by nightfall. However, her early morning check had revealed what she feared most.

Her horse was still missing!

Her papa had left at daybreak to check on the first of the spring calves, assuring her he would help her search for Shadow when he returned. Newborn calves couldn't survive a blizzard, and Laurie understood why he wished her to wait. She also knew letting a hard task go undone just because a man wasn't around wasn't a strength of hers, and she walked the rooms of the house and tramped the grounds restlessly, wrestling with waiting until her papa returned.

Finally, she couldn't wait any longer. No matter what she had been told, she had to search for her beloved mare. She had learned in her Bible readings that God cares for the least of His children, and He doesn't want any of them to suffer. That may not be exactly the way her Bible said it, but the meaning was the same. She had to follow the Good Father's example, didn't she? Finding Shadow was the right to do. Papa would understand, surely.

Laurie made her way to the barn for the second time that day, searching for the stableman. It was with great care and a sound dose of confidence that she approached him about riding Stormy, the black stallion with four white feet.

"Daniel," she said in her most charming voice. "I miss my morning ride. I thought I'd take Stormy out for a quick trot. I won't go too far. You know Papa's left for the lower meadow. I know if he sees any sign of Shadow, he'll bring her right home with him. However, I thought I might ride toward the back meadow, near the edge of the trees a bit, just to see if there's any sign of her. I won't be gone too long. I promise." Her father might not let her go, but Daniel Gates was another matter. The stableman had a difficult time ever telling her no. She ended with her most becoming smile.

Daniel stammered and started with, "Well, Miss

Laurie," but she interrupted with a big hug and a thank you.

Before Daniel could clear his throat, she took off toward the barn to saddle up the stallion. She was outside in only a few minutes. "I'll be back soon!" she yelled as she headed toward the back meadow, smiling to herself. She had packed light provisions in her coat and wasn't concerned about her return or the impending storm. Her only thought was heading toward the mountains to find her beloved Shadow.

She rode across the vast meadow one way, and then came back around the other way, constantly searching for any sign of the young mare, only to be disappointed. She had just reached the first of the pine trees at the far end of the back meadow, where she could barely see the rooftop of the barn. Searching the ground carefully, she thought she saw a horse hoof print. Yes, it had to be! It was a faint print of a horse going toward the mountains, here at the end of the meadow. Questions surged through her mind. What was Shadow doing this far away from home? How did she get out of the barn?

The morning was slipping away faster than Laurie noticed. The sun would soon be high overhead. Dark, ominous clouds were blowing in, threatening to blot the sun from the sky and pull the day into the dimness of night. Eagerly and anxiously she headed into the dense forest as the snow began to gently fall. She needed to hurry if she was to see any sign of the missing creature she loved so dearly.

Despite Laurie's stealthy escape from underneath Daniel's indulgent eye, she was more than prepared. She was armed with her rifle and her ram's horn. Her father and grandfather had taught her to be well equipped for any unforeseen occurrence. At any unusual sounds, she could call out on the ram's horn or shoot her rifle to ward off an impending emergency, and help would come running. They had also taught her to stay within hearing distance of those sounds.

Today, however, was different. She had to take a chance. Knowing she would have to turn back soon, she headed deeper and higher into the mountains. All she wanted was her precious Shadow back. She loved her horse more than anything, except, of course, for her papa.

As her search continued, she began to think how angry her papa would be with her if she didn't return soon. Even that didn't dull the sharpness from her sense of urgency, and she was determined to continue her search. Would her papa expect her to leave one of the worker's children stranded in the mountains during a snowstorm, just because no one was there to accompany Laurie on her search?

As she noticed the stallion's hooves beginning to slip on the mountain rocks, she began to feel disheartened. No matter how desperate she was to find Little Shadow, she might be forced to turn back before the weather got any worse.

Stopping the enormous black stallion, she studied the wind and the heft of the snow. If the flakes were drier, she could advance with impunity. However, once the rocks themselves froze, this moist snowfall would harden into an invisible layer of ice.

She took a deep breath. There was a small place to turn around just ahead. She had been here many times, just not during the cold season. The past several winters, Papa had insisted she stay away from this trail once fall began to slip away. A bear had occasionally been sighted in the area, and there was no need to take unnecessary chances.

Laurie imagined Little Shadow standing against the wind somewhere, the snow and ice pelting her quivering skin, just hoping her mistress would come to rescue her. With a shiver of dread, she decided that maybe she could advance just a bit more. Her Scottish determination ran deep in her veins. This was something she would do, and if her papa complained, she would stand up to him. After all, she had stood up to that bear back at the ranch. It had come at the ranch hands and scared at least one night's sleep off the men. Not Laurie, though. She hadn't been frightened. Not much, anyway, and at her hands, soon the bear was gone.

Her horse climbing a little further, she saw something that made her freeze into place. A cold, haggard breath entered her lungs, and there it stayed. Her hands and feet felt like weights. She could hardly move as her vision narrowed to just one thing, the marks on the ground in front of the stallion.

"No, it can't be," she gasped desperately. Splattered under a scattering of snow was the thing she hadn't even imagined she might find, blood! She dreaded what might be revealed in the cold, dried stains on the ground where the lifeblood of an animal had drained and puddled. It just couldn't be from her horse, her precious mount.

She knew she should turn back to get her Papa and show him, but she couldn't force herself. What if Little Shadow was just around the bend, lying there in the turn-around spot? What if Laurie's precious mount was injured and all alone?

She pushed herself forward, climbing up only a few feet at a time. She looked ahead, searching for the trail, and saw an animal down the side, wedged between a rock and some small aspen trees. Tears made her vision blur until she realized the shape wasn't that of a horse. It was short and bulky, even in its stillness, and she laughed as the tension that had grabbed her heart shattered. The bear! There had been a bear after all! She let out a deep sigh of gratitude. Never in her life did she think she would be thankful to see a bear. It was clearly dead, lightly dusted with snow, and lying with its head to one side and its mouth open. She followed the stream of frozen blood and knew it was the cause of the puddle she had seen. She began to cry softly with relief. Her Christian faith was stirred in her as she sat on her horse, and it poured from her soul.

"Oh, thank you, God. Thank you for not letting me find my horse like this."

Yet, her heart still pounded with the uncertainty of the bizarre scene. How had the bear gotten there, and who or what had killed it? It hadn't been dead long, at the most a day, because the blood was still visible under the thin deposit of snow.

Then, even more puzzling to Laurie was the location of her horse. It surely couldn't be tied in with the death of this bear, and yet this seemed more than coincidental. Little Shadow couldn't have done this, that was for sure.

The big stallion began to snort loudly and stamp his feet. She had little time to think once the smell of the bear finally spooked the horse. She tried to turn her mount around slowly, talking to him gently, but the animal only snorted louder. She knew she had to get off him, or he could hurt her by throwing her. If she were to slide down the steep slope beside the trail, she might find herself in the same predicament as that bear.

She carefully dismounted. A pine branch caught the edge of her cloak on her way down, and the strong wind blew the hood of her robe away from her face. Her mass of cinnamon hair tumbled down. Frustrated, she reached up to get the unruly accumulation under control. Pulling her hair away from her ear, she heard something. It sounded like the faint cry of another horse answering her stallion. Could she be imagining things? She held her breath and listened. Laurie heard it again, only louder. It had to be Little Shadow.

She impulsively shouted, "Shadow, where are

you? It's Laurie. Where are you? I love you, Shadow. Let me know where you are."

IN A NEARBY cave, hidden by the trees that had grown up over the opening, the Cheyenne scout known as Shadow Hawk lay in a semi-consciousness delirium. Somewhere in the deep recesses of his brain, he heard a voice. It spoke in English, the language of his father, and it called his name ever so faintly. He was too weak to respond to the hallucination. After a few moments of uncertainty and wishful dreaming, he faded for a moment back into unconsciousness. He didn't know if he was awake, or if he had dreamed of one of the angels of the white man's God calling his name, breathing sweet things to him as he lay protected in his cave.

A troubling thought tickled the back of his mind, even as he struggled to recall his father's stories from long ago: Why would an angel of the white man's God be trying to find him, anyway? Even as the world around him was frozen into a chilled landscape, his face burned with heat. He was just conscious enough to understand that he was very sick, and without help, he would likely die.

Blackness swept over him, and his world turned inward once more.

LAURIE BEGAN TO anxiously urge the stallion behind her to follow her up the steep side of the mountain, going the direction where she had heard the horse's response. There was a large boulder directly in the path, and the mountain fell away at her side. She had never been this high up on the mountain in this sort of weather, and she was frightened. How bad would it continue to grow? She had no way of knowing.

With the snow crunching softly under her feet, she walked around the icy monolith. A few more strides upward, and with her eyes searching, she located the cave. Her heart stopped for just a brief second as she saw the path the bear had made as he fell.

Then a sharp snort interrupted her thoughts, the sound of a horse. Laurie walked breathlessly toward the entrance. Oblivious to anything but the sound of her beloved Shadow, she stepped inside. There stood her adored Shadow. She began to cry, and warm tears stained her cold, rosy cheeks.

"Oh, Shadow. You're safe. Oh, Shadow, I've missed you. I prayed that you'd be returned to me safely. I love you so much; I thought you'd never leave me. Don't you love me, too?" She sobbed with relief. The tension of worry that had eaten at her nerves and kept her stomach in turmoil was broken, and she walked toward the horse.

Just as she stepped up to her beloved creature, she saw a shape in the shadows. Her heart went to her throat. She stood as frozen as the bear dead in the snow outside.

Was it yet another bear? The mate, or a sibling? Not now, she prayed, not after she had finally gotten her horse back. Please, God, she silently sent to Heaven. She remained still as her eyes slowly adjusted to the darkness. She realized it was not another bear, as she had immediately feared, but something far more dangerous.

A man!

What? How? Was it a horse thief or a trapper? Laurie's mind raced as she considered her possible actions. He wasn't moving. Was he sleeping? He hadn't responded to her in any way at all. Was he even breathing? Had the bear killed him?

She examined the area cautiously, discovering where a fire had been, and a large hunting knife lay unsheathed beside the cold ashes. Stepping softly, she went back to hoist her rifle from the stallion. She was taking no chances with a horse thief, or whatever else he was. She was better off armed, even if he was unarmed.

She cleared her throat to get his attention, but there was no response from the motionless man. She repeated the action, but there was only silence. Ever so quietly she approached the dark shape. The bulk of the person seemed to grow in her mind. She knew she would see movement where there was none if she let her mind loose.

Concentrating, she carefully scooted the knife to the side with the edge of her boot, knocking it away from the stranger. She gingerly picked it up while never taking her eyes off him and put it by her horse. Then she quietly approached the stranger, keeping her steps as stealthy as an Indian.

As she glanced at the prone form, something about him reminded her of a small boy from many years ago. The cast of his cheek, perhaps, or the sheen of his hair. Perhaps the way he was tumbled across the cave floor. She couldn't place it, undecided what would bring that memory alive now. His father had brought the boy to the ranch when she was just a girl, and he had spent the day playing with the other children. His father was a white man, and the boy hadn't seemed especially Indian, at least when she first saw him. Then, in his movements, she'd recognized the signs, his steps taken with the quiet of the caterpillar, and his coal-black eyes that saw everything. She was entranced, even as a girl, when he spoke. His English had burned with the smoky flavor of the Cherokee tongue.

For years she had tried to emulate those feet, and her eyes had tried to see with that boy's agility. The ranch hands had laughed at her, telling her she would become a little Indian if she kept it up. Finally, tired of the teasing, she had let it go except when she couldn't be seen by others. Finally, it had become an invisible part of herself, one that often served her well.

Laurie hadn't made a sound as she approached the man. She nudged him ever so slightly with her boot tip. He didn't respond. Surely, he was dead. He must be. She studied him closely in the dim light. She couldn't afford any mistakes. Pausing and holding as still as a tree on a windless day, she saw his chest rise. She took a deep breath and let it out in relief. He was alive, although she didn't know if that was a good thing or not. She knew she must ferret out what must be done, and she steeled herself for what might happen as she tapped harder with the cold rifle muzzle. This time the young man slowly opened his bloodshot eyes and tried to lift his head, unaware of the gun staring him down.

"Well, at least that tells the story. The scoundrel is awake, as well as alive, for all the good it will do him," she muttered.

In a barely audible voice, the man whispered, "Shadow's well. You can go now." His head fell back onto the blanket covering the cold, hard earth of the cave, having never seen his captor through his infection-laced delirium.

Laurie was alarmed. How did this man know her Shadow? Who was this stranger? And why did he have her horse?

— 4 —

THE MAN WAS either injured or very sick, and in the muted light at the back of the cave, Laurie couldn't tell which was worse. He was a white man, that much she could see by his dress and skin color, and probably a trapper judging by his knee-high moccasins, leather jacket, and long hair.

She knew she couldn't trust her instincts in this situation. She always wanted to help a hurt or wounded animal, and this man was no exception. But what was he doing up here alone with her horse? She shouldn't help a thief, not one that had stolen her beloved mare. What should she do? She felt helpless in her indecision.

"Oh God," she whispered, "Help me. I don't know how to proceed."

Her prayer didn't seem to buoy her as much as she needed, and she sighed in resignation. Her papa would know what to do if only he were here, but he wasn't, and it was up to her to save this man's life. Either that, or she could just leave him to die. If he was truly the horse thief he appeared to be, she might even be praised for her actions.

The more she thought about it, the more she came to the realization of what she must do. She needed to leave him stranded on the mountain and get help. She couldn't help the stranger by herself. It was obvious he couldn't get up without assistance, not even to get on the horse, much less ride back to the ranch.

The young man groaned softly, and the sound caught her attention. He attempted to turn to one side, and as she watched him struggle, she observed what looked like dried blood that had oozed from under his back. Impulsively she bent down and made a concerted attempt to help him to roll to his side. He moved as an outdoorsman might. That would be good if he were injured as badly as he seemed. A strong constitution would help him to withstand the rigors of travel for help. After a great struggle, she finally worked him onto his side.

The back of his coat and shirt were torn and frayed, and she could see claw marks gouged into his flesh. Laurie knew he had killed the bear, but not before the bear had gotten a piece of him. This was a man lucky to be alive. Then, for a moment, she glanced at Little Shadow, and a dark thought crossed her mind. Perhaps not so lucky, if he was a horse thief in the territory of Colorado.

The jarring movements of her inspection roused the delirious young man, and he once again opened his feverish eyes. He found Laurie's face, and he roughly whispered, "Angel with Shadow. Everything be all right." With the ghost of a smile on his lips, he let his eyes close once again.

Laurie's breath escaped her. How could he know her middle name, the one her mother had called her? This was more bizarre by the moment. She stood and stepped to the edge of the cave. She reached to Little Shadow and rubbed her hand along the animal's neck, reassuring her with the small sounds that were Laurie's way of letting her know she cared. The mare turned her head and nuzzled Laurie as if hoping for a treat. Laurie just rubbed her nose, knowing she had nothing to give. As she turned away, her arm brushed her coat pocket, and the bulge there reminded her of the food she had packed and not eaten.

"Here, girl," Laurie whispered, reaching into the pocket and pulling out a carrot fresh from the root cellar. She ran her hand along Shadow's jaw, enjoying the feel of her muscles as the animal hungrily devoured the treat. "Oh, girl. You've not eaten. I wish I'd brought more. Just wait, Shadow. When I get you home, you'll have all the oats and carrots you can eat." She reached to wipe the tears from her eyes with the back of her hand.

She knew she had to leave to get help now, and

she would have to take Stormy. There was only one saddle, and she couldn't take the time to saddle her mare. This man's life might depend on the minutes she could save on the larger horse, and her heart had already committed her to providing whatever rescue she could. She had no choice but to leave Shadow here.

She stepped out of the cave to find a clearing sky, though the wind was still fierce. The storm must have passed over, and the sun was brighter than when she had first arrived. Grasping the reins of the stallion, she embarked on her trek down the mountain. She had only gone a dozen or so steps when she heard a familiar sound. Her heart jumped with elation. It was her father blowing his ram's horn, and the sound was bright enough to indicate a very close proximity. He must know she was up here, and surely, he was coming for her. She looked around for a suitable place to blow her horn in reply, but there wasn't room without spooking her horse, and she couldn't chance the possibility that he might trample or injure her while trying to escape the noise. She didn't want him to stumble and go off the precipice that ran along the side of the trail.

She changed directions as quickly as she could and led the stallion back up the narrow trail to the mouth of the cave. There she grabbed her ram's horn from the saddlebag and took several steps from the horse. Laurie placed the horn to her lips and blew with all her might. She counted to ten and blew the ram's horn again.

INSIDE THE CAVE, the noise aroused the Cheyenne brave from his delirium. He opened his eyes in agony only to view what he thought had to be his guardian angel standing just outside the cave's entrance. Laurie's long auburn hair was blowing in the blustery air, and she held the horn to her lips. Her profile against the snow outside made her look more beautiful than any human deserved to be. With the sun glistening on her face, Shadow Hawk decided this was the loveliest creature he had ever seen. Nothing human could be this perfect. Yes, he thought, she had to be an angel, exactly as the pictures he had seen in his father's Holy Book. Surely he was dying, and she had come to take him to, to . . .

The young brave faded into unconsciousness again, dreaming of the ethereal being he'd glimpsed.

AIDAN KERRIGAN WAS relieved when he heard the ram's horn reply to his own. After four hours of hard riding and climbing over this mountain, his efforts had been rewarded. He had been distraught when he arrived at the ranch house only to discover Laurie had left two hours ahead of him. He had been able to track her closely, but it had been unnerving to turn each corner on the trail, never knowing if he would find her injured or whole. At least now he had located her, and he knew she was alive.

"Thank you, God," Aidan breathed sincerely, and

his eyes cut to the clearing sky above, grateful to know his daughter was unharmed, despite her disobedience. But that emotion only lasted a few moments before his anger began to well up. The more he thought about her youthful disobedience, the angrier he got.

With each jarring step of his horse on the ice-covered path, he muttered, "What's she doing this far from the ranch house? This weather! This season! She's created an unconscionable and heedless danger for herself and for others. She knows better than this, missing horse or no horse! This daughter of mine will be in some serious trouble when I get hold of her. I cannot imagine from where this stubborn independence comes."

Part of the anger boiling into him was frustration at the rising pain in his own body, and yet his private, physical concerns must be aside. His daughter was close, but she still wasn't found. He looked the direction from which he'd heard his daughter's ram's horn. He let his eyes flick over the peaks around him, judging the sounds and how the peaks would throw around the blast of sound before letting it filter into his ears. With a quick frown of a decision made, he turned to the path he knew he must take.

The steep side of the mountain was where this trail led. As his left leg ached from the cold, he was reminded of the time it was broken, much on a day like this. The winter wind whipped around him, fighting its way past the buttons on his coat, as he recalled the scene with a vivid sharpness, as if he were there again. His trusted hand, Daniel Gates, had yet to join him, assuming much of the load of managing the ranch, and Aidan had been responsible for chasing down various wayward livestock. A cow and her twin calves had gotten through the stockade and were missing. He couldn't let them run loose, no matter the risk to himself. After a couple hours hunting, he had finally been able to hear them bawling up on the face of the mountain.

He breathed a prayer of thanks for that long-ago day. It was a prayer he had uttered many times before, and it was from his heart each and every time. "Thank God Jeremiah Hawke was out trapping on the mountain that particular day, or I might have died up there. I wouldn't have been able to save myself, much less the livestock."

A deer had come out of nowhere and spooked his horse. She threw him off and in the fracas accidentally backed up and stepped on his left leg. Aidan hadn't had time to react. The leg had snapped like a dry tree branch. He was there for what seemed like hours in pain, trying to get on his horse, but with no luck. Every hour he would fire off a shot. Jeremiah Hawke came through the mountains later that day and heard Aidan's gunfire. When he went to investigate, there the rancher was, trying his best to make a splint to help himself walk and not doing a very good job of it.

"Yes," mused Aidan to no one in particular, as he navigated his horse up the narrow trail. "I might not have survived if it hadn't been for Jeremiah that day. He got both me and the cows off that mountain." Aidan knew the dangers of this mountain, and he hoped his daughter didn't have to find them out in the same way he had.

That had been over a dozen years ago. They had been casual friends before then and true friends afterward. The men had seen each other three or four times a year after that rescue. Jeremiah would stop at the ranch on his trips to Bent's Fort to trade his furs just to see if the ranch needed anything. Sometimes Aidan would request for him to bring back a few supplies, like coffee or sugar. A few days later Jeremiah would stop on the way back and drop them off.

Then, around eight or nine years ago, Jeremiah had disappeared. Some speculated he had gone back East to marry. They suggested he now might have a new family and simply wanted to forget his trapping days.

Aidan didn't see Jeremiah as that kind of man. He had loved his son and cared about the boy's Cheyenne Indian mother. Aidan did have to admit it was strange how he had vanished. Some folks down at the fort had suggested he had headed to California to the gold rush.

Aidan had known better than that, though. He and Jeremiah knew where gold was, right here in Colorado, and there was plenty of it, too. Seeing how people were willing to kill and die for it, they had decided to keep their mouths shut about what they knew. They had seen firsthand how people acted on the trail to and from California when hunger for gold stole their souls from them. A man's best friend could turn on him. Others than just the miners would discover the lode soon enough. Then, a man must be prepared to protect himself or die trying.

That was one of the reasons Aidan kept so many ranch hands around. He had enough work to keep them busy, but he wanted their presence just in case. The laws here were only as good as a man's power to enforce them.

All in all, he still wondered about the mysterious disappearance of Jeremiah. He had heard later his cabin was empty, and the woman and boy had disappeared. Aidan supposed they had gone back to her people.

His thoughts drifted back to the present moment, and he considered he should be home in front of a roaring fire, not out searching for his daughter on a cold day like this. He reached to his collar and tucked in the fabric tighter to seal off the fingers of cold snaking inside. Only Laurie would do something so rash and cause him to be out on such a day.

The air was heavy with the recent storm. He looked up the path Laurie must had taken, and off to the side, he located the dead bear. It was plain what could have happened to his Laurie had something else not gotten to the beast first. Aidan's heart pounded, picturing his precious daughter lying against that tree. Why wouldn't that girl be more cautious? It alarmed him to think of how he could have found her. He would have never gotten over the loss of his only child.

His mounting adrenalin pushed him faster and faster up the steep slope. His horse whinnied at his urging, and the wind whipped the animal's mane sideways. Trees cracked and popped as they swayed around him.

"Laurie!" he called.

"Papa, I'm up here!" Another shout erupted, "And I've got Shadow! I need some help, Papa," she continued.

Aidan breathed with relief to hear his daughter's sweet voice. Then he bellowed in anger, "You're going to need more than help when I get there." His voice was rough with emotion and physical pain. He heard the gruffness, and he pictured how his daughter would respond. Yet, didn't she realize the danger she had put herself in?

Aidan pressed his knee to his mount's side, and he clicked his tongue against the roof of his mouth to urge it on.

LAURIE PLACED HER ram's horn back into her saddlebag. She squeezed her lips tightly together, and her shoulders tensed up. She knew her papa's voice, and his words had carried with them a sternness that she might certainly regret.

Very seldom did she ever truly disobey her papa, for he could be harsh if she didn't do what he said. He might try to soften his rebuke by telling her his reprimands were for her benefit, but that didn't make the punishments any easier to bear.

However, she was someone who knew what she wanted, and this time, surely Papa would understand. She loved him and tried to please him, but he must know how much her horse meant to her. He couldn't punish her for trying to find her Shadow.

She could hear her papa coming up the narrow trail. Apprehensively, she stepped from the mouth of the cave to meet him.

AS SOON AS Aidan laid eyes on his beautiful daughter, all the remnants of his anger melted away.

"Oh, Lassie, you gave your father's heart a scare. Don't ever do this again, Lareowyn Angelle Kerrigan!" His words were full of love, but he spaced her name out in his sternest voice. He dismounted his horse and grabbed his daughter to him.

Laurie hugged her father and whispered softly, "Papa, I'm so sorry, but I had to find Shadow. I couldn't let her be lost. I truly am sorry I disobeyed you. I just wanted to find her before she was lost forever." She looked at him while trying to blink back tears that were threatening to spill down her face.

Aidan stared down at his daughter's watery eyes and felt a tug at his heartstrings. Despite his feelings of warmth for her, his reply was firm. "Now isn't the time to discuss this. We need to get off this mountain before the real blizzard hits. This little break in the weather is just what we needed. Thank the Good Father above for providing us these few hours. Your things, where are they, inside?"

"Yes, Papa, out of the storm."

As her father stooped to step inside the cave, Laurie quickly recovered her thoughts and spoke up. "Papa, there's someone else here, and he's hurt badly. He could be a trapper, or even a horse thief. He had Shadow . . ."

Her voice trailed off as Aidan made quick strides to where the unconscious young man lay. His eyes briefly scanned the area. "Well, I don't see any traps or furs on him, so that right near rules out a trapper. In fact, what's really strange is that I don't even see a gun. Judging by what he doesn't have, I think he may just be a plain horse thief. Good call, girl."

Leaning down to see just what needed to be done, Aidan took a closer look at the young man in the shadows. He just stared for a second, then commanded his daughter with a firm, no nonsense tone.

"Daughter, I need my tinderbox. I can't see too well."

Laurie went to her father's horse and hurriedly brought the small box to him. Aidan took some of the dried branches the brave had collected, along with his own tinder. and started a small fire. Leaning closer, he gave the motionless young man a thorough inspection. Then mumbled to himself, "Well, I'll be . . ."

"What is it, Papa?" Laurie asked, with a puzzled tone.

"Daughter, what the . . . how long has he been unconscious like this?" he asked a little louder, his tone much more subdued. He reached down and touched the stranger's forehead. "Hot, way too hot, and this cave is cold." Before Laurie could remark, Aidan stood and began to give her very firm instructions. "We've got to get him off this mountain and down to the ranch."

LAURIE MADE NO reply. She was puzzled by her father's change in attitude, especially since he had already as good as accused the stranger of being a horse thief. What use would he have for a man who would walk onto his own ranch and take his daughter's horse?

It was one thing for Laurie to feel compassion as if the man were a wounded animal. It was another thing, indeed, for Aidan Kerrigan to do the same.

— 5 —

ARTHUR HENRY STUART stamped his foot angrily and asked again in his most condescending manner, "Where is Miss Lareowyn? I must speak with her. It's of the utmost importance."

The world around him stood out in bright, brittle clarity, and it burned his eyes with acrid reality. He hadn't been by Slim's Saloon or had a drink in days, and he desperately craved the soothing solace alcohol so readily provided. He glared in irritation as he narrowed his eyes into a squint. He hoped that by emphasizing Laurie's given name, he would make an impact on Mrs. Gates, the Kerrigan's housekeeper.

"I'm tellin' you again, sir. She's not 'ere, nor 'er horse. Go down to the barn and check for yourself. She's gone." The rotund housekeeper went back to punching down dough for yeast rolls, ignoring the fuming shape of the man in front of her.

"Gone?" Arthur latched onto that word and threw it back at her. "Her father wouldn't let her go anywhere without a proper escort. She must be here." Arthur countered the housekeeper's assertion rudely, expecting that by raising his voice, he would force what he wanted from her. "I intend to stay here until her whereabouts is made known to me!"

Mrs. Gates cocked her head at him. "You can spend the night, for all I care. Miss Laurie and 'er father aren't 'ere. When they do get back, they'll be expectin' a hot meal, and I intend to see that I 'ave it ready. So, if you will excuse me," she retorted, and went back to her dough.

"Impudent woman," muttered Arthur under his breath, seething with anger at his casual dismissal.

"Bragging' nincompoop," whispered Mrs. Gates, as she continued her dinner preparations. She glanced at him, as he threw himself from her kitchen.

Storming out of the house, Arthur's words tumbled from him, "As soon as I marry Laurie, we're leaving this forlorn country forever!" He kept his words low, but he wouldn't harbor them inside as he let his frustrations bleed from his lips.

The arrogant man threw himself down the porch steps in the direction of the bunkhouse and cabin, and a gust of wind caught his coat and nearly blew it open. He clutched it tighter. It wouldn't do to let the papers he was gripping in the pocket get loose. Never had he been the kind of man who wanted to work for a living, much less do strenuous labor like mining. He always wanted to get rich off others. Now he had finally found a way. He had with him a marriage license as well as a will. He was leaving nothing to fate. He'd let riches slip between his fingers before, and he was taking no chances this time.

The last time he'd been offered the opportunity for riches like this, he'd been only sixteen, a boy, and circumstances had nearly cost him his life. He'd been with his outlaw gang just a short time, and they'd heard rumors and seen a few people at the fort with gold ore. They'd tried bribing people, even threatening them with their lives, and then there was that trapper they'd killed. The gang had been told by one of their spies at Bent's Fort that the trapper came several times a year with a load of furs and several saddlebags filled with gold. Arthur's gang had waited for him to discover he had only furs, that and one small pouch of gold. They had been sure he would have saddlebags of gold on him. The trapper never said a word about where it came from, not even after being tortured. That was almost nine years ago. When the situation had turned sour, Arthur realized he wouldn't be able to enjoy his fortune if he were dead, and he had been forced to let his "friends" go. The gang had only hung around another year or so and then moved on to California, minus those that had died.

Arthur had stayed, trying to find someone who knew about the gold. It had to be somewhere close by. Arthur was sure there was gold somewhere in the vast properties the Kerrigans owned. With gold now in California, people were searching for it everywhere, even in the territory of Colorado. It was just a matter of waiting until more of the precious ore was found. Trappers? Miners? Arthur sneered with contempt. He wouldn't allow anyone to get in his way. Their lives were nothing compared to the riches he intended to obtain. There were even a few "friends" with him who had paid with theirs, that was if he could call anyone in the outlaw gang he had ridden with by the name of friend.

He'd be more careful on this go round, and he would get both the riches and the girl. Still, if things didn't work out, when all was said and done, he would still have her wealth. Life without the girl? There were always more women to be had. Life without riches? That was no life at all, not to Arthur Henry Stuart. He was determined to have it all, and he was certain Laurie was the key to his future happiness. He was keeping a close eye on this one; nothing would prevent him from getting what he wanted now.

"I'll be in control soon; just be patient," he was muttering to himself, when he almost bumped into the stableman, Mr. Gates. Taking no thought of the near mishap, much less apologizing, Arthur blurted, "Gates, where's Laurie?"

Daniel Gates rubbed his forehead. "I don't rightly know, Mr. Stuart," he returned, in his slow and deliberate manner.

Arthur stared in disbelief at the stableman, unwilling to accept his answer. "What do you mean, you don't rightly know? Has everyone gone mad around here?" He ground his foot unconsciously into the soil, and his breath tore in and out of his lungs faster and faster, as he slung his mandate at Gates. "Where is she? I demand to know, and I want the answer this very instant, not five minutes from now, not a week from now, not a month from now. I want to know where she is immediately!"

Arthur felt his face burn with anger, and he squeezed his fist in his coat pocket, no longer caring if he lost his composure. In contrast, Daniel Gates didn't seem bothered in the least. He continued to walk toward the barn, leaving Arthur behind,.

"Don't you walk away from me," Arthur blustered.

The stableman called out, "Well, she ain't in the 'ouse. Ya've already seen to that. An' Miss Laurie's not in the barn, but if ya' don't believe me, ya' can come down and check fer yourself."

As Gates walked away from his questioner, the wind caught his words and quickly carried them away. Arthur could barely make out what he said, but he had heard enough to know he was being rebuffed. He also could see where this hired employee was heading, and he knew he couldn't go there, not and maintain any semblance of what little dignity he might still possess. These were not barn clothes he wore. Arthur wondered just who this cowpoke thought he was dealing with, trying to make him walk in all that mud and muck. No, he'd had enough of those days. He would never do that kind of work again.

At the top of his voice, refusing to go any farther, Arthur screamed above the wind, "I'm still talking to you, and I am NOT going down to the barn. I haven't had my question answered. Where's Laurie?"

Daniel Gates just shrugged his shoulders and kept walking, leaving the angry suitor standing alone in the yard. The frustrated man stood watching in the direction the ranch employee had gone, his jaw trembling in fury. If he could put his hands on his neck, he knew he could make the man tell him the answers he wanted to hear. However, snow began to fall, and the temperature was dropping. Arthur had no choice but to turn around and go back to the house.

Once inside the spacious ranch house, Arthur clomped rudely to the roaring fireplace that was kept burning in the welcoming great room. His slender fingers were like icicles, and he needed to warm up. He rubbed them and held them close to the leaping flames. He hadn't expected this sudden storm and was ill prepared for it. With a certain determination, he guessed he would just stay here until the storm blew over. The Kerrigans certainly couldn't argue with that.

However, that wasn't the issue at hand. Where was Laurie? She couldn't have just disappeared. Arthur couldn't afford to let her roam untracked. She was to be his, and he would intervene quickly if he even suspected another man was attempting to take his place.

One thing that continually frustrated him was her father. What nonsense could they be doing outside on a day like this? Anything a person needed to do or see outside the warm confines of the ranch house could wait with weather like this. For them to have gone out in these conditions, something untoward must be brewing, and Arthur didn't like the thought of that.

It made Arthur nervous thinking about all the things they could be discussing, or even possibly deciding, and there was nothing he could do about it. He knew Aidan didn't like him. The old man had made that clear many times over. He had said nothing directly, but Arthur was sharp enough to tell when he saw the small facial expressions or heard the critical tone in the man's voice.

That wouldn't matter if Arthur could just win Laurie over. It was certain that she was the most attractive woman Arthur had ever seen. From the first time he set eyes on her, Arthur knew she must be his. She'd never had any real suitors because of her young age, as well as the remote location of the ranch. Any single friends of her father were too old to court someone as young as his daughter. Arthur had seen some of them ogling her a time or two when Aidan wasn't looking, but they didn't dare do more. The Kerrigans were too powerful for that.

Courting the old man's daughter hadn't been entirely easy, though. Her father was extremely protective. It had taken Arthur months to gain permission to sit alone in the same room with her. Then, there was always a watchful eye making sure things were proper and circumspect.

Despite her father's reservations, Laurie seemed to like Arthur's conversation, as well as his company. He had taken his time and been very careful. Already, he had brought up vague proposals of marriage to her, just to flesh out her thoughts and emotions on the subject. Laurie hadn't responded affirmatively, just giggled in a girlish sort of way. That was unlike her, being a strong and independent young woman, but she was still a girl, and as far as Arthur knew, girls did giggle.

In Arthur's mind, her response had been a good thing, because she hadn't said no. She just needed a little more time to adjust to the idea, although he couldn't allow too much time. He was ready to get on with it. She was seventeen years of age, and he was already nearing twenty-four. Still, he cautioned himself, he had to prepare her to approach the hitching post just like with any good brood mare.

Before the storm, today had seemed like a good day to ask her in earnest. His plan had been to go for a walk with her outdoors, and he had chosen the meadow with a specific purpose in mind. He had come to the ranch late enough that he would hopefully be forced to stay overnight, as he had done several times before. This would give him more time to be with her.

A key element in his plan was the hope that this time he could persuade her to be intimate with him, once she had agreed to his proposal. They would be engaged once he spoke with her, and that was as good as a marriage ceremony. Arthur knew he could depend on her innocence and love for him to allow him to compromise her. Once Laurie was with child, her father would have no reason to oppose him, and Aidan would agree to a quick marriage. He didn't dare ask her father for her hand first, not and give Aidan a chance to turn him down. All Arthur had to do was convince Laurie. He knew how headstrong she could be, and if she wanted to get married, her father wouldn't be able to convince her otherwise.

Her strong will would convince Aidan to permit the marriage. Then, Arthur would enjoy breaking her spirit after the wedding ceremony.

There was one other reason to rush this plan along. The sooner they married, the quicker he could get to searching for the gold. Inwardly, Arthur smiled. He wouldn't search himself, but he could hire miners. Then he and Laurie could move back East and have a wonderful and rich life. She would be straddled at home with children, lots of them, and he would be free to gamble and drink and do whatever else he wanted. As he stared into the fire, Arthur's mind continued to wander with all the plans he had for his future.

"Well, I see that you're still 'ere."

The housekeeper's words collided into Arthur's thoughts like a tumble of rocks in a landslide. He looked up to see Mrs. Gates approaching the fireplace, and he glowered at her.

"As long as ya' are goin' to be here, ya' can help by keepin' the fire stoked, while I stay busy with finishin' dinner," she pressed onto him, in a very no-nononsense manner. As Arthur opened his mouth to reply, the sound of approaching horses thrummed through the walls.

"Well, it's about time!" Arthur's snappy remark relieved him of any responsibility for the fire, and he was glad for that. He looked at Mrs. Gates, and his words were venomous, "Now, I'll find out what's really been going on around here."

They both turned at a loud shout.

"Open the door!" Aidan Kerrigan's voice thundered through the wooden front door.

Mrs. Gates made quick strides across the room to open the massive, carved wooden slab, and instead of rushing with her to help, Arthur did what he did best. He stood in the place that was safe, warm, and the greatest distance from danger possible. He huddled in front of the fire, and he let the others do all the work.

— 6 —

MRS. GATES' FACE was in shock when she saw what was being unloaded off one of the horses. As she stood holding the door to observe the goings on, she exclaimed loudly that it looked like it could be a dead man.

Aidan had stepped back outside and was helping the poor creature off his horse, while Laurie was helping to support him. At the housekeeper's words, Arthur stepped forward. He looked over in time to see Laurie's arms around the young man, supporting him; and as they came through the door, inexplicable jealously coursed through his blood.

"What's going on here?" Arthur attacked the unacceptable situation. This was something he needed to get under control quickly. The plans he had for this evening hadn't even commenced, and already this stranger, whether injured or ill, was derailing them with full haste.

"Quick! Help Laurie," Aidan called to Arthur. He left no room for the younger man to doubt that he was expected to jump to fulfill the request. Arthur felt he had no choice but to comply with the command given him.

He walked over with some remorse and helped support the young man, letting the youth's arm wrap around his shoulder, as he helped carry him into the house. Together, they placed him on the oversized, horsehair sofa that filled the space in front of the fire. Aidan asked the housekeeper to bring some blankets and a pillow for the unconscious stranger. It took all of them to push the massive, wood-carved sofa closer to the heat.

Aidan and Mrs. Gates tried to get the stranger arranged as comfortably as possible. Aidan instructed Mrs. Gates to prepare some hot water and to get the vinegar and whiskey out. He would also need the sheep lanolin. As Aidan strode off to prepare, Laurie was left alone with Arthur and the stranger. Arthur immediately withdrew from the man, with Aidan no longer there to command him to give his attention to this piece of trash.

"Is this why you were gone all day?" Arthur's voice cut with an acid tone.

She stared at him with querulous eyes. "I headed out to find Little Shadow, and then this disaster of a young man appeared in front of me. I was gripped with the need to help. Anyone would have done the same, and for that reason, your question makes no sense to me."

"And you found your horse, I presume? Bringing home an injured man was just a bonus." Arthur's quick, venomous retort left no doubt that he didn't believe what she told him. His eyes narrowed as his doubts contorted his face. How could Laurie claim she hadn't gone looking for someone to bring home in this horrible storm, a blustering maelstrom that had darkened the sky and then crashed across the world outside?

LAURIE LOOKED AT Arthur, puzzled. She didn't understand why he was being so pointed with her. She hadn't expected him to show up today. If he made plans without her knowledge, she certainly had no idea what those plans could possibly be, and she couldn't order her life by them. All she knew was that she had recovered her horse, and her papa had wanted to help save the horse thief's life. Now Arthur was angry with her for something she knew nothing about.

She took a deep breath. She would put Arthur aside for the time being, for she had too many other things cluttering her mind to worry about his chattering banalities. After all, this day hadn't made sense at all. The stranger knew her horse's name. He had survived a bear attack, and then he had killed the bear. Unexpectedly, her father had come and found them both. Laurie was just grateful to be home and warm. She also needed to change out of her damp clothes. That would surely lift her spirits.

"I'll be back in a minute," she said to Arthur. "I need to dress in something warmer." She glared at the man who seemed determined to become her fiancé, making sure he understood, with her narrowed eyes and firm mouth, that she found his line of questioning disturbing. She turned without looking back and headed up the stairway to her bedroom.

ARTHUR PEERED DOWN at the man who might possibly come between him and his life of ease. He had seen his Laurie holding the stranger in a caring and tender manner, and she had never taken Arthur in her arms. Even if the man had needed help, Mrs. Gates could have assisted him into the house.

The fireplace crackled as a log shifted, the sound magnified in the relative silence of the room. From outside the walls, the wind whistled in fitful bursts. The front door rattled, and Arthur glanced around to see the flames from the fire leap, forcing shadows to jump around him. He didn't appreciate being left alone in the room with this unknown interloper.

He considered the off chance he might know the man, perhaps a gambling acquaintance who'd attracted more than his share of trouble. Sometimes those who gambled and lost didn't appreciate the outcome of the game. Arthur had helped himself to more than one winning player's gains lifted from his warm and freshly dead body. This man just might be one of those unlucky gambling acquaintances, although this person wasn't suffering any retribution of Arthur's. As he leaned down for a closer look by the firelight, his heart stopped, his jaw dropped, and his knees went weak.

His brain cried, "It can't be; that man's dead," as his lips mouthed the words in a silent cry of the impossibility that lay before him. A person doesn't forget the face of the first man he's killed. Yet, as impossible as this had to be, here that very man lay in the Kerrigan fortress, even if he did seem to be barely alive.

Arthur jerked up in surprise as Aidan Kerrigan walked back in.

"DO YOU KNOW this fella?" Aidan had been watching from the other side of the door, and he had carefully noted Arthur's reactions.

"N-n-no, I can't say that I do," Arthur stammered.

However, Aidan could read body language, and in dealing with men over the length of his life, he had become quite good at it. His instincts told him this youth on the sofa was very familiar to Arthur. That meant something wasn't right. The scared, pale look he had noticed when he walked in the room, and the nervous reply Arthur had made to Aidan's innocent question were out of character for the suitor.

"So, you've never seen this man before in your life?" Aidan asked his question slowly, looking straight in the eyes at the man who was clearly attempting to court his daughter.

Arthur regained his composure and cleared his throat, speaking with an uninteresting lift of his eyebrows. "I assure you, Mr. Kerrigan; I've never seen this man before in my life."

His words were spoken a little too blandly for Aidan's comfort. He knew Arthur's reputation as a gambler and card player. He had no doubt about the man's abilities, and this was definitely a poker face.

"Well," the older man started, "I thought maybe you could help us out with information about him. Laurie found him up in the mountains without his horse and wounded from a bear attack. She tried her best to nurse him back to health. You know how sweet she is. She can't turn away a stray no matter how 'ornery it is." Aidan had played a few games in his lifetime, too, and he could match Arthur verbal ace for verbal ace. He carefully studied the look on the man's face. He could tell the turn in the conversation made Arthur even more uncomfortable by the way he tapped his foot and rubbed his hands. Aidan decided to push a little harder.

"By the way, what brought you out on a day like this? It must have been important to want to weather such a storm."

Aidan appeared to be making casual conversation, the words simply inquiring into the activities of a normal day, as if Arthur would naturally have a very good reason for traveling out to the ranch. As he asked the question, he laid down several cloth strips to bind and cover the stranger's back.

ARTHUR GROPED FOR a quick reply. This wasn't the time to reveal his motives, and he hadn't thought to come up with a cover story. With relief, he saw a distraction at the door, and he brightened his face as he nodded at the welcome intrusion. The focus of attention shifted to the young man on the sofa when Mrs. Gates came in with the hot water, and Laurie soon followed in fresh, warm clothes. The bright chattering as the wounds were uncovered and cleansed seemed to divert Aidan's attention.

THE YOUNG BRAVE lay placidly on his side, as he struggled to listen to the voices and noises going on around him. He had been unconscious most of the trip from the cave and had only heard bits and pieces of conversations. From the portions he did hear, he had become even more confused and disoriented.

He wasn't sure where he was or how he had gotten here. At times he couldn't hear his angel's voice, filling him with moments of despair, as the deep tones of men talking about strangers, bears and horses surrounded him. Another voice filled his head, and he hoped, but it wasn't his angel. Maybe he was already dead, and perhaps this was his father's white man's Heaven, the one his father's Holy Book had spoken of. He listened for the sweet voice of the creature he had seen back at the cave. Things would be okay, if only she was here.

"Well, gentlemen. We need to get to tendin' 'im if we're going to save 'im." Mrs. Gates spoke with a booming voice that matched her large size. "Fer all we know, those claws have put some manner of poison in 'im. I can think of no other reason for 'im to be this bad." She clucked her tongue. "'E is in a bad way, men. I don't know if we can pull 'im through, but try to save 'im, we must."

"Oh, I certainly want him saved, Mrs. Gates." Aidan's voice gave no room for options. "He has a lot of unanswered questions to account for, and he cannot die here on my sofa."

"Papa? Shouldn't we get started?"

Finally, Shadow Hawk had located the voice he listened for, the words of his angel. She was here. She hadn't abandoned him, after all. The valiant Indian brave struggled to open his eyes to see her just once more. As he did, the scene around him was a blur, yet his ears directed him to her voice, and there she was. She was indistinct, and he knew she was certainly one of his father's angels. She was standing before a great fire, radiant and glowing.

Then, as he watched her, she slowly came into focus. Her loose hair cascaded around her shoulders. The light from the fire made her tresses glimmer like a luminous waterfall. However, where did this enormous fire come from? Was she protecting him from the Holy Book's death place, from the white man's Hell?

He opened his mouth and struggled to whisper, "Angel," before he slipped back into his tortured delirium.

NO ONE SEEMED to notice but Laurie, who had been watching him closely and thinking about the possibility of him dying right here in the great room, alone and without any family for comfort. Certainly, he couldn't just die after all the work she and Papa had gone through to bring him down from the mountain to save his life. Surely Mrs. Gates and her knowledge of healing could get him through this.

"Well, there's nothin' more we can do fer 'im 'ere. The rest of life's got to be lived, and we better get to it," commanded Mrs. Gates. "Supper'll get cold if'n we don't get a move on." She stood from where she had been with the injured young man on the sofa. "This'n's barely more than a boy. I can see it myself now that 'e's cleaned up a bit."

When Laurie and her father turned to follow the housekeeper to the dining room, a loud voice stopped them in their tracks.

"Surely you jest!" boomed Arthur in shocked surprise. "This man you don't even know is on your sofa. Are you seriously planning to leave him alone in here with no supervision?"

Laurie smiled. "Why, Arthur. You're so concerned for us. You can see he's injured, and severely, too. He's no harm to anyone."

Arthur stood, his mouth agape, "Mr. Kerrigan,

think. You can't be offering hospitality to a total stranger, possibly even a horse thief. He should have been left where he was, or at the very most, thrown in the barn. Why, this could all be a ruse, a set-up to rob you. I've heard of this thing happening."

Arthur continued his complaint, giving perhaps more detail than someone unfamiliar with the specifics of the deed should know. "Once he's in the house, he becomes familiar with the layout and gets to know your routine. Then when he leaves, he tells his friends, and they can come back and raid the entire place later. No, I won't have it. It's too dangerous. I'm sorry for all your hard work, Laurie, but you'll see that I'm looking out after your safety."

ARTHUR RUSHED ON, certain he could force complete compliance. He truly wanted this man dead. If he could get him out of the house, he soon would be, too. He was driven to ensure it was so, and he'd risk the sharpened edge of insult to Aidan's authority to accomplish his new goal. He couldn't believe this stranger looked just like the man he had killed all those years ago. A younger version perhaps, but just the same. That first kill had been burned in Arthur's sixteen-year-old mind, and it had all come back in a rush when he had looked into the face on that sofa.

To aggravate the situation, no longer than the stranger had been here, Laurie seemed to have developed some attachment to him, like a stray puppy. Arthur couldn't let anything except their pending engagement preoccupy Laurie's thoughts.

At one point, he thought he'd heard the stranger say something, but he hadn't quite been able to make it out. Laurie had seemed to know what he'd said. He'd seen the way she had looked at him and compassionately smiled. Those emotions were to be Arthur's, only. He couldn't let anything come between him and his future happiness. This vagabond, no matter who he was, must be eliminated. Arthur felt he had made an excellent argument and could see no reason for anyone to want to save the stranger's life. He stood with a satisfied expression on his face, waiting for the others to come assist the man to the barn.

Aidan Kerrigan had a different opinion.

"Last time I looked, Arthur, my name was still on the deed to this ranch." The words blasted the room in a steely voice. Arthur found himself being glared at by the broad-shouldered rancher. "As long as I own this place, I decide what happens on this side of the door. If you don't like it, there's the outside of the door, and you're welcome to it."

Arthur felt himself burn with humiliation, and his jaw trembled in anger for just a second before regaining a semblance of his poise. "I only meant it as a protection to Miss Laurie, of course. I would never presume otherwise. You know I'm constantly concerned about her safety, being a defenseless female."

Arthur had finished his defense lamely, and he knew it. However, he had spoken the words, and it was too late to believably recant them now. Not only was Laurie's father looking hard at him, but now Laurie was staring a hole through him, too. Arthur recalled how violently she had responded to such allegations about being defenseless in the past.

"That's not exactly what I meant." Arthur made a valiant attempt to backpedal.

Laurie stopped him. "I've never been defenseless, and you of all people should know that. Who shot that mountain rattler on our outing earlier this fall? It was me! So, before you start telling me about strangers and being afraid, you'd better think to whom you're speaking."

With that, Laurie turned to Mrs. Gates and said, "Mrs. Gates, I seem to recall a large splinter in one hand. Shall we remove it before we partake our meal?" She looked at Arthur to make her point. "Let's get started. How can I help?"

Aidan looked on, smiling at this demonstration of strength from his daughter.

Flustered, Arthur stepped back into the shadows. Now, especially, there was no way he was leaving, not until this stranger was gone. And as for Laurie's attitude, there was something to be said for that, also. He'd enjoy breaking this one's spirit once she was his wife, that was for sure, and break it he would. She'd get a real taste of submission in reward for the little number she'd just pulled. No one went against him without feeling his wrath.

His thoughts were halted by a blood-curdling male voice. He turned to see Laurie holding a cloth, ready to staunch the expected flow of blood as Mrs. Gates pulled the deep splinter from the stranger's hand. As it was drawn out, Mrs. Gates applied pressure, and blood and puss oozed out into the basin. Deafening words that Arthur was certain weren't English spilled out of the stranger's mouth. He listened closely to the guttural, anguished sounds and was able to catch a word or two, and in them, he found a language he recognized. The man was speaking in the language of the local Cheyenne tribe. "Help" and "sorry" he had learned from years in the territory, especially at the fort when the Indians traded. This was strange, indeed, that this white man spoke in Cheyenne.

The man he killed those many years ago had been white just like this youth, and he had pleaded for his life in English. Now this youth pleaded in Cheyenne. This was a unique twist in this series of events, and maybe it would be interesting, at that, to discover just what was going on.

— 7 —

I WAS RIGHT all along, thought Aidan to himself.
This is Jeremiah Hawke's son. His mother is Chey-
enne. He just cried out for forgiveness in his native
language, and for his mother and father's help.

Aidan fought a smile of justification in bringing
the young man back to the house. With his parentage
confirmed in Aidan's mind, the big rancher was more
adamant than ever to save his life.

"Laurie, do whatever Mrs. Gates tells you. We've
got to help this young man." Aidan turned to Arthur,
who appeared stunned by the whole scenario.

AS FAR AS Arthur was concerned, something had to
be done.

"You can't possibly want to help him now that

you know he's a probable horse thief and an Indian. You need to get rid of him as soon as possible. You should haul him out of the house and let nature take its course. He'll be dead in a matter of minutes, with the weather like this."

Arthur bit off what he really wanted to say, that no one would condemn the shooting of an Indian horse thief, and he would be glad to offer his own services to complete the deed. With desperation starting to color his actions, Arthur moved toward the injured man.

"Let me help you toss him outside where he belongs."

LAURIE WAS BEWILDERED by the unexpected words that had come out of the stranger's mouth. She had heard Cheyenne spoken on the ranch all her life and could even understand a little of it. She glanced to her father, who seemed not the least bit surprised by this revelation.

As Arthur's remarks soaked in, anger welled up in her at the thought of letting any helpless creature die, much less a human who lay completely defenseless and in a state of delirium, as well. She lashed out at him, wondering how she could have ever considered him a potential suitor.

"How dare you to think such a thing, much less say it!" Her voice shook with the intensity of her emotions, and there was no mistaking at whom the violent thrust of her words was aimed. Her grandfather Kerrigan's fire burned like coals in her eyes as she continued to rip her words from her heart and fling them across the room. "He just might be Indian, but we can't know for sure. All we know is that he can speak a little Cheyenne. You would throw him into the cold for that? We don't know who he is or who might be looking for him. He's sick and needs our help."

Laurie turned her attention back to the injured man who had so recently been stranded in a high, mountain cave, and she leaned over to wipe his brow. He had been found with her horse, but he had also been gravely injured by a bear. In addition, she remembered her papa's reaction to this young man. There was some sort of connection there, although she didn't know what. She would, though. Just give her time.

She spoke softly and reassuringly to the feverish man, "Now, don't be afraid. Everything will be all right. That splinter is out of your hand, and the poison that surrounded it is gone, too. Finally, it can heal. Just lay here and rest. *Nothing's* going to harm you."

Laurie emphasized her intentions with the strongly stressed word, and she jerked her eyes to Arthur. In that one action, her emotions lashed irately across the room, and there could be no room for doubt in what she meant. Who did he think he was?

AIDAN, TOO, WAS angered by the remarks. He was also curious as to why this man who so desperately wanted to become his daughter's suitor was so anxious to see this particular stranger dead. Aidan knew there were folks who didn't like Indians. That was a part of life in this land where the two disparate cultures had clashed for centuries.

However, Aidan had a belief in something much higher than the white man or the Indian. He knew God had created everyone, and they all mattered to Him. Aidan had brought up his daughter to believe in those same principals, and he was proud to see her espouse them in such a confident manner.

Surely, Arthur had better sense than to voice his prejudices, knowing how the Kerrigans believed. Aidan allowed that jealousy could be a factor driving the man to behave is such an irrational manner. He was trying to court his daughter, and while bringing the injured man inside the house, Laurie had hardly spoken to Arthur.

Laurie's actions seemed understandable to Aidan, though. It was simple expediency, a fact of life for anyone who lived in the Colorado territories. In the event of any calamity, personal feelings had to be put aside to deal with matters that involved saving human lives or ranch properties. That didn't mean love and consideration were forgotten. It just meant that life sometimes demanded action that was immediate and sure, and the love was set aside until life allowed it to resurface.

On the other hand, the more he thought about it, he was convinced there was more to this than jealousy. Earlier, he had seen true fear in Arthur's face. The man hadn't known he was being watched, and he had let his raw emotions flood his countenance. It was as if he had seen a ghost.

Something was wrong, and Aidan intended to find out what it was that made Arthur react the way he did. The sick young stranger would have a few questions to answer, as well. Right now, though, the best thing for him was to get bandaged and be allowed to rest.

"Men," Mrs. Gates interrupted. She drew in a deep breath and then released it. "I do believe this 'and is finished. I suppose we might as well do the back while we're here. Supper'll keep. If'n it's too cold by the time we get to it, then it can go back by the fire fer a bit of warmin' up. Come now, and let's get 'im on 'is stomach. That back won't wrap itself."

Aidan stepped forward and reached to help move the injured man, while Arthur sulked quietly from the dimly lit corner.

AS HE WAS moved, the young stranger grimaced in pain. The hands of his benefactors grasped his body, and he endeavored to sit up and concentrate on his surroundings. While his hands flailed, his eyes fluttered opened for a moment as he struggled to focus. He had only one connection with anything familiar in this place, and he knew he had to find her or be lost.

In a fleeting glimpse around the room, he caught sight of her, and he whispered in English, "Angel, do not leave. I need you."

His medicine man's beliefs had never truly been a part of Shadow Hawk's life, and the young man had never found what he had needed in his father's white man's God. However, this day he had seen the truth in the stories that had been read to him. He wondered if the others in the room could see his angel, too, or if she was there for him alone. Shadow Hawk's ragged rasp faded as he closed his eyes again. The agony of his injuries swelled over him once more, but he knew he could not dishonor himself or his people by crying out another time.

It was all he could do to endure the pain, but it was a necessity.

ARTHUR STOOD IN the shadows, deeply disturbed. He had been surprised at the vehemence of Laurie's response, and he could feel his own anger boiling inside. He also knew he couldn't release that anger just yet. The stranger's earlier outburst had obviously been in Cheyenne, and the man had just spoken clearly in English. Was he an Indian or a white man? A trapper was Arthur's most logical guess. Yet, the fluent Cheyenne was too perfect, and that had him puzzled.

Mrs. Gates spoke matter-of-factly. "We've done all we can do. It's up to the good Lord now to decide if'n 'e lives or dies. I do need to get cleaned up and put dinner on the table. I assume there will be three to eat." She looked in the direction of Arthur.

Aidan Kerrigan answered with resignation, "If he

wants to stay, he's welcome. I wouldn't turn anyone out on a night like this. I figure he'll need to spend the night as well."

Her eyes lingering on the man who had tried to turn this boy out into the cold, it was a moment before Mrs. Gates turned her gaze away. It was very clear to everyone in the room who she thought needed to be shown the door.

MRS. GATES FINISHED PICKING up the rags and soiled clothing. Without looking up, Laurie joined her and helped carry the basin of bloody water to be dumped out. She couldn't understand everything that was going on. Her papa didn't seem the least bit concerned about the stranger. That was so out of character for him. He was always so overprotective of her and everything that had to do with the ranch. Now, suddenly he seemed fine with the idea of keeping someone no one had ever seen before ensconced in their home.

Laurie could also see that Arthur didn't care for the stranger. That was also odd, because Arthur said he'd never seen him before and didn't know him. Why did he dislike the stranger so? Another puzzling thing was how the stranger kept calling her Angelle.

AS THE THREE gathered and seated themselves at the table, Aidan Kerrigan bowed his head and asked the blessing. He included kind words for the stranger as well. Afterward, Mrs. Gates began serving the meal. As she placed the plates of food in front of each person, he or she moved aside politely, but the supper was a rather quiet affair. Everyone seemed wrapped up in his or her own thoughts. It was the stranger that was on everyone's mind in some way or the other. Aidan was finding great relief and perhaps even pleasure at knowing this young man was safely within the walls of his home. The pleasure was more immediate to his daughter. She had actually found the young man in his mountain cave, and her instincts were calling out to protect him at all cost, to perhaps even claim him as her own.

Arthur was of two minds as he sat at the table with his host and his daughter. It had already been made abundantly clear to him that his opinions about this young man would not be reciprocated, and for that reason, he was glad he could paint cordiality on his countenance, an expression that wouldn't hinder his plans with Laurie. On the other hand, this man in the other room, a boy, if Mrs. Gates was correct, might have come here with a purpose in mind. If it was truly his father that Arthur had watched being tortured and then had killed, this man might have come for revenge.

Arthur glanced across the table to see Laurie concentrating on her plate of food, and he thought of what else might happen. She might find this new man an attractive alternative as a suitor. She was so young, and she didn't listen to others, especially not to the men in her life. Arthur sensed the oiliness of the new situation, the impossibility of holding onto his plans as long as this man was in the house. He wanted to scream his frustration to those at the table. Just one more day was all he had needed, and this girl would have been his without question.

Only Aidan seemed relaxed and content through the entire affair, and he showed no signs of being perplexed about the household's injured visitor. Finally, when the fruit cobbler was brought out, Aidan spoke aloud to the contingent that had joined together for the meal.

"Once again, Mrs. Gates, you have outdone yourself with this delicious spread. The venison stew was delicious, and the rolls were the lightest I've ever eaten."

"It was nothin' special, just hot food on a cold day. But I'm glad ya' was pleased." The housekeeper beamed with pride, and having expressed her pleasure, she went back to cleaning up the dishes. It was obvious to everyone that her employer's remark had pleased her immensely, and when she thought no one could see as she disappeared back into the kitchen, there was a broad smile on her face.

Aidan smiled and winked at his daughter, tipping his head toward the housekeeper. Laying his napkin on the table, he got up and went to check on the stranger, leaving Laurie alone with Arthur.

"Finally, at last I get some precious moments alone with you, sweet Laurie," Arthur's honeyed voice undulated across the table. He had a smile on his face as if nothing untoward had been said earlier in the great room.

LAURIE STARED AT him. She didn't understand this man at all. What was he saying now? She was exhausted from the day, and she really wanted to go to bed and get some rest. She was in no mood to be wooed by this suitor tonight.

"Really, Arthur. Don't you think we had better retire for the evening? I've had a long day searching for my Shadow. With her being lost, I was able to think of little else, and now I need to let my thoughts go." She rested her elbows on the table and closed her eyes as she sank her chin onto her upraised palms.

Arthur stood, scraping his chair legs on the wooden floor, and he made his way to the empty chair next to her and put his hand around hers.

"Pet, don't you mean stolen?" His voice purred softly. "It's obvious to me this stranger is probably an Indian and, at best, a half-breed and a horse thief. The sooner he's out of here, the better." He paused for effect and, after a moment, finished his thought, "Before anything else is stolen."

He looked at Laurie with greedy eyes, as if she should sink into his arms for safety, calling to her papa to throw the injured man from the sofa and into the storm. That was all it took for her. She stood up pulling her hand from his.

"I don't know who he is, but I do know that Papa has made him welcome, just as he has made you welcome. This is our home, and we invite whom we will. Our guests are none of your business. If you aren't happy with his presence under our roof, then I'm sure you're free to go. So, if you'll excuse me, I bid you good night, Arthur."

With those words, Laurie strode from the room.

AIDAN HAD REMAINED very still as he listened to his daughter's side of the conversation from the great room. He smiled to himself. In his most private moments, he had asked for his daughter to see Arthur as he saw him. It seemed God had heard and answered his prayers. Yes, his little girl would be okay in this world. He had taught her well, and with her Kerrigan iron and a belief in Jehovah God, she would do very well, indeed.

— 8 —

THE NEXT WEEK dragged slowly without much activity, except what centered around Shadow Hawk. The stiff winter winds continued to whistle, and the blowing snow had the ranch at a standstill. Mrs. Gates stayed with the young stranger each evening until a little after midnight. Then Aidan came down and got a report on the youth's condition before he sent her away. He claimed the rest of each night in the great room as his time to watch the twitching, anguished body of the young man. Laurie took the midday shift, often watching the youth wistfully, as if she saw something in him no one else did. Sometimes the youth's delirious voice would moan and mumble in Cheyenne, and other times in English.

As the week wore on, Aidan was puzzled by the

whole situation. The questions sifted through his mind. Why would this young brave be here, stealing a horse from this ranch, especially if he really was Jeremiah Hawke's son? After Jeremiah had disappeared, Aidan had lost track of the entire family, but this young man was a dead ringer for his old friend. That was what really had him thinking. If this was that boy, and Aidan had little doubt of that, he had spent time here years ago.

Something else that concerned him was his daughter's growing infatuation with the man she'd rescued from the mountain cave. Aidan wondered if it was turning into something deeper than simple affection. He had known people to fall in love over less.

As far as that horse he'd been found with, Aidan knew the Cheyenne were known for their horsemanship and their pride in their ownership of their four-legged animals. The tribes owned large herds. Why would he be here without one, forcing him to take one from the Kerrigan stables?

There was one last thing that weighed on Aidan's mind. Where were the young man's parents? Were they both dead? Questions clouded Aidan's mind while his visitor continued to sleep fitfully.

On the seventh day, after numerous sketchy hours when the boy's survival was in doubt, at last he heard a deep sigh from the young man, and his tormented body seemed to finally lay still. Aidan went to him and touched his forehead to find sweat on his brow. He got a damp cloth and wiped his head. The older man smiled. If he was guessing correctly, the fever had broken, and that was a good sign. Maybe this stranger would live to answer his questions after all.

Aidan continued to keep a close watch on him and on the fire as well. The room had to be kept warm for the injured youth's sake. As the fire crackled, he stepped forward and adjusted the wood, and when the flames burned low, another log was pulled from the woodpile and set into the coals to keep the blaze at its best.

The room stayed warm and cozy while the night etched its story across the mountains, and then just before the break of dawn, Aidan heard stirrings upstairs. He smiled to himself. Laurie was just like her mother. She had to know what was going on and then be right in the big middle of things. He knew what she was thinking. This was her stranger, just like with her horse. She needed to be in charge of what happened to him. Only then would she be satisfied with his care and recovery; and that was something Aidan loved about her.

He thanked God every day for his daughter, and as he had done daily for years, he once again prayed for wisdom in raising her alone in this vast wilderness. Without a mother to guide her, she could have turned out wild and uncontrollable. As a tribute to the grace of God, she seemed to be following the right path, always trying to be involved in everything that was good and commendable. She had a great sense of responsibility and continually tried to help in any way she could.

Aidan sat across from the injured stranger, and he chuckled as he thought of those words. Yes, she continually tried to help, even if she did overdo it at times, like taking off to rescue her horse and bringing this young man home with her, and now, spending every waking hour with him, tending to his every need. However, Aidan admitted he would have brought the youth home even if Laurie hadn't wanted to, once he suspected he was Jeremiah Hawke's son.

WITH THIS STRANGER to care for over the past few days, Laurie was awake earlier than her usual time. She hadn't slept well, worrying and praying for the ailing young trapper under their roof. The first question that ran through her mind made her as skittish as a new colt.

"What if he—"

However, she couldn't think about that now. She knew Mrs. Gates had been downstairs, and her father had surely been there, too. He had gone through a few rough days, but they would have let her know if a downturn had occurred. Climbing from her bed, a knot in the pit of her stomach continued to torment her. She had to know how he'd fared through the night.

She quickly dressed and bounded down the stairs, keeping her feet as quiet as possible on the treads to not disturb the household. Despite her efforts, she feared she wasn't really quiet at all. Pausing at the great room entry, she slipped softly inside so as to not disturb anyone sleeping.

Her father looked up. "I thought a herd of buffalo were coming down the stairs. I'm surprised it's only you." His eyes twinkled with his words.

"Oh, Papa, I didn't think that would wake him. Besides, I was in a hurry to get a report on the stranger's health." She looked anxiously at her father and moved to be closer to the man she had helped rescue the week before.

"Well, he had a hard night of it. But, I reckon his fever broke about two or three hours ago, and he's finally getting some rest."

A feeling of relief flushed the young girl's face with warmth. "Oh, I thank God for that. After a week of this, I was so worried, and I prayed for him to get better."

"Well, it looks like the Good Lord heard your prayers and still has a plan for this young man's life on earth," her father answered with a yawn. "I think I'll go up to my room and get a little rest before breakfast. With the remains of this blizzard still hounding us, there won't be much to do once again, today. Do you mind watching over him for a spell?"

"Not at all," Laurie softly whispered. She was already seated next to the young man listening to him breathe, and her eyes were focused on his face. "He does sound better," she said excitedly.

"Shh," her father retorted, a smile softening his rebuke. "You'll wake him up with that loud voice of yours." Aidan yawned again and stretched, and with a wave at his daughter, he headed for the stairs.

Alone in the soft radiance of the firelight, Laurie could examine the stranger, her stranger, without fear of being disturbed. His hair hung across his distinctly chiseled features, and his eyes were tranquilly closed. His coloring had improved, too. The glow of the fading embers against his lightly browned skin gave him the appearance of an ancient, mythical warrior. As he breathed, his chest rose and fell. His arms lay at his side, with his upturned hands in an unconscious position of supplication. It was his face that had her mesmerized, and it seemed to hold her captive.

She tried to guess his age. He couldn't be much older than her, judging by the smooth contours of his jaw. She remembered what Mrs. Gates had said. This morning, even Laurie could see the boy in his face.

This was the first time she had seen him with a completely peaceful expression. The pain he had endured during the week was dulled with his exhaustion. It was good for him to sleep. With the color of his skin, her father must be correct about his fever; surely his temperature was now close to normal.

Laurie stared at the stranger's rich, dark brown tresses. Broad waves flowed through the thick strands. His hair had come unbound when they were cleaning his wounds. It hung in long strands, curling slightly on the ends. She brushed it from his face without thinking, enjoying the silky texture.

She gasped as she felt an iron grip suddenly grasp

her wrist. She immediately dropped the stranger's hair and saw two driving, dark orbs spearing her with intensity. Her response was one of surprise and embarrassment. Even as ill as he was, his strength was alarming.

"I-I-I'm sorry. I didn't mean to wake you," she stammered softly. "I was just pushing your hair from your head, so I could check for a fever. I'm so glad you're feeling better," she continued.

The Cheyenne brave released the pressure of his powerful grip on her wrist, but he still held her hand in his, even as she tried to pull it away from him. He continued his penetrating stare into the depths of her eyes. Then he slowly let his eyes run along her clothing as if unfamiliar with such materials.

Laurie looked at him, embarrassed but saying nothing. She had seen Arthur look at her in a similar way, and it had made her feel dirty. This inspection gave her a different feeling, indeed. Only a few seconds passed, but it seemed like eons to her before he finally spoke.

"Are you not my guardian angel?" he asked roughly. He continued to hold her hand, and as he spoke his words, she felt him squeeze her hand softly, his hand relaxing as his words came to an end. She was taken aback by the question.

Trying to speak without stuttering, she replied in words that were barely above a whisper, "No, no. I'm not a guardian angel. I'm not an angel of any sort, even if it is part of my name. I'm," and she paused, wanting to word her answer carefully, "I'm just a person like you." There was another long silence. He looked perplexed and maybe a little confused, all the while continuing to hold her hand.

Then he inquired again, "You're not taking me to Heaven with you?" He paused for a lengthy moment, and just as the silence started to become interminable, he slowly began another question, "You're not protecting me from the flames of Hell?"

Laurie took a deep breath. She hadn't expected anything like this. It was exciting that he thought of her as his angel, but as for the flames of Hell? She didn't like that at all.

She prompted him, "The flames of Hell?"

His face looked distant for a second, then he added quietly, "I remember I was dying in a cave, and I prayed to my father's God. Then you appeared and said you were taking me with you." He continued to look into her face and waited as if challenging her by the intensity of the look in his eyes, making Laurie even more uncomfortable. After all, she had done that, at least the part about taking him with her. She wasn't sure if she had said exactly that, but that had certainly been her intent.

"Well, uh." Then she relaxed and smiled, "That part is true; I did find you in a cave. And I did help bring you here . . . but don't worry about that right now. You need to rest. You've been here a week, and you're just starting to get better."

The young brave peered at her and gently whispered, "If that's so, then you're the angel I prayed to. The God of the Holy Book must be real, just as my father said."

He closed his eyes and slowly released her hand, and as he gently drifted back to sleep, Laurie sat beside him, barely able to breathe. She was bewildered by all that had just transpired, and questions erupted in her mind. Why did he consider her an angel, more importantly, his angel? How did she feel about someone thinking about her in such a way? And, why had her heart jumped into her throat when he touched her? Where were all these emotions coming from, and from someone she had known less than a week? He had been able to speak even less time than that.

"I must be feeling relief that he's going to live," she murmured aloud, as she reached one hand and rubbed the skin on her arm where he had touched it. "I've been so nervous about my horse, and then I had to worry about him. I haven't been able to think clearly since he's been here. That must be why I'm reacting this way."

She heard the back door open, and she realized it was time for Mrs. Gates to prepare breakfast. She sprang to her feet and headed toward the kitchen. She needed something to get her mind off their visitor. Her injured young man was sleeping peacefully, and being busy would be the best detraction for her right now. She would offer to help with the meal preparation.

"Well, good mornin' Lassie," Mrs. Gates rumbled, with an early-morning and indulgent smile. "I see you're up and chipper. I hope it's good news comin' from that young man in there. Either way, we've got work to do."

Mrs. Gates' words tumbled from her as she made her way into the kitchen carrying the foaming milk bucket. She winked at Laurie as she stood in the doorway between the kitchen and the dining room.

"Oh, it is good news! It's the best news," cried Laurie. "The trapper's going to live. Papa said his fever broke early this morning, and when I came downstairs, the stranger woke up and spoke for a moment." She paused in her excitement, remembering what the stranger had shared with her. More subdued, she continued, "And I wish to help with breakfast, too."

"Well, praise be to God! That is a good report, both about the boy and ya' helpin' me with breakfast. I'll be sure to tell Daniel the part about the boy. 'E was a mite worried about the stranger and all. I was a bit worried last night myself. When I left 'im with yer Pa, 'e could have gone either way."

Even as Mrs. Gates finished her last statement, her hands were already in motion getting out the eggs and venison sausage for breakfast. She had prepared the biscuit dough before leaving the previous night, and all Laurie had to do was roll and cut them out before putting them on the massive wood-burning kitchen stove. They would be ready by the time the sausage and eggs had finished frying.

Reaching for the coffee, Mrs. Gates added, "I

reckon there'll still be three for breakfast in the dinin' room, even though I haven't seen or 'eard you speak of yer feller yet. Seems strange, 'im bein' here the week, but can't say as I'm surprised, deep as the snow is."

"Arthur's not my feller," Laurie replied hotly. "He's just someone who's a friend of mine . . . like you. He's just a friend—nothing more." Laurie felt her face warm at her brusque reply, but there was a new surge of denial making her adamant about her lack of sentiment toward Arthur.

"Well, at least I don't make moon eyes at ya' like 'e does," Mrs. Gates interjected, smiling wryly, and taking no offense at Laurie's attitude. "I know my girl, and I'm glad to hear yer remarks. I'm sure there's no love lost between Mr. Kerrigan and that Arthur feller, either." She smiled even more broadly as the girl retorted to the old woman's words.

"Ooh, you know what I mean," Laurie shot back. Her hands reached for the rolling pin to press out the second batch of dough, and she threw her arms into the activity with a vengeance. She was perturbed at the idea of Arthur as her suitor. Yet, until the past week, she really hadn't thought much about their relationship. He came to see her, but she had never tried to lead him into thinking there was anything more than a friendship. She knew he wanted more, and she felt a tug at her conscience as she admitted she had never given him a reason not to pursue her.

She began to reflect over the past few months of

their friendship. There wasn't a lot to consider, because most of their conversations had centered on Arthur and his opinion of things as well as his plans for her future. He had talked vaguely concerning marriage, and she had just laughed about it. She enjoyed his company to a point. He was always quick to compliment her, and he usually behaved as a western gentleman. She enjoyed the flattery, even if sometimes she knew it was false.

What made her feel so differently toward him now? They had never talked about each other's personal beliefs and convictions, but she knew he wasn't a Christian from things he had said. However, a lot of the hands and men her father knew weren't Christians. That had never really bothered her about Arthur until now. She couldn't fathom why it suddenly concerned her so much today. Her thoughts were cut short by Mrs. Gates as she tapped her on the arm.

"Yes?" Laurie attempted to smile as she shifted from her reverie.

"Dear, are ya' with us this mornin'?" Mrs. Gates smiled at her. "Ya' aren't respondin' to me at all."

"Oh, I'm sorry. What did you say?" Laurie's face warmed, with no idea what Mrs. Gates was talking about. "Did you ask me something?"

The older woman just reached an arm around Laurie's shoulder and gave her a quick hug. "Ya', my dear, are more worn out than ya' know. I can tell that. Ya' are concerned and all that. The boy will be fine, and ya' might think about going back to bed once breakfast is over. Nothin' will be happenin' today, my girl, not with this wind still ragin' on the other side of these stout walls. I'm just prayin' for the sun, so's I can feel my hands and feet begin to thaw."

Laurie just looked around, aware that she still didn't know what Mrs. Gates had wanted from her. "Your question, Mrs. Gates? What was it, if you don't mind me asking."

"Oh, my dear," Mrs. Gates laughed, setting the milk jar down on the counter and covering it with netting. "I was just asking if'n ya' was goin' to pour the milk or just stare at it. Look, though. I've already done it for ya'." She turned away to call to the rest of the house, "Breakfast is hot. Come now if'n ya' want it."

Laurie smiled. With Mrs. Gates, nothing was out of control. All she needed to do was to take charge of things herself, and there were days when Laurie was glad to let her do just that.

This was one of them, too.

— 9 —

BREAKFAST WAS ALWAYS a noisy event. Mrs. Gates' rule was to cook once for everybody, family and ranch hands alike. She wasn't cooking in two places, either. The ranch hands came and carried their part to the bunkhouse. Over the past week, they'd battled the snow and wind, and Mrs. Gates knew to give them warning when it was about ready. She rang the bell when she started the gravy, and the workers knew it was almost time. For them, it was pretty much the same fare every day. She had a heaping platter of fried eggs, a plate piled high with venison and pork sausage, biscuits, and of course lots of thick, peppery gravy.

On Sundays, she made flapjacks from batter she prepared the day before. Mrs. Gates didn't believe in working too hard on the Lord's Day, so the hands made their own coffee. They kept a pot boiling all day. It was a black, steamy brew that the cowboys had told Laurie would put hair on her tongue. She tried it once when she was only seven to see if it really would, in fact, put hair on her tongue. It was so hot and strong, she couldn't even swallow it. It had burned her entire mouth. That must be the secret, she had decided back then. If you could get it down, maybe then it would put hair on your tongue.

Today, the ranch hands were already standing at the back door waiting to carry the food across the snowy stretch back to the warm bunkhouse. They were particularly ready today for the hot breakfast Mrs. Gates had prepared. All of them had already been up working for hours in the aftermath of the blizzard with only coffee to go on. On a frosty day like this, they were anxious to get out of the snow. With three platters of food and a big steaming crock bowl of gravy, they never went back to their labor hungry. Mrs. Gates made sure of that.

Once the ranch hands and her husband were supplied with food, Mrs. Gates started on the house breakfast. Many times, it was the same cooking she had done for the rest of the ranch. Other times she served bacon, ham, poached eggs, French toast, fried pork chops, and apple or cherry pie. Besides gravy, there was always fresh butter with a special home-made jelly or jam for the biscuits or toast. Mrs. Gates would offer up a large pitcher of fresh milk and steaming cups of coffee with heavy cream to cool it down.

Today they would eat what the ranch hands had, with wild plum jelly to go along with the hot, fresh biscuits. That suited Laurie just fine. She was pouring the cream when she heard Papa coming down the stairs. As a creature of habit, he was used to being up at daybreak. Arising at dawn no matter what time he turned in was one of his well-known traits. Today was no different. The smells from the stove had apparently awakened him, even though he had only been asleep two hours. As Aidan approached the kitchen, Mrs. Gates greeted him with a jovial laugh. Then his daughter gave him a kiss on the cheek as he headed for the coffee.

He poured himself a cup of coffee, drawing in the steaming aroma, and he turned to face the women.

"Well, I'm glad to see you two in such good spirits. I guess it's the stranger's wellbeing that's brought it about. I certainly don't think it's the continued cold weather," he ended dryly.

"Yes, it's good the poor young man is goin' to survive. Thank God for that," Mrs. Gates replied, as she carried the mouth-watering biscuits to the dining table.

"I'm certain he'll be hungry when he wakes." Laurie's eyes followed the steaming plate, as Mrs. Gates marched by, barely able to resist snatching one for a bite.

"Eat it while it's hot," the housekeeper called out

in her usual banter. Those who were joining around the table for breakfast knew she was true to form as she set the biscuits out. "Don't let my good food go to waste," she finished. Laurie and her father made their way to the dining room, while Mrs. Gates began filling the plates. "I guess there will only be the two of ya' this mornin'," she observed.

Setting his cup on the table, Aidan Kerrigan replied, "Well, that's his choice, and it's his loss, as well. We don't stand on ceremony here in the Kerrigan household. Arthur's been here a week, long enough to learn our schedule, and he can eat a cold breakfast if he wishes to sleep in until the day's half done."

Up until that moment, Laurie had dismissed the errant suitor from her mind, thinking only about the health of the young brave in the next room and the exchange they had experienced earlier. She wasn't thrilled to have Arthur's name brought back up, but at least he was sleeping in, and she could enjoy her breakfast with her father in peace.

Laurie nodded at her father in agreement. She concurred with his remarks about Arthur not showing up, and she was amused to see a twinkle in his eyes. Together, they sat at the table and bowed their heads while her father offered thanks to God for the providence of the day.

Once the prayer had ended, Laurie reached for biscuits and gravy, hurrying through her breakfast, cutting her food quickly, and taking large bites. Aidan glanced at her as he ate, noting the obvious pace at which she downed her food. He pressed his napkin to the corner of his mouth, and as he laid it on the table beside his half-full plate, he crumpled it into a ball and cleared his throat. He waited until Laurie slowed and looked at him.

"Yes, Papa?" She held a corner of biscuit halfway to her mouth, and a dab of gravy fell to her plate.

"I know there's a young man in the other room, and he will need some looking after. I assume from your frenetic clearing of your plate that you hope to get the privilege."

"I'm sorry, Papa." Laurie felt herself warm with embarrassment, but she did manage to slow down. Her last few bites were larger than she would normally take, but she chewed slowly, and her plate was finally emptied. After she finished clearing the last of the gravy from her dishes, she excused herself and stood to head toward the great room.

With a smile, Aidan called out, "Oh, I guess I was right. I thought all this rush might be for Shadow, since you haven't gotten to ride her the past week, but then you'd be heading through the kitchen, if you were on the way to the barn."

Laurie stopped and turned, realizing how obvious it must be that she had bolted her meal. Her father's plate still half full.

"Papa, don't embarrass me." She glanced toward the great room and to the staircase, grateful no one had overheard. At her tender age, embarrassment in an unfamiliar romantic encounter could still bring a flush and warm cheeks, and she pressed her hands to her face and dropped her eyes. She understood from people's remarks that she could be headstrong and independent minded, but she was still seventeen. She simply wished to offer her aid to the injured man.

Her father smiled when he saw the blush on her cheeks. "I can tell deeper concerns when I see them."

"What? Oh, don't be silly, Papa. I thought I heard something in the other room, and I was just going to check on—"

"How sweet of you, Laurie," interrupted a male voice from the stairwell, as Arthur made his entrance into the dining room.

THE PREVIOUS WEEK hadn't gone well. Arthur had thought that by being firm, he would get the results he desired, and instead, he had come very near to driving a wedge between his future and himself.

He had decided during the night that he could catch more flies with honey than he could with vinegar, and that meant he would have to be more careful with his words. He'd rethought his battle plan, and yes, this was a war to him, an all-out assault on the Kerrigan fortune. He planned to win every battle along the way. On the night of the stranger's arrival, he had lost his battle to have the intruder in the great room thrown from the premises. But, it was a new day, and he had made more purposeful plans as he lay in bed late into the night. He had gone over every detail, and things would go his direction from now on.

"I presume you were waiting on me. I usually don't arise this early, but I know how prompt Mrs. Gates is with breakfast, so I awoke and came right down. I thought, perhaps, I'd be the first one up, but I see I was mistaken. It's nice to hear you were coming to check on me." Arthur looked approvingly at Laurie as he finished in his newly sweet and placating tone.

Aidan looked with amusement at the man stepping down from the stairs. "So, both men and demons deign to arise from their slumber when they smell the temptations of Mrs. Gates' cooking." He grinned at his black humor as he glanced at his daughter.

"Laurie," Arthur smoothly ignored the spicy gibe and spoke to his hoped-for fiancée, "surely you haven't eaten, yet. Come sit by me and tell me all about your injured savage in the other room." He smiled as he sat next to Laurie's customary place at the table. Turning to smile an unctuous and bright greeting to her father, he continued, "I suppose your daughter's new interest made it through another night without incident. However, I think it may all be for naught when we find out the truth about him."

Arthur flashed another one of his winning grins.

ONCE AGAIN LAURIE felt her protective instincts bristle within her. She jerked her head around and shot back, "As a matter of fact, Arthur, I *have* already eaten. I was up early this morning, so Papa could get some rest before breakfast. He stayed up most of the night with the stranger. I'm heading to check on his well-being on my way out to check on my Shadow. So, if you will excuse me," she finished hotly, and she started for the great room.

Arthur was left with no choice but to sit and eat breakfast with Aidan, who was decidedly taking his time, apparently enjoying every minute of both the excellent breakfast and the spicy tête-à-tête between his daughter and Arthur.

IN THE OTHER room, the young brave had been listening to bits and pieces of the conversation since Aidan had arrived downstairs. He, too, had been awakened by visions of his angel and the savory smells of breakfast, an aroma he remembered from his childhood. His father had always enjoyed fried eggs and venison sausage. The memories and pleasant odor caused Shadow Hawk's stomach to rumble from hunger.

Then he heard his name mentioned.

He thought his name being discussed by these white men was very strange, indeed. How could they possibly know him? No one had asked his name, and he hadn't told anyone. Only a guardian angel could already know a person's name without being told beforehand. Shadow Hawk remembered that the beautiful young woman had said she wasn't one, but he still wasn't thoroughly convinced. How could anyone that lovely be from this place where only men lived? Shadow Hawk was lost in his thoughts of the angel, when suddenly he felt her near him. Even before he opened his eyes, he knew she was there, staring down at him.

"Are you well?"

The whisper that floated to Shadow Hawk's ears was so quiet he was certain no one else could have possibly heard it. Opening his eyes, he looked into her face as if trying to discover who she really was, human or angel. It was as if he was looking at someone he had known for a very long time, and the certainty of it made his heart pound. Finally, he broke the silence.

"How do you know my name?" he asked, his voice barely audible.

LAURIE WAS CAUGHT off-guard by the question. She didn't know him, and that was the point. He was someone fresh and new in her life, and he had been there for her to rescue. She had to think a minute before she could reply.

"I-I don't know you, not really," she stammered, feeling very warm and a little nervous under his constant gaze. "If fact, I don't know you at all. You were on the mountain, and I had gone to find my horse. When I found her, I found you, also."

"I heard you say my name when talking in the other room. How do you know it?" Shadow Hawk pressed her insistently for an answer in his soft, Indian way.

"I don't know your name, and we haven't been introduced. However, you have seemed to know my Christian name. It's Angelle." She smiled, "My complete name is Lareowyn Angelle Kerrigan. My papa calls me Laurie. Now, how have I called you by your name?"

The young brave blinked his eyes several times and looked away, with a puzzled expression.

"What's the matter?" He seemed upset, and Laurie had no idea what she'd said.

He murmured, "This name of Laurie is like the name my father once called my mother. She was known as Lari. It surely must be a common name among the white man."

"My name Lareowyn means Lover of Horses in the Scottish language. Little did my parents know how true that would turn out to be! If it hadn't been for my horse, you might not have been found."

"Your name is Angel, but also Lover of Horses, and Lari, like my mother." He kept his gaze from her, and Laurie felt herself getting warm again. She was a little self-conscious, too, and finally unable to stand the awkward silence any longer, she blurted out, "What's your name, if you don't mind me asking?"

"Yes, what is your name? If, in fact, you'll be telling us the truth."

Laurie turned to see Arthur step in just in time to interrupt her question. She jerked up in shocked surprise. She hadn't realized anyone was listening to their discourse.

"I didn't mean to alarm you, my dear. I was just

coming to check on the stranger, myself. After a week of your care, I'm certain he must be fully recovered. I'm so glad you have such a helpful nature." Arthur's words smoothly flowed from his throat, like warm butter over a stack of hot hoecakes.

Laurie looked at Arthur in astonishment. He had become some sort of two-headed snake in the past week. Just moments ago, he had been degrading the poor man, and now he was coming to check on his health. She felt it was odd, even for Arthur. She just shook her head as she wondered how she could have ever let him spend time with her, especially discussing a possible future with her at his side.

There was one thing she didn't have to wonder about, though. Until the past week, she had never really thought about Arthur's motives. Now it was like a curtain had been lifted, and she could see him for what he was. She didn't like the view, either. He had always been charming, if a little tactless at times, or so she had thought. Now she felt she was beginning to see the true Arthur, a rude and obnoxious person only interested in himself. What had she ever seen in him before?

Then she felt a twinge of guilt. She was a Christian. Maybe she was being too judgmental. With a flash of guilt, she knew there was no maybe about it. She *was* being judgmental, and God wouldn't approve. After all, she wasn't perfect, herself.

Allowing herself to retrace her concerns, she recalled that even Arthur had never been rude like this before. In the past, he had generally been polite enough, maybe even boring at times, always talking about getting rich and moving back East. She had told him on more than one occasion that she was never leaving this part of the country. She loved the mountains, the trees, and even the winters. But he would go on about how much she would love Boston and New York, and he seemed to ignore her plainly stated concerns, rambling on about moving away. It had never really mattered to her, because she didn't plan on leaving. This place was her home. Arthur could certainly go those places if he wanted, but she wouldn't be going with him.

"Are you listening to me?" Arthur's words broke into her thoughts.

Laurie turned to see he was speaking to her, and his frown from the previous evening had returned to his face.

"I'm sorry, Arthur. You were talking to me?"

Arthur snorted in frustration, but he smoothed his expression. "Yes, my dear. Surely the weather must be clearing after a week of this atrocious cold, and I thought I would sit with the young man while you went for your morning ride. There's no reason for both of us to be tied to this burden of caring for him. I can remain here in the great room while you enjoy your daily frolic." Arthur began to walk around the room, and as he did, he ran a hand across the back of the sofa. "I know how much your morning jaunt means to you. You were willing to risk life and limb for the sake of your horse. That was very commendable of you, Laurie. Dress warmly and have an enjoyable ride, and I shall be waiting for you upon your return." He flashed her an engaging smile as he finished.

Weather clearing? She could hear the wind outside. Arthur's remarks were strange, but it was more like the men she was familiar with. Maybe she had been a little rushed in her earlier assessment of him. After all, he had always been a gentleman in her presence, and he seemed to continually look out for her best interests. He had never done anything she was aware of that would intentionally harm her or her family.

With her reassessment, Laurie began to see the way it must be. She had been overly tired the past week, in addition to being upset over Shadow. The stress of the days had worn her patience thin. She had overreacted to some of the comments Arthur had made. His words hadn't been an attack on the man in front of the fire, or even at her. He had truly been concerned about her safety.

And shouldn't she be generous if he'd overreacted, in any case? Who wouldn't on such a climatic and tense occasion? It was just a big misunderstanding on both their parts, and it was a relief to have the old Arthur back. She understood everything, now; she had rescued this strange man, and that was why she was so wishy-washy in her feelings.

Laurie turned to face the fire, and she rubbed her

arms, soaking in the warmth of the flames. There had been too much going on in the past days, and the stress had certainly been there. A ride would do her good, at that. Thinking of Shadow, she felt her mood brighten. That was what she needed. It would help her sort out her feelings. She couldn't understand why the stranger made her feel the way she did, why she was so drawn to him, but soothing Arthur's bruised ego could do no one any harm.

She turned from the fire to face him with a smile on her face.

"Why, thank you, Arthur. That's very sweet of you. With the cold outside, I won't be gone long. It won't be good for the animals to be out long in this weather, either, so I'll also keep that in mind. If you need any help, Mrs. Gates is in the kitchen, and Papa will be around someplace. He can't do too much because of the weather."

Laurie reached for her coat and scarf.

She shouted over her shoulder as she exited the house toward the barn, "I'll be back soon!"

WITH LAURIE'S ATTENTION shifting to her beloved Shadow, she left a smoldering young man lying on the sofa, thinking dark thoughts concerning Arthur.

— 10 —

AIDAN FINISHED HIS cup of coffee, and he slowly
set the mug on the table. He, of course, had been listening to the entire conversation from the other room.
It had him puzzled, too. Things weren't adding up.
Arthur was behaving as a different man today. What
was he trying to pull?

Aidan moved his coffee cup absently from spot to
spot on the table as he mulled over the scene. One
thing was for sure, Arthur was somehow tied to Jeremiah's son. He knew him or something about him.
No man turns as white as fresh fallen snow and shows
such fear without something behind it.

"Well, I see our patient is recovering somewhat,"
drawled Aidan as he stepped into the great room, pay-
ing particular attention to Arthur's intent scrutiny of

the sleeping stranger. The man's actions just doubled Aidan's determination to know the final answers here. He cleared his throat when Arthur didn't answer immediately.

Arthur jerked as if startled out of a deep concentration. Then he looked over and replied, "Yes, he does seem better than when he was brought in last week. I thought for certain he wouldn't make it until the first morning, but I see I misjudged his stamina."

"Despite some of our efforts to ensure otherwise." Aidan drilled his eyes into the other man.

Arthur ducked his head, cleared his throat, and walked over to the fireplace. "I'm glad Laurie is out of the room, so that we can talk plainly. I didn't want to give her cause to be upset after all that's happened over the last few days."

"What's on your mind?" Aidan calmly moved closer to the fire. His words were those of a gentleman, but his adrenalin was already flooding him with readiness. After all, Arthur had been very adamant the first evening in his intentions about the stranger. Aidan knew he intended to brook no nonsense from this man, no matter how flowery his words sounded.

"We both know that this man is a horse thief. Why else would he have had Laurie's horse? In addition, he's more than likely an Indian masquerading as a white man."

The smirk on his face showed Aidan he considered his pronouncement one that the older man probably wouldn't have arrived at without his help.

"You have a point, I'm sure." Aidan reached for a poker, and he shifted a log in the fire. He turned his head to look at the younger man. "You may get on with it without the melodrama."

Arthur paused for a moment, and after a bit, he continued dramatically, "What I want to know is why you're keeping him here, in your own house. Why would you put your daughter's life in danger?" Arthur shuddered dramatically and looked at Aidan as if for clarification.

The big rancher stared at the younger man as if to size him up. The ranch owner chose his words carefully, but he intended to make no bones about his meaning. "The Good Book says we are to help our brothers in need."

"Surely you jest." Arthur's mock look of horror, intended to show total confusion at Aidan's actions, was transparent. He even raised his hands in the air as if pleading for help. "You couldn't possibly think of this man as a brother, knowing he stole your only daughter's beloved horse. Why, Mr. Kerrigan, to allow such a man in your home is almost unthinkable, and yet here he is under your roof, a horse thief, and God knows what else he's done. I'm truly taken aback, and I'm surprised at your revealing character, sir. I wouldn't have thought you would put your daughter at risk like this. Who knows what this man is capable of?" Arthur closed his brief performance with a dramatic flourish and stepped away from the fire.

"Well done, Arthur. I see you're truly an accomplished actor." Aidan's dry comment was accompanied by a rueful grin.

Arthur turned with a look of shocked surprise on his countenance. "I assure you, sir, this is no act. I've only your daughter's best interest at heart." His emotional rebuttal was quick and forceful. "I'm wounded that you'd think I didn't have Laurie's well-being always paramount in my thoughts and actions."

Aidan kept his composure, all the while wanting to expose Arthur for the fraud he was. The older man's eyes narrowed as he rallied in a scathing reply.

"To answer your questions and lay your burdens at ease, I assure you I plan to keep a close guard on anyone who enters my home. I have them watched so that I know where they go, with whom they go, what they do while they are gone, and when they return. I wouldn't dream of putting my daughter in danger. Should someone ever threaten to do so, they would have seen their last sunrise on the morning of the day they tried to harm or cause discomfort to her in any way. An eye for an eye, a tooth for a tooth."

ARTHUR COULD SENSE the implied threat and felt it was directed more at him than the stranger. That made him even more guarded than he had been the past week. He had always felt that if Aidan surmised anything amiss, he would no longer allow him to court his daughter. He would have already called him out and exposed him, and that meant the old man was

— 123 —

probably bluffing.

With that determination made, confidence rushed into Arthur's blood, and his composure again relaxed. He knew this might be a game of poker, but he was superior at sleight of hand. The ranch owner wouldn't get the upper deck. Arthur could beat him at his own game.

Arthur took in a deep breath and continued, not at all perturbed, but reassured by his own vain self-confidence.

"I totally agree that you should scrutinize anyone coming near your daughter," he persisted smugly. "I'm relieved to know this is being done for her safety. I've had my apprehensions in the past, but now I can rest easy knowing our Laurie is receiving the utmost protection and guidance. Thank you so much, Mr. Kerrigan, for enlightening me with this information. And should you ever need my assistance, I will be happy to make inquiries for you regarding any person you should like to investigate."

The young man on the sofa tried to move, and they turned their attention away from one another and noticed he was awake.

"Well, I'm glad to see you're much improved over yesterday." Aidan's countenance lit up as he began to speak. "Here, boy. Let me help you sit. You'll never get any better if you just remain there all day."

He knelt at Shadow Hawk's side to give him a hand, wrapping one arm underneath his shoulder to take away some of the strain. Even so, the injured young man winced at the shifting of his wounds underneath the bandages. Immediately, he caught himself, and all signs of pain disappeared from his face. In the Cheyenne way, he refused to deface his tribe in this white man's home.

Arthur's eyes caught the older man's sudden change in expression, and he thought it strange that he would seem so relieved to see the stranger awake after staying with him so many nights. He also noticed just how quickly he had moved to assist the injured lad. Arthur was certain something was churning under the surface that he didn't know about. Either that or the Kerrigans knew this stranger and hadn't divulged that. At least they must know something about him. The possibilities were nerve wracking, for if they knew this young man, were they aware of the man his gang of friends had killed those many years ago? Nothing could be more troubling to Arthur. After all, Arthur was attempting to woo Aidan's daughter, and with a nefarious scheme in mind, as well. If his past came back to haunt him, all could be lost.

Aidan interrupted Arthur's thoughts as he spoke to the young man on the sofa in an excited tone.

"I'm sure you must be hungry, seeing you haven't eaten more than liquids in several days. Let me see what Mrs. Gates has out in the kitchen." Aidan headed out of the great room with a broad grin.

IN ADDITION TO Aidan's behavior confusing Arthur, it was also confusing to the young brave, who wasn't sure where he was and who the people were who were helping him.

Then, there was the man in the room with him. A foreboding look of dislike was written all over him. Any Cheyenne could easily see that, even in a white man. Shadow Hawk's eyes flickered past the things in the room as he tried to use the tracking skills he had practiced as a Cheyenne brave. He wasn't outdoors, and he was seeing things and actions that were unfamiliar to him. However, noticing small signs and movements was the same, no matter where he was. He just had to work harder at it in these unfamiliar surroundings. The young man was combing his mind for answers when Aidan appeared shortly with a steaming cup of coffee, holding it out to Shadow Hawk.

"This will get you warmed up until Mrs. Gates heats up some of her venison stew from last night. She made up some extra just in case we had additional company. I'm glad it worked out. You eat some of her cooking and you'll feel better in no time at all." Aidan smiled and glanced boldly at Arthur. "It seems as though this young man will make a full recovery."

Shadow Hawk was very thirsty, and not having eaten solid food in some time, he was very cold, even in front of the fire. He reached for the proffered cup carefully, seeing the steam coming off the top. The brew smelled bitter and very strong, perhaps even stronger than the concoction his medicine man had made him drink when he was approaching manhood.

The steam told him it would be very hot, and he was glad to see a handle on the side. The handle would be cooler than the rest of the container. Shadow Hawk wasn't totally unfamiliar with the white man's drinking cups. He just never used them, not since returning to the tribe after his father's abandonment.

He wrapped his free hand as closely as he dared around the outside of the bowl, desiring the heat from the cup against his skin. He wasn't sure he would like the flavor, but he would drink it down. It would be a bad omen to refuse a gift from these strangers.

Shadow Hawk started to speak, but Aidan interrupted him and said, "Save your strength. You'll need it for later. Let's wait until you get some good grub in you before you start talking. I know you understand what I'm saying, because I heard you talking in both English and Cheyenne. You've got a lot of explaining to do, and I'll be asking you some very pointed questions."

The young brave had many questions to ask, and he was uncertain why he wasn't allowed to do so. The two men were confusing to him, he wasn't sure where he was and who the people were who were here helping him, but he knew his angel. He had prayed for her to come to him, but she had left earlier on her horse. He didn't know when she would return, either.

Before Arthur could comment about the strangeness of not letting the young man speak, Aidan added, "Arthur, why don't you go find Laurie? I'm sure she'll be thrilled with the news. She'll want to be here when this young man shares his story with us."

With that, Aidan went to the oversized, hand-carved hall tree and handed Arthur his coat and scarf. Once again, Arthur had no choice but to oblige. He bundled up as Mrs. Gates came in with a warm bowl of broth crowded with venison and vegetables.

"Hurry along, now, Arthur. Laurie wouldn't want to miss a thing," Aidan said, as he escorted Arthur to the door.

AS SOON AS the door was closed, Aidan went straight over to the young man. He pulled up a chair close to him.

"While you let that cool, I'd like to introduce myself. I'm Aidan Kerrigan, owner of this ranch, and from all accounts, you must be the son of Jeremiah Hawke." Aidan watched as the young man inhaled a startled breath, which verified what he had guessed all along.

"You look just like your pa, except you're a little darker; you'd get that from your ma. I met her a couple of times. I also remembered he had a son just a little older than my Laurie. Once I looked at your face in the light, I knew it had to be you.

"Your father was the best friend a man could have. I thought it strange that his son would steal a horse. If you'd asked for one, I would have gladly given it to you.

"I also wonder why you're traipsing about without protection in a snowstorm. I know that you have better skills than to do that. What happened?"

Aidan kept his attention squarely on Shadow Hawk, who sat very still and said nothing. From the expression on the young man's face, he was still recovering from the shocked surprise of the revelation that this man knew so much about him.

"I want to ask a whole lot more, but our time is limited before my daughter comes rushing in. So, these questions can wait, because there are other unanswered questions I have about your father's mysterious disappearance. Jeremiah was a trusted friend of mine, and I valued his friendship. He would have never left this part of the country without stopping by the ranch and saying good-bye. This much I know. Do you have any idea what happened to your pa?"

The young brave looked at the man sitting across from him, with disbelief turning his face pale. Aidan surmised the young man remembered their family had known one another, or else he wouldn't have traveled this distance to abscond with one of the ranch's horses. It was as obvious that he didn't realize Jeremiah and Aidan had been close friends. The young brave might be frightened of his immediate future, as he was at the ranch's mercy, but he needed to trust him. After all, they had taken care of him so far, and they could have left him in the cave or even killed him if they had wanted.

The youth's face shifted, as if a choice had been made, and he began to speak.

"My father went to the fort to trade furs and never

returned. He abandoned my mother and me. We had no choice but to return to my mother's people. We have lived with them all this time. I have changed. I am now a Cheyenne Wolf Soldier." He finished his words with his teeth clenched in anger and a sneer on his lips. "I am no longer the son of a white man."

Aidan was surprised by the tone of the young man's voice. He never thought he'd hear this from the son of Jeremiah. Even though he could see the hurt beyond the sneer, he couldn't believe it. The thought was ridiculous to even suggest Jeremiah Hawke would ever desert his family. That just wasn't in him, not the man Aidan knew, and here this pitiful young man thought he had been abandoned by his father.

The Jeremiah Aidan knew had loved his wife and son. He had worried for them when he was gone for more than a few days. Nothing was adding up, just like it hadn't added up those years ago when he went missing.

"The Jeremiah Hawke I befriended loved his family and worked hard trapping to provide for them. He wanted to create a good life for his wife and son. He was saving to build a house where his trapper's cabin was located. Jeremiah was planning on starting to build the spring he disappeared. He had come over to ask for my help with the plans and the construction."

Aidan looked at the young man, waiting for a response.

Shadow Hawk's face hardened. "I see my father told you the same untruths he told me. He must not have thought as much of your friendship as you thought he did," smirked the young brave.

Aidan made no comment. He was still puzzled by the strength of the anger from this son of his friend. How could this boy think his father would ever lie to him? Jeremiah was one of the most honest and peace-loving men he had ever come across. This would have to be gotten to the bottom of, and soon.

There was silence between them as Aidan digested this new information.

The aroma of the food began to have its effect on the young man, and Shadow Hawk could wait no longer for the stew to cool. He reached to the bowl and dipped a finger inside, looking up as he did so to see an eating utensil hovering between his face and the stew. He grabbed the spoon, and without hesitation, he began to ladle the food into his mouth.

He hadn't eaten for days, and he closed his eyes, absorbing the flavor and warmth.

Aidan watched the young man as he inhaled the food. The boy would feel well enough to ride and fulfill his destiny soon, if he continued to eat well. He could see his old friend there, and he could see Jeremiah's Indian wife there, also. However, he couldn't see why he would be so filled with the anger. Surely, even if something had happened to his father, his mother would have told him of his father's strength, courage, and kindness toward others. Nothing this boy was describing sounded like the friend he had known all those years ago.

As he walked across the room to a comfortable chair, Aidan pondered what he'd observed. There was another thing that kept interweaving itself through this boy's stories. In Aidan's mind, something ominous linked Arthur to each and every strand of events as the boy told them. That was also puzzling. Aidan would eventually pin it down, too. The looks Arthur had given him, and the desire to let the youth die in the cold were essential elements of the mystery.

Aidan stood from his chair, and he observed the flames of the fire as they jumped and crackled. It would be warmer closer up, but where he stood, the air was cool. It was the chill of the snow and the strength of the wind just outside the thick log walls. They infiltrated even the massive exterior of the hulking stronghold during winter's worst. He would be more comfortable nearer the flames. However, this gave him room to think without having to be involved in a conversation.

He was resigned to the fact that everyone in this household would soon know all about this young man's words. However, he was anxious that Arthur not know them all. It seemed important to shield some of the facts. Something about Arthur's strange behavior toward the young man was tied to the words the boy was saying, and it made him think he needed to keep this mystery about Jeremiah Hawke quiet. He didn't want anyone knowing the identity of the young man, yet. If the youth's father had come to a sad demise, the same could happen to his son. Aidan wanted

Arthur to play his hand, if he did indeed have one to play. The man would return soon with Laurie, and Aidan needed some plausible story for the events that had occurred since Arthur's absence. He needed it quickly, too. Turning from the fire and focusing on the young stranger, Aidan began the conversation in a different vein.

"What I don't want is for you to be telling anyone about yourself. Arthur, my daughter's suitor, is strangely alarmed by either you or something about you. Perhaps it might even be someone who looks similar to you. When he first glanced at you, his face went white as a sheet. Do you recall ever seeing him before?"

Shadow Hawk looked up from his food, with puzzlement on his face. "What is a suitor?" he asked innocently.

"That would be the young man trying to win her hand in marriage." Aidan laughed.

SHADOW HAWK STOPPED eating to let those words sink in. Laurie, his angel, would soon marry that other, much-disliked man. He felt an uncomfortable twinge in his stomach. That couldn't happen; she was an angel, his angel.

Aidan stepped back to the young man, pulling the chair up to sit directly in front of him. He began to question him again, pushing him as he tried to put all the information together. "Have you ever seen Arthur before?"

Shadow Hawk shook his head no and went back to the food. Even though it was mainly broth and had been satisfying before, now it tasted differently. He could feel the distinction in his mouth, with a flavor like that of old leather. His angel was getting married, and the thought of her being with any other man made him nauseous. He could feel his stomach churning, and his head began to spin.

His face must have reflected his emotions, because Aidan said, "Hey there, boy, you need to take it easy on the food. You haven't eaten in a while. Also, there was poison in you that we squeezed from your hand. Eating too fast or eating too much can make you sick. Hand me that bowl, and you lie back down. You're not ready to conquer the world, not just yet. You'll need to stay here a few more days and recuperate. No sense rushing things. However, I'd like to know your name; it will be easier than calling you young man."

Shadow Hawk blindly offered him the bowl and then began to reply, "My name is Shadow of the Ha—"

Before he could finish, Aidan interrupted, startling the young man once again. "Of course, I remember. You were named after your Pa because you favored him so. Shadow Hawk it was, but all I ever heard him call you was Shadow."

That was true; it was what his father called him. Shadow. His Shadow. More painful memories emerged, flooding his mind like a swollen river in the springtime, rushing everywhere with surging abandonment. Memories he had carefully tried to erase and forget were surfacing again, wanting to remind him of his past. His father would often say, "Where's my Shadow? I need him. I'm going fishing." When he called, Shadow would drop whatever he was doing and go running to his pa, ready for an adventure. Then, how was he repaid for his devotion? With the ultimate betrayal, abandonment. The bitterness rose in him like gall.

Shadow Hawk looked up to see the man scrutinizing him expectantly. It was as if he was waiting on an answer Shadow Hawk was expected to give. Shadow Hawk hadn't even heard what he had asked. He had been too busy nursing his memories of hurt and anger.

"What did you ask? I didn't hear you."

"I asked if it would be acceptable if we called you Shad, which would be short for Shadow. I don't want anyone snooping around trying to figure out who you are or why you're here. If anyone asks, I'm telling them you're a new hired hand."

Shadow Hawk felt the same way about one thing this man had said. The fewer people who knew him, the fewer who would be suspicious of him or his actions. It would also be good to have a place to hide, and if he were here working on the ranch, what better place could he want?

"Yes, I approve of the name Shad," he said slowly, trying it out for the first time. What Shadow Hawk thought was very different, though. *That will be a good name to use among the white man when I go to search for my father and get my revenge.*

"Good, and you can call me Aidan, like the rest of my friends. I do believe you found that horse and were bringing her home when that bear got hold of you, right?" He gave Shadow Hawk a wink and finished with a warning, "There's no sense in letting the whole world know our business. Let's just let that story stand, and then we can settle up later."

Shadow Hawk looked at the man who had given him the perfect lie to prepare for his revenge. This man who thought he was being generous to Shadow Hawk didn't need to know what Shadow Hawk's true intent was. With a deep breath, the young brave nodded in agreement.

"Good, boy. Shad. Now, you lie back down, there, and finish resting. From the looks I saw on your face, I'd say you're not as well as you let on."

SHADOW HAWK GAVE him a silent nod and lay back down. With a full stomach and a warming body, it was only minutes before his eyes closed, and he was back asleep.

— 11 —

IT HAD ONLY been a short forty-five minutes since Aidan had left the room to let Shadow Hawk get some much-needed rest, when Laurie came in with Arthur, her cheeks rosy from the cold and laughing at a humorous story he had just shared. The young brave jerked awake, and he glanced around, momentarily disoriented. Through the open shutters, he could see that the sun had finally broken through the dark clouds, and to him, Laurie's face was a vision of loveliness. She glowed from the sunlight that had burnished her skin as she stepped into the house. Spending time on Little Shadow must have invigorated her spirit, and the crispness of the blizzard-laced air had surely cleared her lungs. She appeared bright and fresh, as if there was nothing she would criticize about her world.

Even Arthur seemed charming and personable. He was in top form for Laurie, and he was putting on his best show. He was doing everything right, so his dream for his future wouldn't be lost.

However, his time alone hadn't been the peaceful respite Shadow Hawk had needed. He was troubled by thoughts of his father as Aidan had described him. Shadow Hawk did remember the man the rancher described, and he was the one Shadow Hawk had worshiped as a child. Then he had gone, and Shadow Hawk's world had dissolved into an Indian campground where he was a second-class citizen, no more than a half-breed.

Even more disturbing to the young brave was his angel. In his father's Holy Book, angels were from a place called Heaven. How could she be marrying a human? She was an angel, she had come to rescue him from the cave, and she had known his name. His preoccupation with seeking revenge against his father had faded with his thoughts of Laurie. He could hear her soft voice and feel her gentle touch, even when she was gone. She belonged to him, for he had prayed for her to come. God had answered his prayer and sent her to rescue him.

Somehow, Shadow Hawk knew, his angel had been made into a human, and he also wrestled with the knowledge she was to marry this hated man. His mind had been wrestling with confusion earlier when he heard the kitchen door open and her voice had preceded her into the room. He resisted the urge to call out to her; instead, he stilled his body and withdrew into himself, practicing the Cheyenne way, listening to the chatter of the cheerful couple. The Cheyenne people were strong, and he wouldn't disgrace himself. He would be the white man he must be, so that he could accomplish his mission, but he would also be the Cheyenne that gave him his strength.

LAURIE PEELED OFF her heavy coat and handed it to Arthur as she stepped into the great room. She looked around, her eyes sparkling, and then she saw the injured man. Arthur's attempted distractions were forgotten as she hurried to the young warrior's side, leaving her suddenly disgruntled suitor to hang up their coats and wraps.

"Oh, you're awake. I'm so glad. You must be getting better. Did you get anything to eat?" She looked up to see Arthur had moved to the back of the sofa, and he was obviously not happy to see his girl fawning over the intruder. She looked at him pointedly and then glanced back to Shadow Hawk, speaking gently, "I'll go find you something."

"Laurie, my dear, he's clearly doing fine," Arthur began, when Laurie froze and held up her hand for him to stop.

"Remember whose house this is, Arthur. My father's. This young man is his guest, and I will see that he's cared for."

"As you will." Arthur let out a heavy sigh.

Laurie rushed headlong toward the kitchen. Stepping inside, she called to the housekeeper, "Mrs. Gates, pardon me. Do you know if the stranger has eaten anything? He must be starved by now." She shifted to the counter to lift a heavy cloth, and she opened a pot of stew that was simmering over the fire. "Venison?" She smiled at the thought of how much their guest would enjoy that.

"Dearie, your pa has already seen to Shad. 'E was restin' until ya' and that beau of yours came in, but I am pleased to know ya' are concerned about 'im." Mrs. Gates' hands were occupied with her preparations for dinner, but she rolled her eyes at Laurie to make sure she got the older woman's point.

"Shad, is that his name? Are you sure? How do you know?" queried Laurie, feeling a little miffed that Mrs. Gates knew his name, yet she didn't.

Mrs. Gates chortled to herself, "Your pa up and asked 'im 'is name, and even offered 'im a job fer the favor he did ya'."

"What favor did he do me?" questioned Laurie, baffled by the housekeeper. Laurie had found the man, and it seemed to her, she had done *him* a favor instead.

"Why, 'e found your horse and was bringin' 'er to the ranch when 'e got attacked by that bear," Mrs. Gates asserted, as she continued with the noon meal. Mrs. Gates was one of those talented people who could carry on a conversation and work at the same time. She was cutting slices of cold ham and thick wedges of bread. Some cheese would be laid out along with glasses of milk or coffee. "There are still some apples in the cellar and dried cherries, if'n anyone wants somethin' sweet," she added. "Perhaps, dear, ya' could get me a platter full. But I'll be reminding ya', dinner during the week's never meant to be a big affair, just something to hold the ranch hands 'til supper. I already put the beans and pork fatback on to cook for the evenin' meal, so that's what we'll have. All I need to do later is stir up the cornbread. "

Laurie was still focused on their guest, and she questioned the housekeeper again, "The stranger was doing *what*?"

"Why, ya' heard me, dearie. That boy, 'e was returning your 'orse. That was what your Papa told me, anyways." Mrs. Gates reached out with the massive knife, and she pulled it through the ham once again, causing a bright pink slab of meat with strikingly uniform dimensions to fall to the side. "Just returnin' your 'orse. What a good man! Imagine that, and in this weather, too. Ya' was a lucky girl. Anyone else, and they'd just 'ave taken that horse, beautiful as she is."

Laurie shook her head. Everyone in this house was nuts. Her Papa seemed to know all about this stranger, now known as Shad, while she still knew nothing, except his name. Shad was almost like part of a name, a nickname. Shadrach. That could be his full name, she guessed. His real name. Shadrach something. And even that information had come from the housekeeper.

Well, she had a few questions of her own, and she strode from the kitchen toward the great room.

ARTHUR HAD WORKED on his demeanor since returning to the house, and he was determined to put his best foot forward. He hadn't been able to clearly hear the conversation coming from the kitchen, so was unsure what Laurie and Mrs. Gates had discussed, but when Laurie entered the room, he hoped she was in his corner once again. When they returned from outside, she had seen the intruder, and she had changed the heft of the reins. Arthur had felt her begin moving away from him again, and he didn't want his hard work undone.

Now, the look on her face as she returned from the kitchen added a new layer of worry to his concerns. He sensed all was not well, and he had to find his firm footing in her good graces once more.

"Is something wrong, my pet?" he cooed at her.

Laurie tensed up and her eyes narrowed, and he knew the pet name was a poor choice. She wouldn't want to be called pet names by anyone, especially not with her aggravation with whatever happened in the kitchen.

"YES, SOMETHING'S WRONG," Laurie burst out. "Everybody seems to know what's going on but me. For just once I'd like to be aware of what's happening in my own home, especially before the housekeeper does."

"Well, you'll have to hang around the house more often and not go gallivanting across the countryside," came her father's booming voice, as he approached from the staircase.

Laurie spun on one foot, caught off guard by her father's presence.

"Papa, you're going outside? I can see you've changed your boots."

"Very observant, Daughter. When things happen around here, we can't say, 'Oh, don't let that happen until Laurie gets home.' Things happen when they do. Besides, what is it you missed? Also, whose fault is it you've missed whatever it is? I told Arthur to go get you, all because I knew you'd want to hear what Shad had to say. You certainly can't blame me that you took a leisurely ride on your steed."

Hearing her papa say Shadow Hawk's name again only increased Laurie's frustration. She should have been told his name first. She found him, after all. And why didn't Arthur tell her to come straightway to the house, she wondered.

"Arthur!" She stamped her foot. He had only mentioned her father's request a few minutes before they returned, and only after spending some time outside. She glared her frustration his direction. He could be so insensitive. Charming? Yes, if he chose. Then, he would do something like this, and she couldn't stand him.

ARTHUR VOLUNTEERED, "I could see how much you've missed your morning rides, Laurie, and I didn't think a few minutes pleasure would hurt anything. I'm sorry if that's the cause of any unhappiness. It certainly wasn't my intention to keep you from enjoying time with your houseguest." He truly made an effort to appear contrite, and he was pleased when Laurie reddened with embarrassment at the scene she had caused over the stranger.

"Oh, I suppose I have seemed a little short about this. It's just that I thought I would, well, you know, since I found him and all, that I would, well, get to know who he is first." Laurie began faltering as she spoke, and she turned a deeper shade of red. She let out a vanquished sigh.

Aidan stepped to his daughter and took her hand. "What you mean to say is you feel about him like everything else around here, that he belongs to you. It's your horse, your house, your ranch, and now, your stranger." Her father smiled with affection as he gazed into her youthful face.

"OH, PAPA," LAURIE said, feeling her face burn, and certain she was turning an ever deeper and more intense shade of red. "It's not just that. I don't know how to say it, but, but, I guess . . . I don't know what it is." She was still embarrassed with the awkwardness of the whole ordeal. Her papa was looking at her, almost laughing, while Arthur was glaring at her in a more disapproving manner.

Worst of all was the intense stare Shad was giving her. The pain in his expression was clearly not from any physical act of injury. He seemed hurt, as if he carried an emotional ache, one coming from somewhere deep inside. She wondered what had happened in the brief hour she was away. She stepped up to her papa, grabbed his arm, and looked up at him with a distraught need for information that must be written on her face.

"Papa, what happened while I was out riding?"

"Shad and I got to know each other a little better, isn't that right, son?" He nodded toward the young brave. Aidan reached to pat his daughter's arm, letting her know he cared about her concerns, but that there was really nothing untoward going on. Things were as they should be, and she shouldn't be concerned.

"Yes," Shadow Hawk replied to Aidan's question. His eyes remained riveted on Laurie. She noticed his look, and she warmed once again with embarrassment. Shadow Hawk continued, "Aidan and I have had a short conversation."

"Arthur, is there a problem?" Aidan called to him with a teasing tone, as though laughing.

Laurie turned to see Arthur frowning, as though insulted or bothered by something recently said. His muttered reply surprised her.

"Yes, you actually called this horse thief your son. You've never referred to me in such a manner, though you've known me for quite some time. The fondness with which you've addressed this man is inexcusable." Arthur's pressed his lips together. and his brows drew together in a knot. Then, he must have realized what he was doing and self-consciously smoothed his features.

"Arthur, are you feeling well? You seemed to feel a pang, and I think perhaps this weather is doing you ill." Laurie smiled at him, but she didn't step to him, and he just waved her question away.

THIS WASN'T THE way Arthur had planned for this situation to go. What was most intolerable was the way in which the stranger had addressed Mr. Kerrigan.

Never had Arthur ever been offered the opportunity to call Laurie's papa anything but the more formal Mr. Kerrigan. Now, here was this half-breed horse thief calling him the ever-so-casual Aidan, with not so much as a by-your-leave. This couldn't be believed! How could he take such liberty, and with Mr. Kerrigan smiling the whole time? Arthur found the whole scene incredulous.

Either unaware or not caring what his daughter's suitor thought, Aidan filled in the story smoothly, his comments directed to everyone in the room, but most intently at Arthur.

"It seems I knew this young man from some years back. However, in the shape he was in, I couldn't be sure. He had worked with my ranch hands for only a short time, and then he left due to a family matter.

He's returned, looking for work again."

Arthur raised an eyebrow at the revelation. The intruder was very young, and he hadn't been at the ranch since Arthur had courted Laurie. He turned to Aidan to question him, but the man preempted his query by continuing his revelation.

"I can always use a dependable and trustworthy hand. Why, when he saw Laurie's horse, he knew it had to belong to the ranch and was headed this way with her. That was precisely when he caught up with that bear. It's a good thing my sweet Laurie Angel came along when she did." Aidan flashed a smile at his daughter.

At the name Angel, Shadow Hawk winced ever so slightly. No one else in the room noticed the motion, and it would have gone undetected, even by Arthur, had he not seen Laurie watching Shadow Hawk intently. She seemed to be interested in everything there was to observe about the dark-eyed, soft-spoken warrior.

"How convenient for all of us," Arthur remarked sourly.

This was the way it was going to be. The horse-thief, or whatever he was, was here to stay. This couldn't be good, not for Arthur's future. He would have to act fast if he wanted to protect his assets, and that meant Laurie and the Kerrigan holdings. He needed time to plan and to think clearly. He couldn't stay here indefinitely trying to build a blockade against this intruder, Shad. He needed to get back toward the settlement. Besides, it had been too many days, and he hadn't had one drink of alcohol. He was starting to feel the effects of the deprivation. He knew, because he was more on edge than usual. This turn in events hadn't helped his nerves, either. The Kerrigans didn't drink and only kept a bottle around for medicinal purposes. Medicinal! That was a word Arthur was warming to. He could use a little "medicine" right about then. It would soothe him, and he needed to clear his mind to come up with a plan to get Laurie out of her father's clutches and away from this Shad character. Only with this Shad out of the picture would he be free to enjoy himself in the lifestyle he thought he truly deserved. So, number one on his list must be to get rid of the half-breed. It was time to move out of this house until he had his new plans up and running.

His brain churning with all he needed to do, Arthur excused himself from the rest of the day. "I'm sure you all have a lot to consider, and I'll just be in the way. I believe that with the sun now out and the blizzard past, I shall take my leave."

A look of relief peppered the expressions of each person in the room, further irritating Arthur. No one was sorry to see him go. So, he thought, having him here had put a strain on a usually relaxed household. He guessed his absence would help put back some semblance of order to the estate. So be it. One day, the estate would be his, and he would order it to his liking.

Stepping closer to Laurie, Arthur murmured, "I always enjoy our precious Laurie's company and treasure the time we are together."

He took her hand and brought it quickly to his lips. He brushed across it ever so lightly. Laurie immediately pulled her hand back in barely concealed disdain.

LAURIE WAS FAMILIAR with the gesture. It was supposed to be a gentleman's way of greeting and exiting. However, she had never enjoyed those types of mannerisms from Arthur, or any other man, for that matter. Without thinking, she let her eyes flick to Shadow Hawk's face, and she wasn't surprised to see fury smoldering in the coal black orbs buried beneath his brows. This new addition to their household certainly seemed capable of a wide range of unexpectedly intense emotions. She recognized irritation when she saw it, and it was clear he didn't like what had just taken place. However, she was unsure if the irritation was at her, or if it was aimed at the man who had just taken her hand and brushed it against his lips.

Seemingly unaware of what was going on outside of his own actions, Arthur wasn't dissuaded by Laurie's gesture of displeasure, and he droned on.

"However, I do want to get back before sundown, and it will take a little longer traveling through the snow and slush. I shan't stay for lunch. I wouldn't want to burden this gracious family any longer, as I feel I have imposed enough. Thank you so much for your generous hospitality," gushed the suitor, as he started for his coat and wrap.

"A man's gotta do what a man's gotta do," boomed Aidan, as he stood up to escort Arthur to the door, making sure he didn't forget anything that might encourage him a speedy return. Reaching her hand to her mouth so her reaction remained unseen, Laurie grinned at her father's remark.

"ABSOLUTELY! I'M GLAD we both agree." Arthur's parting words evaporated into the frigid air as he headed for the barn stables, his brain already calculating, trying to contrive a plan to get rid of that half-breed once and for all.

— 12 —

THE SORENESS IN Shadow Hawk's hand had slowly diminished to just a nuisance, and his back was
healing nicely. It was his knee that still caused him a
great deal of discomfort. He had been up and around
the Kerrigan's home for five days; and living in their
expansive household involved a pattern he was finally
getting used to.

His angel would come down every morning before breakfast, before her morning ride, to change the
bandage on his back. She would talk softly, reassuring him she wouldn't hurt him as she washed it and
put on a fresh dressing. He would silently endure the
torment of her proximity, knowing she was betrothed
to another.

He could never reach out to her, only ask himself

why his angel would save his life and care for his wounds, when she belonged to another man?

Shadow Hawk questioned his loyalties every day. He had grown up for many years with the white man's God from the Holy Book, and then he had spent many years since learning of the Indian spirits, the gods that ruled the Cheyenne world. He had come to accept the medicine man and the things he taught, at least until that day in the cave. Then, his father's stories had come flowing back, and he had remembered the angels.

Now, his Holy Book angel was to be someone else's. What manner of god would do that to a person? Shadow Hawk's father had told him that God was full of love for everyone. But, he realized he had been told that by his father, a white man, who was a liar, just like all white men. Shadow Hawk knew that should tell him the truth. If his white man father had lied about how much he cared for Shadow Hawk and his mother, he had probably lied about the God of the Holy Book, too.

Each day he spent at the Kerrigan estate, Shadow Hawk started with a new resolve. He would be the Cheyenne warrior, the scout that could travel through life unobserved, and the hunter that would take his prey where he would. He would be the tribal chieftain that showed his strength by his severe manners, and he would never give in to the pressures of emotions. Then he would see Laurie, and all his good intentions would melt into a pool of muddled hopelessness.

There were also the glances of confusion she gave him. Sometimes he saw tears welling up in her beautiful, turquoise eyes. Never had he felt so helpless or desperate, not even when the bear attacked him. He would recover from that. It was easy compared to what he was going through now. If it had been a matter of a hunting expedition, he would have killed a feast for the tribe without question. Or, if he had been challenged to swim in the swiftest of rivers, he would have fought against the waters without hesitation.

Instead, his angel had changed that. He wanted to be close to her, to spend time in her presence, and that alarmed him. He could feel his vulnerability every time she stepped into the room. He felt protective and wanted to defend her forever.

Never had he felt such strong emotions for a woman, even the most beautiful of the girls in his Cheyenne tribe.

LAURIE HAD FELT a change in the Kerrigan's houseguest since the day she first rode Shadow after returning home. Her father had gotten better acquainted with Shad, although she wasn't sure what their conversation had been about. All she knew was he no longer spoke of her as being his angel. He never offered conversation, and when she asked a question, his answers were either cryptic, or he ignored her altogether.

His apathetic attitude toward her made her sensitive and depressed. They emboldened her to try even harder to be pleasant to see if he would respond to her. Instead, the harder she tried, the angrier and more verbally abusive he became, and she would feel the urge to rush away just to keep from bursting into a shower of tears in front of him.

She couldn't understand why she valued his approval so badly. All she knew was that she had to see him every day. Regardless of what he said to drive her away, she needed to be near him. His rejection was making her crazy. She didn't know how much longer she could stand it without completely falling to pieces.

SEAN AIDAN KERRIGAN had been watching Jeremiah's son, and he had a few troubling issues of his own. He could see the sparks flying whenever the two young people thought they were alone. Watching, he could see nothing his Laurie was doing to cause Shad's constant anger. However, Shad must be saying words to cause Laurie to go racing out of the room and up the stairs in tears. He had hoped they would become friends, but it didn't seem it was working out that way. They seemed able to tolerate very little of one another.

When he asked Mrs. Gates about it, she just smiled and said, "Who knows about two people in love? Every couple is different. They must find it out fer themselves. Neither one of them seems to know it yet, but it's written on both their faces."

The remark took Aidan by complete surprise.

Love? Friendship between the two, yes, was something he had hoped for. He hadn't expected love, and he wondered what Mrs. Gates could see that he couldn't.

However, the more he observed the two of them together, the more he came to sense that love must be what was building. His daughter would be eighteen this year, and he knew Shad was only a little older, two or three years at the most. Aidan and Laurie's mother had been about their age when they fell in love, but Aidan wasn't prepared for this. He wasn't ready to lose his Laurie, even though he knew it would happen someday whether he was ready or not. Just to think of it was very sobering.

SHADOW HAWK WANTED to recover as quickly as possible, so he could leave the emotionally charged environment that had embroiled him. The young brave realized he couldn't suffer much more of his sweet angel's presence so near him without reacting in some serious way. Then, all would be lost, and she would hate him forever. He didn't think he could walk the path of his life alone if she truly despised him.

On this morning, after Laurie had changed his bandage in stoic silence, Shadow Hawk softly spoke.

"I want to ride with you today."

LAURIE'S HEART FLOATED to the clouds. This was what she had hoped for, prayed for, even. Was she sure she had heard him correctly?

"Shad, are you sure? Do you think your knee will be able to take the strain? I don't want you to do anything that will hurt you," she told him gently.

TO SHADOW HAWK, her voice sounded like the sweetest honey from a honeycomb. For a moment, he silently basked in the thought of her concern for him and the tenderness of her presence at his side. Her voice was so comforting, he would never tire of hearing it. It only made him want more, although he knew it was more of something he couldn't have. That thought jarred him back into the cold reality of things as they were.

"I want to ride. No harm will come to my knee." With that, he shrugged off her concern and slowly stood up, being careful to keep his balance. He couldn't let Laurie see how fragile his knee was. There was some pain as he stood, but nothing he couldn't take without a complaint.

LAURIE GAVE HIM a wounded glance and replied, "I understand, Shad. If that's what you wish, I'll ask Daniel to get your horse ready."

She was still pleased. Even if he didn't enjoy her company, he would still be riding with her. Just that caused the hurt she had felt earlier to vanish, while her heart leaped with excitement. She would be alone with him doing something that was the substance of life to her. The thrill of being with him was worth the short wait that it would take for Daniel to get a proper mount ready.

She pondered once again the reason for his abrupt change in attitude from worshipful supplicant to tense adversary. She hoped it was no more than being enclosed in this house that had him constantly on edge. Once he was outside on a horse, hopefully some common ground could be found, and perhaps they could become something more than enemies. She smiled in anticipation.

SEEING A SMILE brighten Laurie's face caused Shadow Hawk's resolve to soften. That's all he wanted, to please her forever. Knowing he was responsible for some small happiness in her filled him with a flush of satisfaction.

Yesterday he had made himself strong in the realization that he would never want another woman. This one must be his. He thought it might even be the white man thing called love, but he had no experience in that. He had only his mother and his white man father, and he knew what had come of that. However, as much as he reasoned with himself and tried to deny it, he was certain something had begun to bind them together, at least on his part. It could only be this love.

He had also come to the overwhelming and repulsive revelation that she was everything he didn't want. She was a white man's daughter, she was betrothed to another man, and her family was wealthy in land once belonging to his people. All these qualities were things he should despise.

None of that seemed to matter to his emotions. From the instant he had seen her in the cave, he was smitten. He had tried to brush it off as a symptom of having been near death and of her being an angel. Over the last week, he had argued with himself to decide the reasonableness of the matter. Maybe it was the fantasy of the moment that had blended with a hallucination, one that had happened in his thoughts only. Regardless, he became emotionally intoxicated with his angel. He was disappointed, yes, and relieved when he found out she was only human. That had been the deciding point. Once he had accepted that she was no angel, he realized he could truly be allowed to care for her.

That was why he also knew he had to leave soon. He couldn't trust his feelings. He couldn't care for her so intensely without letting it slip out in some way. The sooner he could handle a horse, the quicker he'd be gone.

It was of paramount importance to him, now.

AIDAN HAD HEARD Shad telling Laurie he wanted to go for a ride. He knew the young man was still not in any condition to leave. He wanted to make sure that wasn't Shad's intention. A small discussion over his expectation with the boy was certainly in order.

Aidan stepped down the stairs and into the great room, stopping near the fire that still burned heartily in the massive, stone fireplace. He rested one foot on a dwindling pile of cut firewood to the side, waiting until the two children gave him their full attention.

"Shad, how's that knee of yours?" Aidan inquired politely, all the while noticing how he favored the one, putting his weight only slightly on it when he tried to walk.

"Papa, he wants to go for a ride." Laurie seemed to glow with pleasure.

"I'm sure he's missed the outdoors, as I would, if I were stove up indoors on a beautiful day like this. The weather's certainly changed for the better. Let's get the young man outside and see how he's doing."

Together, they gave the brave the small assistances he needed to locate his leather footwear and clothing warm enough to embrace the chill outside the thick log walls. Soon, he was prepared, and Laurie headed through the kitchen to request the horses be readied for a ride. Aidan studied the young man as he walked toward the front window and observed the scene outside. In the distance, the mountains shot up from behind towering trees, and the sky was a clear blue with faint clouds dispersed across the heavens like milk poured into a cup of steaming coffee. Now that he was walking, Shad looked even more like his father, for he carried himself the same, even to his gait, even though it was hampered with his healing injury.

Laurie burst back into the room, her face bright with excitement, and the three headed outdoors. Aidan infused the occasion with a jovial, approving air, telling them he wished to cheer them on, while his real goal was to ensure the boy could successfully do this.

SHADOW HAWK SLOWLY hobbled toward the steps where he could see his angel bringing up the horses. He would have to position himself carefully if he was going to mount without help. Once the horses were in full view, he felt disappointment surge. Of course, she had both horses saddled, a difficult situation from which to extricate himself. He hadn't ridden with a saddle since his father had disappeared. Perhaps, he considered, it would make it easier to mount. The saddle might also give him more stability.

He approached the steps off the high porch slowly, moving down them with care, uncertain whether this was something he could successfully do.

LAURIE TOOK ONE look at his face and knew something was wrong, that he must still be in pain. The thought hadn't occurred to her that he might be an Indian and not familiar with using a saddle. Dismounting, she hurried over to him.

"Are you sure you're ready to do this?" She held a bated breath, awaiting his answer.

"Yes, I want to ride. I just do not know if I can mount easily," he answered in his soft, low-pitched voice.

SHADOW HAWK PAUSED in his efforts to mount his animal. His angel might have been easy to persuade, but Aidan had known him before Shadow Hawk had even spoken aloud. This white man would possibly see through any deception he tried to put over him. He rested his arms on the horse's shoulders, and he ducked his head, asking for Brother Horse to let him mount easily, and not to whinny or jump at his presence.

"Shad, son, you need any assistance? That leg going to be a problem?"

Aidan's booming voice startled Shadow Hawk into raising his head and studying the animal's coat. The short hairs glistened in the sunlight. Shadow Hawk said simply, "It's getting better, and I feel it wise to test it out on a ride today."

He took a deep breath, knowing he mustn't show weakness, or he would fail, both in this man's eyes and in Laurie's.

AIDAN WALKED UP to Shadow Hawk and put his hand on his shoulder. He looked the youth directly in the eyes, and he saw more than simple honesty there. When it came to men, Aidan knew how to read them, and this young man's father, he knew even better. However, he also knew there was much of this boy's mother inside of him. His Cheyenne words told Aidan of that. This boy would need his space. All the older man could do was offer to help him, and if the boy would accept his help, that was fine. If he wouldn't, there was nothing Aidan could do about that.

"Well, that sounds like a good plan as long as you don't stay up on the animal too long. If Laurie's set on a long ride, you stop and take a break. There's no sense in re-injuring that knee. It'll take twice as long to heal. Also, just so you know, I'll need your help in the late spring calving season. So, plan to stick around to help out." Aidan finished with a long look. Then he grinned before continuing, "You have months yet before that, so you'll have plenty of time to get completely over any injuries you have."

"I have no intention of getting hurt again. Also, you are right. We shouldn't ride too long on my first day out." He gave Aidan an equally long look back, causing Aidan to grin even wider.

"Just so long as we understand each other." Aidan released the boy's shoulder, winked at Shadow Hawk, and called to his daughter, "Laurie, I suspect you need to make this easier on our friend."

The big man laughed, turned away, and then strode toward the house.

SHADOW HAWK WAS confused by what Aidan said. The rancher was expecting him to stay for quite some time. He would have to tell him soon that he was leaving as quickly as he could ride.

"Papa, it's no problem." Laurie called to Shadow Hawk, "I'll bring the horse up to the porch, and you can mount from there. Do you think that will do?"

Shadow Hawk smiled to himself. My angel still

hasn't figured it out. She doesn't realize I'm an Indian, and I only ride bareback. Laurie saw his smile and with only a moment's hesitation started to lead the stallion up to the porch's edge.

"Angel, I mean Laurie, would you mind if I rode your horse?" Shadow Hawk questioned her in his deep, soft voice, not caring about his slip when he called her by the white man's term.

Laurie colored slightly and replied, "No, I never thought you would want to ride Shadow, since she's smaller than most horses."

Shadow Hawk froze with the realization that he had been badly mistaken. "What did you just call your horse?"

Laurie laughed, "I thought I already told you. She's called Shadow."

This one thing Shadow Hawk now understood. It was almost a relief, although it was also a disappointment. It also meant the angel from his father's Holy Book was nothing more than the story that his medicine man had laughed at when Shadow Hawk had first gone to the tribe with his mother.

Back in the cave, Laurie hadn't been calling to him. She had been calling to her horse. The inrush of knowledge confirmed he hadn't been truly delirious. He had heard her call the name of Shadow, just not to him. She was telling her horse how much she had missed and loved her.

Now he wasn't sure how he felt. He was no longer confused about the scene in the cave, thinking an angel had come to him, then having to accept that she was only human. With a surge of elation that he could barely keep off his face, Shadow Hawk understood that his angel had always been human and not some creature sent to haunt him.

He turned to her with new strength in his voice and said, "I prefer to ride an Indian pony. The horse you call Shadow will suit me just fine. I can mount with care from here."

LAURIE BEAMED. Arthur had never liked her horse, but Shad said he preferred her animal to the stallion. She knew the stallion was worth much more than her horse, but she loved Little Shadow all the same. It would seem that Shad felt the same way as she did.

No one had ever ridden Shadow except Laurie, and now of course, Shad. He approached the horse and spoke softly to it, keeping the pain that had earlier been a limp carefully disguised.

SHADOW HAWK CONTINUED to speak in low tones and a calm manner as he mounted the horse, relaxing in the saddle once it was finally under him. It would be easier to keep his balance and lead without using his injured knee. He breathed a sigh of relief once they started to ride. Laurie said she loved to ride in the lower meadow. So, there they would be.

— 13 —

THEY HAD NO sooner left the yard than Laurie
started into a full gallop. Immediately, Shadow Hawk
wasn't sure if he could keep up. He prodded his small
mare to go faster, and she seemed to do so with abandon. Her hooves clipped the soil with a thumping res-
onance that echoed in Shadow Hawk's bones, and the
brisk wind brushed his face, pulling his hair back and
burnishing his cheeks. He was soon relieved to find
he was able to ride in the saddle easier than if he had
been bareback. His knee wasn't having to work to
control the animal underneath him.

He let the horse go at an easy clip as they traveled
farther down the mountain and into the valley. The
sun caused a blinding light that reflected off the melting snow, and since Shadow Hawk wasn't familiar

with the terrain, he didn't need to end up getting thrown or letting the horse get hurt because the brightness of the sunlight had blinded him. He slowed the animal's pace, the best way to ride properly under these conditions. Laurie had stopped up ahead and waited for him to catch up.

"Are you having problems? Am I going too fast?" She was breathless from the cold as well as the ride, and her skin glowed from the excitement. She did look like an angel with her long hair cascading down. She sat on the tall stallion with her breath coming out in smoky puffs in the crisp morning air, and she was the picture of beauty.

"No. For this first ride, I feel this slower pace is a good one. However, I've not ridden far enough," Shadow Hawk answered, still adjusting to riding in a saddle. He was used to reading a horse's thoughts and intentions through the motions of its back and the flexing of its muscles underneath its skin. The saddle forced him to interact with the animal differently. "Let's go a little farther before we turn back," he suggested.

"Oh, good. I love to ride as much as I possibly can." With that, Laurie took off like a shot. Shadow Hawk had no plans to follow quickly, but his horse did. The mare leaped forward trying to keep up with the stallion. The lunge caused his knee to make a noticeable cracking sound, and he felt numbing pain for a few seconds. With urgency, he gritted his teeth until he could slow his horse to a walk. Finally stopping altogether, he knew he needed to get off to check his leg but wasn't sure if he could do it without losing his balance and falling.

LAURIE LOOKED BACK and saw Shad just sitting while Little Shadow was twisting her head in the cold. Clouds of steam flooded from her nostrils. She noticed how natural the young man seemed on her horse, as if he had ridden her before, as if they could easily be one with each other. She smiled. He must be waiting for her to return so they could head home. There went their time together, she thought sadly to herself. However, he had cautioned her he needed to start slowly. She turned the big stallion around and trotted up to Shad. His face was drawn in agony, and Laurie could tell something wasn't right as soon as she reached him.

"What's wrong? What happened?" she questioned quickly.

"My knee snapped when my horse took off after you," he said through his gritted teeth.

"Oh, Shad. I'm so sorry. Let me help you." Removing one foot from its stirrup, Laurie swung her leg across, dropped to the ground, and was off her horse and heading straight for Shad and her beloved Shadow.

Shadow Hawk was very careful as he began to dismount. Laurie smiled, careful to ensure it couldn't be seen. He didn't want to fall in front of her, and that was very brave and sweet. Gently he pulled his leg across the top of the horse and began to slide down the side of the saddle. Laurie stood and helped him keep his balance as he reached the snow-patched ground.

She felt guilty that her quick gallop had caused Shad to suffer even more pain than he had already faced over the days since she had found him. She had only just arranged an opportunity for him to spend time with her, hopefully to build a friendship of some sort. Now, after everything she had done to be his friend, this had to happen, and she wouldn't be surprised if he blamed her. He was on her horse, after all. She didn't know why everything had to go wrong when it came to her trying to win his friendship. Frustration began to flare up inside her, and tears welled up in her eyes.

"I'm sorry. I didn't think about my little Shadow trying to keep up with me. I would never want to hurt you intentionally; I hope you know that," she softly uttered, her voice barely above a whisper, trying not to let out a sob. "It's just that, that . . ." She could hold back no longer, and a flood of tears started down her innocent face.

TEARS. PLEASE DO not cry tears. Shadow Hawk couldn't stand to see his sweet angel cry, and it was worse to have been the cause of her weeping. He could barely maintain his pretense of bravado. What was worse, his instincts were telling him to turn and leave now, before she learned his feelings for her, though his heart said something entirely different.

What he felt inside won.

"Oh, Angel, don't cry. It's okay, please, sweet Angel. Don't cry," Shadow Hawk whispered to her, with his voice shaking from emotion. Laurie looked up, and he wanted to wipe the tears from her dark eyes. He kept his voice soft and comforting, not cold and distant as it had been during the past few days.

She took one more step, and his coat was almost touching hers. In that moment, Shadow Hawk reached to her face, one thumb poised to remove the signs of her distress from her golden cheek.

A torrid of emotions raced through him. He knew he shouldn't do this. He shouldn't force his feelings on her. He was desperate to tell her how he felt, despite knowing she was promised to another. Only the fear of rejection made him hold back. Even with the knowledge she would never be his, he couldn't abandon her. Not yet.

Finally, Laurie mumbled between sobs, "Why do you hate me? What have I done to make you not like me anymore? I hoped we would be friends."

Shadow Hawk didn't want her to misunderstand why he was distancing himself from her. He forcefully pulled himself away from her, using all the willpower he could rally, and he peered at Laurie's watery eyes and tear-stained cheeks. He could never hate her, but he could not be allowed to love her, either. His emotions were shredded knowing this was all he would ever have. He cupped his hands under her chin, tilted her head up, and stared into her sweet, childlike face. Very slowly he spoke to her.

"I have been drawn to you. From the moment in the cave, I have found you beautiful beyond my dreams. Everything about you, your hair, your eyes, your smile, makes me want to spend time with you. You were an angel sent from Heaven." He dropped his hands from her face and looked away. He could feel his eyes brimming with sorrow. He wouldn't cry though, not now, and not ever. She was not his to cry for. He had spoken too deeply of his feelings, and he didn't want to be ashamed of what he'd done.

"What is it, Shad?" Laurie lifted her hands, and with slender fingers, she brushed her distress from her elegant lashes. "You're speaking Cheyenne, and I caught a few words, but I can't understand everything in your beautiful language. What are you not saying that I should know?"

"Your father said you've already given your heart to another. But know this Angel, I will never care for another woman as much as I care for you. I want to be only with you. It's you I have grown to love."

Shadow Hawk kept his eyes on the distant mountains, forcing his feelings into a crevasse deep inside, one that would never know his voice again.

LAURIE STOOD IN stunned and confused silence. What was he saying? She barely understood the Cheyenne language, except to recognize a few words of it when it was spoken, and Shad was speaking fluently to her in the Indian tongue. Spoken quickly, she understood even less. She knew it must be important, because he had refused to look at her and had spoken so gently and tenderly. He had to be telling her something he wanted her to know, and she couldn't understand why he didn't just tell her in English.

"I don't comprehend your words, Shad. What is it you're trying to tell me?" She reached and wiped one eye as she inquired quietly, giving him time to respond. When he didn't, she reached to touch him, and he held up his open hand. Gently and slowly, their skin made contact, and they pressed palm to palm.

"I know you don't understand my language. That's why I said what I did in Cheyenne. I had to let you know how I feel before I leave. I couldn't go without saying something. My heart wouldn't release me."

Again, his words were in Cheyenne. Laurie was more puzzled than ever. Was he ever going to speak to her in words she could understand? She questioned him again.

"Why are you still speaking in Cheyenne? Why won't you talk to me in English? I'm sorry. I only know a few words, and I didn't recognize any of them because you were speaking so quickly."

SHADOW HAWK SAID nothing more, just wrapped her hand in his and leaned his forehead against her fingers, never wanting to lose this moment with her. Holding her hand in his brought the greatest contentment a man could hope for. This was what he wanted for the rest of his life. Nevertheless, he knew it was a false emotion; she didn't belong to him and never would. He needed to leave as soon as possible, or he would be forever doomed by what this love would force him to do.

Using his warrior determination, Shadow Hawk gently pushed her from him.

LAURIE COULD FEEL the difference in his demeanor. His moodiness was one thing she couldn't understand. Something had once again changed in him. She didn't understand why, and it made her sad.

She whispered dismally to herself, her words so soft as to be for her ears alone, "The moment's gone. His fondness for me is like a leaf caught in a wind gust as it wafts away."

When Shadow Hawk finally spoke, he was once again like the Shad of the past few days. His back was straight, and it was with great effort that he kept his voice flat and emotionless.

"Angel, I need to go back to the ranch. My ride has come to an end."

AS SHADOW HAWK turned to limp back to his horse, he was surprised that his knee no longer hurt with the knifing pain he had felt earlier. The jolt and the standing here as he spoke with his angel seemed to have worked the joint back into place. He gingerly turned it, but felt no sharp pain racing down his calf.

The numbness seemed to be fading, as well. He might soon be able to walk, run, and ride again as before.

Knowing he would be able to make his escape was a relief. Finally, there was something good he could smile about. He could ride a horse bareback without fear of losing his balance or suffering pain. This would be his first opportunity to truly enjoy riding since he had left the Cheyenne camp. He would show his angel what kind of rider he really was, and he would push his body to do it, even if it brought the pain back to his leg.

Without giving a clue to Laurie, he jumped onto Shadow Hawk and shouted, "I'll race you to the house."

LAURIE STOOD IN stunned surprise, as Shad took off as though he were racing the wind. She wondered what was going on, at how he managed to mount and take off so quickly. She thought he had hurt his knee again.

The thoughts tumbled wildly in her head as she mounted the stallion and begin to goad him to run at his top speed. She would show Shad she could ride as well as any man, especially him. She, too, went in hot pursuit of the ranch house and home.

FAR FROM THEM on the northern slope, Aidan Kerrigan pulled his small viewing telescope from his eyes. When it came to his daughter, he was most protective. He wanted to be sure Jeremiah Hawke's son was the same quality of person his father was. He knew better than to trust a person based on another's character. Every man stood on his own merits.

He had observed the entire scenario. He could tell there were heated emotions coursing between the two, even from as far away as he was. He was pleased to observe nothing had happened that he didn't approve of. More importantly, he knew God was not displeased by their behavior, either.

He was thankful he had judged correctly. This was a quality young man. He might have some issues to settle about his father, but overall, Aidan was quite pleased.

He was confident God had sent him their way.

— 14 —

THE RACE TO the house had cooled both of their charged emotions. As soon as Shadow Hawk arrived, he took the horse to the corral. He wanted to be away from Laurie as soon as possible, before she figured out what he had said to her. She was only seconds behind him. His back was to her, but he could feel her presence as she approached the corral. He knew she must be waiting for him to make some comment.

"You ride well for a woman. Or a man, for that matter." Shadow Hawk turned to face her as she dismounted. He brushed a hand along Little Shadow's neck, and he patted the thick muscles under the tight, damp coat.

Laurie smiled, giving him a pleased expression. "I'm pleased you admire my horsemanship. I have a question that needs answered. I thought your knee was still hurt. How did you manage to walk so quickly and ride so fast?"

"That last lunge from the horse possibly moved something around inside. That must have been why it hurt so much before. However it repaired itself, the improvement was the best thing that could have happened. Now, I feel like myself again. I'll be able to leave here sooner than I had hoped." He felt his heart race. She was still beautiful, even if she couldn't be his. He studied the fasteners on the saddle, and he began to work the straps free. Once the saddle was draped over the fence, he tied the reins to a post, found a brush, and began to curry Little Shadow's flanks, not understanding the impact his remarks would have on Laurie.

LAURIE FELT HER heart stop for a moment, and when the world had turned still and silent, she sensed dread coursing through her veins. Shad was leaving. Her stranger wasn't staying.

Her world went gray with his words.

She knew one thing for sure. He couldn't just up and go. Not yet, not when she was finally starting to understand how much she truly cared about him. Today on the ride, she had felt happier than she could remember. Now, all this would be taken away from her if he left. She had to convince him otherwise.

"But, why do you want to leave so soon? You haven't been but here a few weeks. Don't you like staying with my family, Shad? With me?" Laurie questioned him anxiously.

SHADOW HAWK KNEW it would be easy to stay and become a part of the ranch life, and Laurie would be a part of it, too. He would be close to her, and they could find time together, if they truly desired it. Yet, these were feelings Shadow Hawk must keep to himself. She was betrothed, and he had vowed to avenge his and his mother's abandonment. This could not be his life, just as life in the tribe had not been his life.

"I have other things I need to do, a journey I was on when I ended up here. I have to finish what I started." He drew in a rough breath and looked at her, letting his eyes become hard. "Besides," he growled, "nothing here belongs to me."

LAURIE WAS TAKEN aback by the angry tone in which he had answered her. Questions shot through her mind like the arrows from a bow. Why did he speak to her like that? What had she done to irritate him so soon after their riding trip? What was she doing wrong?

Also, she had no idea what should belong to him. She let her thoughts unwind for a moment. What had he borrowed that wasn't his? Then she remembered that he had accepted some clothes from some of the ranch hands, because his shirt and jacket had been shredded by the bear. However, that was no reason to leave.

Then she remembered something else. Shad had come here with nothing but a leather satchel, not even a horse. Maybe that was it. Perhaps he was thinking about a horse.

Yes, he definitely needed a horse.

If that was the issue, she was certain Papa wouldn't mind if he borrowed one of their horses until he had one of his own. That had to be it. Men were prideful when it came to the animals they rode, or the lack there of.

"Is it because you don't have a horse of your own?" Laurie asked quietly, as they left the stable and headed toward the house.

NOW EVEN THIS white woman could see the foolishness of his ways, and Shadow Hawk almost laughed out loud with her sudden realization. Of course he would need a horse. He and his mother owned several horses, all good stock. He had left them because he was angry and didn't want anything from her or his father. He had wanted to prove his manhood and show that he could make it in the world without either of them.

It hadn't quite worked out that way, to his chagrin and embarrassment. He smiled before he realized what he'd done, and he forced it from his face.

"What did I say that was so funny? I see you trying to hold back. Are you laughing at me? Did I ask a dumb question?" Laurie looked at him with questioning eyes. Shadow Hawk glanced at her and said nothing. Ahead of them the log house reared above them, inviting them to take advantage of the warmth evidenced by the smoke from tall chimney overhead.

Shadow Hawk felt transparent before this woman, and that could be very dangerous. He wouldn't be able to trust himself around her unless he got control of himself, and at this point, he wasn't sure that he could if she remained near him. He was Cheyenne, and he would be strong, but he felt his heart warming toward her more than ever.

All she needed to do was tell him she felt some tender emotion for him, and he would be dedicated to her forever. Yet, he knew that would never happen. His angel had already promised herself to Arthur.

That he couldn't bear.

Shadow Hawk couldn't entertain nor tolerate the thought of anyone holding or loving his angel. He wouldn't stand by and watch that happen. He knew himself too well. If that were to take place, there would be a fight. He would cause bloodshed. Laurie would hate him forever, because he would take her lover's life.

He felt the world darkening, and he tried to focus on the path they walked.

LAURIE COULD FEEL another change in Shad's mood as they approached the kitchen's back door. His brooding attitude was what she was always concerned about, and she stopped him before they entered the house.

Placing one hand gently on his chest, she asked pensively, "It's me, isn't it? You are leaving because of me. That's what you were telling me in Cheyenne on the ride this morning." She waited, breathing shallowly, praying he would say no, but dreading the words that would confirm her assessment.

SHADOW HAWK LOOKED at her with a heartrending and crushed feeling inside. How could he tell her? He paused for a long moment before he answered.

"Yes, Angel, because of you I have to go. One cannot take another's betrothed." With that remark, he slowly removed her hand from his chest, gently caressing her fingers as he let them go.

Laurie's face went white with shock. Shadow Hawk stepped into the house, leaving a stunned and bewildered Laurie on the back porch.

LAURIE'S HEAD REELED, her heart pounded, and she couldn't breathe. He was engaged to someone already. Why hadn't she known that? She should have known that. Why hadn't he spoken up before now? Why had he waited until she was practically in love with him to tell her?

Her body felt lifeless as she opened the door and stumbled into the kitchen. A roaring in her ears, like a thousand rivers at once, deafened her. Inside her head, the pressure of a thunderstorm exploded, driving every thought from her.

However, it was her heart that ached the most.

She felt listless and dead. All she wanted was go upstairs and lie down. When the housekeeper asked if she was ill, Laurie just said she wasn't feeling well and left Mrs. Gates puzzled, agape, and without words.

SHADOW HAWK HEARD Laurie coming into the kitchen, while he stood anxiously in the great room in front of the massive fireplace. He had hoped, no, a better word would be to say he had prayed to the white man's God that Laurie would come in and tell him it wasn't true, that she had made a mistake. She didn't love Arthur, but him, Shadow Hawk. Instead, she bypassed him and went straight to the staircase. She avoided him altogether.

That was her response. For Shadow Hawk, nothing else mattered now. She hadn't tried to deny or even say she cared for him in any way. She even looked surprised that he knew. She must have been trying to keep it a secret, but why? Did she want to hurt him in some way? Was she like the other white person he had loved in his life, his father? Would she have never told him until it was too late? She had remained on the back porch until she could go straight to her room without having to face him again.

None of this made any sense to him or to his heart, and the pounding of a thousand horse's hooves in his veins left him in emotional torment.

He had to leave, and for that, he must find Aidan.

— 15 —

AIDAN WAS NOWHERE to be located on the ranch. Shadow Hawk learned he had left shortly after Laurie and Shadow that morning, heading out the opposite direction. He still hadn't returned, and Shadow Hawk couldn't delay any longer. Being rejected by his angel was more than his heart would allow. He must leave today. He couldn't linger so near to her, knowing Laurie was avoiding him.

To fill the time, he wandered to the corral and offered to help with the horses. The other ranch hands appreciated having the extra assistance, and it only took a few minutes before they realized he was a natural with the animals. All the beasts seemed to respond to his low, gentle voice and his sure touch. Even the most spirited, Desperado, was calm around him.

During his handling, they could easily see that the animal that appeared to have a special connection with him was Little Shadow, Laurie's horse. She was usually shy and backed away from most of the workers. Mr. Gates and Aidan were the only two outside of Laurie who could get the horse to mind. Today, however, she tried to follow Shadow Hawk from the moment he entered the corral. He had to push her out of the way more than once.

It was as if they were bonded by something greater than that of horse and trainer.

LAURIE NEEDED TO shut out the light that seemed to be making her head hurt even worse than her heart. She rose from her voluptuous feather bed to close the curtains. At the window, she glanced out to see her Little Shadow in the corral.

She smiled to herself at the sight of the animal until she recognized the man her horse was chasing. It was Shad! Her little Shadow was trying to get Shad's attention. The animal never did that with anyone but her, and she hadn't done it in a long time even with Laurie. Not since she was still a young colt had she seen her little Shadow try to capture someone's interest with such enthusiasm. Laurie's heart felt even heavier, knowing not only she, but even her horse wanted Shad's attention, yet he intended to leave. Poor Little Shadow would be brokenhearted, too. With an aching heart, she threw herself across her bed in a fresh and unstoppable flood of tears.

"How will I ever forget him? How will I be able to erase him from my heart?" Laurie's anguish poured from her shattered heart into her pillow. "O God, help me. I know you love me and only want the best for my life. Why did you bring Shad into my world, if you were only going to take him from me? Help me understand your plan for me. I love him so, and I don't know how I'm going to get over him. Please help me. I ask this in Jesus' name, amen."

Laurie finished the prayer with a deep sigh. She felt better now that she had at least come to terms with her feelings. She had finally admitted to God and to herself that she loved Shad. Crying softly, she soon fell asleep, exhausted from the emotions of the day.

AIDAN RODE UP to the corral a short time later, having observed from a distance the treatment Shadow Hawk was giving the horses. He was truly Cheyenne, all right. No one else could handle horses better than they. Shadow Hawk was no exception. Aidan surmised that the young warrior must have a few horses of his own to be this adept in their care and management. He got the horses to do in just a few minutes what it normally took three men to accomplish over the course of an hour or so.

"I see where your real talent lies," Aidan called out amiably as he approached the corral. "I thought you were just good at handling bears and such." He grinned as he stepped down from the large chestnut stallion he had taken out that morning. As Shadow Hawk approached, Aidan handed the reins to him. Shadow Hawk took them and spoke to the horse in whispered and elegant Cheyenne, speaking low comforting words. The horse immediately began to respond to the young brave.

"So, that's your secret. Cheyenne. A man must speak Cheyenne to be able to manage horses well. I guess you'll need to teach my cowboys how to speak your language," laughed the rancher.

SHADOW HAWK WARMED at the compliment. He wasn't used to praise for a job anyone in his tribe could do. However, he was pleased knowing his skills were appreciated and that he had pleased Aidan even in this small way.

He would be sorry to leave the ranch and the start of their friendship. This man was one white man who truly seemed to care. Shadow Hawk could see the rancher's concern evidenced through the loyalty of the workers at the ranch. He appeared to treat everyone fairly and with respect, and in turn, his ranch hands treated him with dignity and respect. Each ranch hand pulled his weight whether the owner was on the estate or not.

Shadow Hawk could see why his father had liked him and valued his friendship. In the man's words to him, Shadow Hawk had been able to tell that the ranch owner had been saddened by the loss of his friend. Even though it had been years ago, he must still miss him. For the first time, Shadow Hawk saw his father in a different light, one based on the memories Aidan had shared. Shadow Hawk's new understanding of the two men's friendship made what was necessary more difficult and painful.

"Ai-Aidan, I need to talk to you," Shadow Hawk stammered nervously. He stood very still, keeping his countenance as immobile as possible. He wanted to show only the utmost respect with his request.

"Sure, son. What's on your mind?" Aidan clasped a hand on the young man's shoulder. "You seem a mite apprehensive."

Shadow Hawk had a difficult time facing his benefactor. He tried to keep his head up, but he eventually let his eyes study the ground, trying to frame the sentences as he spoke.

"I appreciate everything you've done for me, bringing me here after I stole, uh, took Angel's, I mean, Laurie's horse. You got me back on my feet and told me things I didn't know or remember about my father." Shadow Hawk paused for a moment. This was a more arduous task than he first realized.

"Go on," prompted Aidan.

"Well, hmm, well, I need to leave, and I need to leave today. I must finish what I started, and I'm well enough now to do it. I do have one request, if I may be permitted, one that I would like to ask for my father's sake. I would like to know if I could perhaps, maybe, borrow a horse?"

"A horse, huh? To borrow?"

"I will return it as soon as I get back to my people. I have several horses there. I give you my word as a warrior." Shadow Hawk paused, and then in a rush, he finished, "Also, as a friend."

Shadow Hawk's face was hot with embarrassment. He had never asked for anything from anyone other than his mother in his entire life. Now here he was asking a white man if he could take a horse.

Aidan was silent for a moment. Shadow Hawk considered the long intermission must be because of his request for a horse. He attempted to amend his appeal, "If you cannot loan me one, I understand."

It would be hard to trust someone who had stolen something from you, especially your daughter's horse, and he wouldn't be surprised to have this man turn him away without a second thought.

Aidan shot back, "Oh, no, Shad. You can have your pick of the horses. I wasn't even thinking about that. Take two if you need them. What I was wondering was why you felt you had to go today. Since you just started walking, don't you think you had better rest a spell and get used to the pace again? How about tomorrow? I'll let you have a horse in the morning. I think that knee of yours needs a little time off, too. You've been on it most of the day, I suspect."

Shadow Hawk felt a small measure of disappointment surge through him, and yet, there was relief at the same time. He was being encouraged to stay. Aidan wanted him to wait one more day. He could do that, tolerate it here for one more night. The self-torture wouldn't be unbearable. Laurie didn't want to face him, and he could possibly avoid her completely.

Besides, he really needed that horse.

"I believe one more day will not hurt my cause. As you have put it, I *reckon* I can stay one more day."

This time when he spoke, Shadow Hawk let a smile hover around his mouth. He looked to catch Aidan's eye, and he could see the same look on the older man's face. That was when they began to laugh. The word "reckon" was clearly a white man's word, and Shadow Hawk had never used it before. That was obvious, and his emphasis on the word was equally obvious.

THAT THE MOMENT struck both of them as funny amused Aidan. He hoped it was a good sign, and he decided to take it that way. When Jeremiah's son laughed, he thought that perhaps he just might be able to, also.

— 16 —

AIDAN INQUIRED IF Shadow Hawk knew the whereabouts of his daughter.

"U-upstairs in her room, I suppose," the younger man fumbled, in an awkward and stuttered response as his face hardened, leaving the laughter and camaraderie fluttering in the wind.

Aidan watched Shad's demeanor change as he answered the question. Once again, he was the distant, brooding young man he had first laid on his couch weeks ago. There was no point in trying to talk to him now. It would be wasted communication. So, with a grunt, Aidan set off in the direction of the house, leaving Shadow Hawk to tend to his horse and his thoughts.

"So that's what this is all about. I suspected Laurie might have been the motivation for Shad desiring such a hasty departure," Aidan muttered to himself as he stepped onto the porch. "What has that daughter of mine done now?" As he entered the back door, he could smell supper cooking on the stove.

"Well, it's about time," said Mrs. Gates. "No one in this 'ouse keeps regular hours anymore. Not one person had dinner today, mind you. Not a one of ya'. Laurie's sick upstairs, and Shad said 'e wasn't 'ungry. Ya', the man who should be settin' the example to them others, well, ya' were nowhere to be found."

Hearing of his daughter illness, Aidan headed straight to the stairwell without giving another thought to the housekeeper. He arrived outside Laurie's door and tapped lightly. Hearing no response, he opened the door to the dimly lit room to find Laurie asleep. He could see her puffy, swollen eyelids, and he knew that had come from crying. Something was amiss between her and Shad, but at least it didn't appear to be life threatening. Whatever it was, it could wait until she woke up. It was good for her to rest.

He quietly exited the room.

When he came down the stairs, he went directly to Mrs. Gates. "Do you know anything about what's going on with those two?" Aidan's question was direct as he reached for a cup of coffee.

"All I know is they was talkin' until they reached the 'ouse. It was after their mornin' ride and gettin' nigh on to dinnertime. They stood on the back porch fer a few minutes, and the next thing I witnessed was that boy stompin' through the door alone and goin' to the great room. A few more minutes passed, and Miss Laurie came in and rushed up the stairs, sayin' she didn't feel well. When I went to check on 'er, she was bawlin' 'er eyes out. She never would say what happened exactly. All I got out of 'er was that she truly loved 'im, and why did she have to feel this way."

That left Aidan totally confounded. He could tell from the scene he had viewed in the spyglass that his daughter was on the precipice of love. The last thing he wanted was for her to experience a broken heart. He couldn't imagine what Shad could have said or done that might make her feel so distraught. Laurie was always in God hands, and right now Aidan felt his own hands were tied. Something about this just didn't figure right. After all, he had watched the pair, and Shad had seemed to like his daughter well enough. Aidan was certain Laurie liked the young man, and he had no doubt God had sent Shad into their lives just in the nick of time. Arthur had begun to get very possessive of Laurie. Aidan wanted his baby girl happy, and if Shad proved himself to be what Aidan had seen so far, he was the man for her.

If he was to help fix this, Aidan needed to hogtie this problem fast. For his first step, he had a lot of thinking and praying to do, and he had best get started now. He headed to where he always went when he needed to pray for Divine guidance: his bedside. It was also the place where he most often found it.

SHADOW HAWK CHOSE to remain outside until Mrs. Gates rang the supper bell for the cowboys two hours later. He accepted he had no choice but to head to the house for the evening meal. He had already washed up at the water pump with the ranch hands, leaving his damp hair unbound so that it could dry in the fresh air, and it had curled and waved in its natural way. He dreaded the evening looming before him. This was the first time he didn't want to be here as a part of this family. Once inside it was easier, because no one except Mrs. Gates seemed to be around.

"Evenin'." The housekeeper spoke without looking his way.

"Good evening," he replied in little more than an uncomfortable whisper. As he reached for a cup to pour some coffee, Mrs. Gates glanced his way. A smile of astonishment crossed her face.

"Where on Earth did ya' get such pretty hair? Is this what ya' have been keepin' bound up all this time? If I had locks like yours, I'd let the whole world know. I tell my sweet little Laurie she should thank God every day for havin' such thick, wavy hair. When I was young, I'd 'ave given my eye teeth to 'ave 'air such as 'ers, or yours, for that matter." She laughed, "I can't believe God wasted such glory on a man. All I 'ave is this straight little grey mop on top, barely enough to pull up in a bun. At least ya' have the good sense to grow yours long so ya' can enjoy its beauty." She turned back to the stove and continued turning the meat.

Shadow Hawk smiled to himself as he sat at the kitchen table. Warmed by the coffee and the conversation, he deliberated about what the housekeeper had said. His hair was long, too long for most white men. Usually only outlaws, trappers, and bounty hunters wore their hair like his. Most civilized folks took pride in their short, cropped hair.

However, the white man didn't consider Indians to be civilized and called them savages. Shadow Hawk wasn't ashamed to be a Wolf Soldier of his tribe. He had always taken special care of his long hair, even though it wasn't as dark or straight as the other members of the Cheyenne band.

His mother's deep blue-black hair had a few waves, also uncommon for Indians, but it was his father's head that had been covered with thick, shaggy blond curls. Shadow Hawk had inherited many of those waves and curls. His hair color was a combination of both, rich with motion and colored a deep, shimmering brown.

Despite that knowledge, he really hadn't given much thought to his hair since he had been here. No one had commented that it was too long until now, and even then, he had been given a compliment. Still, if he were leaving to spend more time in the white man's world in the morning, it might be time to take the next step. His hair would have to be cut abruptly short, if he intended to fit into polite, white man's society. He knew he had to blend in if he was going to complete his destiny.

He took a deep breath and quietly asked, "Mrs. Gates, I'm looking forward to supper, and it does smell very tempting. However, I would like to request a favor of you once we've enjoyed our meal."

The housekeeper shot a curious glance his direction. "Well, it depends on the favor. What is it ya' need me to do?"

"I need a haircut, like your husband's, if you would be so kind. I would be much obliged," Shadow Hawk responded.

"After I just told 'ow nice your hair was, why would ya' want to go an' cut it all off? My 'usband keeps it short so it won't be in the way when 'e's workin' with the cattle or the 'orses. But yours is long enough that ya' can keep it pulled back like it's been all along. It won't be in yer way while ya' work here on the ranch." Mrs. Gates reached into the oven and pulled out a pan of bread. Placing it on a cooling stone, she continued to question the young man at the table about his hair. "What 'as made ya' want to do it so sudden like?"

"I've been needing to get it cut for some time now," Shadow Hawk said quietly. He patiently waited for an answer from the housekeeper and was caught off guard by her next question.

"Does Miss Laurie know what ya' are plannin' to do?"

He had never considered Laurie's thoughts about his hair. He guessed she might have an opinion, and then again, maybe not. Surely it couldn't matter much what she thought about his hair. Still, if the river flowed the opposite direction, he would never want his angel to cut her beautiful tresses. He couldn't visualize her without them.

"What I remember is that while ya' was sick, all she did was admire yer hair with 'er eyes. She couldn't seem to keep out of the great room, or away from ya', fer that matter."

Mrs. Gates turned back to the stove to adjust the meat, and Shadow Hawk smiled at her. He wasn't sure if her suddenly red face was from the heat of the stove or her comment to him. He wasn't about to ask, either. He was glad she had turned away, because he felt his face warm at the memory.

Yes, his angel had been at his side the entire time. Her gentle presence had relaxed him and helped him rest. He remembered falling asleep with her delicate voice tenderly encouraging him and even singing his cares away. More than once, she'd spoken of his hair and how beautiful it was. But, that was then, before he had learned about Laurie and her engagement. This was now. Shadow Hawk's attitude once again changed to quiet resolve. How she felt about his hair didn't matter to him. It must not matter to him, and so he asked again, insisting this time.

"Mrs. Gates, you will cut it for me? I ask you for this one favor. You must do this for me."

"If ya' are sure that's what ya' want." She hesitated. "I'll do it first thing after the dishes are washed."

"I'll help wash the dishes, if you'll allow me. The

sooner I get it done, the better." Shadow Hawk had no sooner ended the sentence than Aidan Kerrigan made an appearance.

"Well, I see I didn't miss a chance to enjoy Mrs. Gates' good food. I didn't realize how long I'd been upstairs. I spoke with Laurie, and she said she'd be down to eat later, as she still doesn't feel well." Aidan smiled at Shadow Hawk and asked, "Are you ready for some grub? I'm so hungry I could eat a bear, or at least the better part of one."

Shadow Hawk nodded yes and stood as they headed for the dining room. He had missed the mid-day meal but still wasn't very hungry. Now, with Aidan's words, he was concerned about his angel. Maybe she really was sick and not completely avoiding him. He didn't think her father would lie about that.

After Aidan paused and waited for Shadow Hawk to bow his head with him, he offered his words of thanksgiving to the Father above for the blessings and bounty his ranch had been given. He also made a point to say a special word of thanks for the young man who had joined them on the ranch. He pointed out during the prayer how much he was thankful the Lord had given Aidan the opportunity to share with Shad about his misplaced father, whom Aidan considered an old friend. After he was finished, he raised his head to give the young man across from him a long and meaningful look. It took several minutes for Shadow Hawk to raise his head after the prayer was completed, because he knew his eyes would be red.

They cut into the juicy and tender venison steak and buttered potatoes Mrs. Gates had prepared. Shadow Hawk usually enjoyed the cooking the housekeeper provided and had thought he could get used to eating like this very easily. Not tonight, however. The atmosphere was quiet, and the dining room felt empty without Laurie's presence. Shadow Hawk could feel her absence, like a hollow cavern that echoed with loneliness. He felt dried by a summer wind of despair and emotionally dissected by the burning sun of circumstances out of his control.

Aidan paused in his meal, holding his knife and fork in opposing hands, and swallowed a substantial chunk of venison steak before he commented, "I hope you're not getting sick, too. Laurie looked none too good, and now after observing you for the past few minutes, son, you look a mite peaked yourself. I don't think you better go anywhere for a few days until I know you're up to snuff."

Shadow Hawk warmed at Aidan's reference to him as son. It was comforting to be addressed in such a manner. However, he wasn't sick, at least not in the way Aidan was thinking. He also knew the only way he would get better was to leave. With his angel here, and her heart intended toward another, he would never get better under this roof.

Instead of revealing the truth, he guided the conversation down a deceptive trail that would never lead the big rancher back to his real motivation. "I'm fine. I didn't eat dinner and worked a little harder than I've been used to over the past week. I'll be well enough to travel tomorrow." Shadow Hawk emphasized the word tomorrow.

"I can't hog tie you and force you to stay, but I think for your own good, you should wait a few more days until you're completely recovered. It's foolishness to take chances like you do, Shad. You're too smart of a young man to be risking your life the way you seem to enjoy. Riding that horse as fast as you did the first day you were out could have really caused some permanent damage. It would have made me sick to see you fall and get hurt. Besides, you aren't even used to a saddle."

"It was the saddle that helped me. It didn't put as much pressure on my leg as if I'd been bareback." The youth wondered how Aidan knew so much about their ride, and that also made him wonder what else he knew.

"All I'm saying is to be careful. I care about you and don't want to see you gettin' yourself all bunged up."

Mrs. Gates came in and refilled their cups with coffee to go with dessert. Shadow Hawk didn't care for sweets much and was pleased that Mrs. Gates had noticed and didn't place a slice of pie at his place. She had given him an apple, instead.

With dinner over, Shad stood and offered, "Show me what to do, Mrs. Gates, and I'll get to it."

AIDAN SQUINTED HIS eyes in a questioning manner, wondering just what that was about. He could certainly expect his Laurie to help Mrs. Gates from time to time, but Shadow Hawk? Now, that was strange. The ranch hands never came inside to help, and rarely did Mr. Gates make the offer. It wasn't falling true for a guest to step into the kitchen to give the housekeeper a hand without some ulterior motive in place.

And there was one more thing puzzling him. Where was Laurie? She should have been to the table already.

He got up and left the room in search of some of the answers, and he had a pretty good idea where to make a start.

— 17 —

MRS. GATES DRAGGED the dining room chair closer to the kerosene lamp sitting on the buffet next to the table. Shadow Hawk had just come back in from dampening his hair again to make it easier to cut. This would be the first time in almost ten years since it had been trimmed. When he was young, his father had kept it cropped short. To settle his score with him, Shadow Hawk would need it short again.

He sat nervously, awaiting the first sound of the shears.

"Now, Shad, I don't want ya' upset if ya' don't like the 'aircut. I'm not used to workin' with such thick wavy 'air as yours. Remember, ya' asked fer this." Mrs. Gates lifted a section of his hair, and she started to cut.

LAURIE OVERHEARD MRS. Gates' final comment as she approached the dining room, wondering what they could be talking about. With her curiosity piqued, she stepped into the dimly lit room. The view she discovered horrified her. There stood the house-keeper butchering Shad's beautiful, long hair. Laurie let out a shocked gasp. She blinked to make sure what she saw was real.

"What are you doing?" She huffed her question at Shadow Hawk, and then she repeated her words to Mrs. Gates.

"I am tryin' to cut 'is hair and not doin' a very good job at it, dearie," came the placid response. "I told 'im I didn't know how to cut 'is kind of 'air. But 'e asked me to do it anyway."

Laurie stepped to them, her feet carrying her forward without conscious thought, her mind in a fog at the damage that had been done to the young man's much-admired locks. She reached out and touched a strand that hadn't yet been shorn. This was her Shad's hair, soft and silky in her hands. Why was he taking even that away from her?

"Mrs. Gates, please continue." Shadow Hawk moved his feet impatiently on the floor, and his voice was sharp at the end.

"But, why Shad? Why would you want to cut your beautiful hair?" Laurie questioned him sadly, with her voice barely above a whisper. He said nothing, just sat in icy silence. His back was straight, and his Cheyenne stoicism made him as immovable as an ancient rock promontory.

Once over the initial shock, Laurie felt even more deeply miserable. Her eyes started to water with tears. She blinked hard to keep them from surfacing on her cheeks.

The housekeeper eyed her and saw she was visibly upset. "Now dearie, don't start that frettin'. Ya' have been ill all day. That's what's makin' ya' feel so bad. Let me get ya' some supper. Ya' will feel better once ya' have eaten." Mrs. Gates studied the mess she was making of Shad's hair and commented, "It's only hair. It will grow back, ya' know. No matter how bad it's been cut, it will grow back." With that, she turned and headed into the kitchen, leaving the young people alone in the dining room with Shadow Hawk's partially clipped mane.

Laurie sniffled a couple of times trying to regain her composure. Standing behind Shad, she stared at his hair, glad to see most of it was still there. She was grateful to have come in just as the housekeeper had started cutting the first long strands.

The initial cuttings lay on the floor. Laurie reached down to pick up the silky threads. In doing so, she inadvertently bumped the chair, causing Shadow Hawk to turn to see what she was doing.

"Leave them where they are," he said between clenched teeth. Laurie stared up at him in hurt surprise. He wouldn't even let her have his hair that he was cutting off and throwing away. She stood up, still holding his hair in her hand.

"Why, Shad? It's useless, now."

"It doesn't belong to you, just like I don't belong to you," he hissed venomously.

Laurie was devastated. How could he be so cruel, reminding her that he loved someone else? Her hand went limp as she let the strands drop carelessly beside her. Her heart was torn. How could she still love him despite everything, she wondered, as tears began to pool at the corners of her eyes.

SHADOW HAWK STARED into her poignant face and realized he had pushed her too far. He had hurt her again. He wasn't trying to; he just wanted her to connect with the emotional torment in which he was embroiled. He wouldn't be able to maintain this hardened exterior if he saw tears like he had earlier. He knew where that would lead, and he wasn't strong enough to endure it again.

He took in a deep breath as he felt his composure crack, and he whispered, "Oh, Angel, Laurie, please do not cry." It was a softer, sensitive voice than he had hissed at her before, and it caused her to look at him. "If having my hair will make you happy, then take it. I don't care, really. Just don't cry, if you please. I don't want you to be upset because of me."

"I don't understand. Why would you cut it? It's so beautiful."

He pointed to the hair strewn around him. "I've been making plans to get it removed for some time, and this has been my first opportunity. Now seemed like a good choice—"

Before anything else could be explained, Mrs. Gates stepped back in with a plate of food, along with a glass of milk. She started to hand it to Laurie. One look at the venison steak, and Laurie blanched.

"Maybe just the potatoes, Mrs. Gates, and the milk. I still don't feel very well. I'm only downstairs because Papa insisted I eat something."

The housekeeper looked at her and smiled as she handed her the milk. She patted her and replied, "Of course, Laurie, honey. Whatever ya' want to eat. I'll just put that steak back. Then I've got to get back to my 'air cuttin'."

That remark caused Laurie to look franticly at Shadow Hawk. Her eyes pleaded with him, but Shadow Hawk's countenance revealed nothing. He maintained his impenetrable silence.

"I can cut his hair, Mrs. Gates. I trim my own, and Papa's, too. I'm used to dealing with the thick waves. Let me do this, so you can get your work finished." Laurie let her eyes plead desperately.

"Well, I don't know. I told 'im I'd cut it like my 'usband's, but Shad's 'air is a whole lot 'arder to manage than my Daniel's. The final word will be up to Shad. I'll be relieved to go on home fer the evenin'. But, I don't mind stayin' and tryin' my 'and at it, if 'e wants me to." The housekeeper let out a sigh as she spoke and looked at the young man in the chair.

Shadow Hawk was annoyed by the discussion. Either way, he wouldn't like it. He could let Mrs. Gates finish the job and probably emerge a scruffy coyote, or he could force himself to be in the presence of his angel only to be inundated by her proximity.

He looked at both women facing him. One wanted to finish her day while the other desired something more, but he couldn't discern exactly what. Why was Angel so willing and even anxious to cut his hair? How could this benefit her? Shadow Hawk stared at one woman and then the other before he made his decision.

"Thank you, Mrs. Gates, for being willing to take on such an arduous task. I appreciate everything you have done for me while I've been here. But if An—, Laurie," catching himself before finishing Angel, "is willing to attempt the chore, then she may do so."

Mrs. Gates let out a big sigh, reaching and tugging repeatedly at the front of her dress.

"Thank ya' kindly. I'll be taking my leave of the both of ya'. Have a good evenin'. And, don't forget to eat, Miss Laurie. Ya' have to keep up your strength." Mrs. Gates removed her apron and grabbed her coat, as she headed for the back door.

LAURIE BREATHED A sigh of relief as the housekeeper exited. Finally, she could find out why Shad wanted to cut his hair. She had heard his words earlier, but that lame explanation simply hadn't been enough for her. Keeping Shadow Hawk's attention, she absently picked up the scissors and toyed with them while she spoke, holding them next to her own auburn tresses.

"How would you feel if I cut my hair?"

Without hesitation Shadow Hawk grabbed her wrist in a granite-like grip and immediately wrenched the shears from her. "You will never cut your hair, do you understand? Nothing that beautiful will ever be touched. Don't ever try, Angel. Neither you nor anyone else will ever cut your hair."

Laurie blinked back sudden tears of pain and anguish. He was hurting her arm with his hand, and he was hurting her soul with his anger. Plus, he was speaking in Cheyenne. Why, when it was something important that she wanted to know, did he always revert to Cheyenne?

"Shad, my arm," pleaded Laurie, trying not to let him know how powerful his grip was and how badly it was hurting her. He relinquished his grasp instantly, his eyes on the imprints where his hand had just been.

Shadow Hawk reached to her, taking her arm in his hand as he examined her already reddening wrist. A guilty flush washed over him like a flash flood thundering down a mountainside streambed. He held her arm ever so tenderly. She knew he wouldn't intentionally hurt her, but there on her wrist was the evidence of his temper and his inability to control it. Laurie didn't know what made him this volatile and out of control. He would never touch her in anger. She was confident of that. Something inside must be roiling in his heart to cause such a visceral reaction.

Laurie stood quietly staring into his dark eyes as he held her arm. Why would he care if she cut off her hair, but would have little or no regard for her feelings about his own locks being shorn off? He loved someone else. He had as good as told her that. Why did her hair seem to matter to him? The questions in her mind were cut short by the approaching sound of her father on his way in from checking on the ranch and locking things up for the night.

AS AIDAN STEPPED into the kitchen, he noticed the lighted dining room, but he heard no voices. That was unusual in itself. Oil for lamps was too costly to let rooms remain lighted when they were empty. He went to investigate.

As soon as he walked inside, he took one startled look at Shadow Hawk and let out a deep belly laugh. The young man looked like a half-shorn sheep, and he was still holding scissors in his hands. Laurie had a look of sheer fright on her face.

"Did you do this to Shad?" her father questioned. Laurie silently shook her head no. Humor danced in her father's voice this time, "Did you do this to yourself?" The laughing inquiry was directed at Shadow Hawk.

"No!" was Shad's strongly worded comment.

Aidan looked at one and then the other. Both appeared guilty of something. "Well, who in tarnation got a hold of your hair? A goat?"

"Mrs. Gates!" they blurted out in unison.

Aidan chortled and then paused, "Well, from the look of your head, I'd say she'd better stick to cooking. She can do that a whole sight better than what she just did to your head. Have you seen yourself?" Shadow Hawk miserably shook his head no. "Hmm. Maybe you should have a look-see. Laurie, honey, run upstairs and fetch your looking glass."

Laurie threw a glance at Shad before starting for the stairs. Aidan observed the movement of her eyes. Shadow Hawk just stared back at her, indicating nothing. Although his countenance reflected a look of remorse, Aidan couldn't tell what it was for. Something was going on that he couldn't figure out without asking a few questions.

Aidan positioned himself across from Shadow Hawk. "What possessed you to up and cut your hair? Your father was a trapper and wore his hair long. Maybe not as long as yours, but no one thought anything about it."

"I'm not a trapper," came Shadow Hawk's somber reply.

Aidan deliberated a moment, then he took another path with his words, hoping still to garner the information he sought. "You've been living with your mother's people, and long hair is part of their heritage, and yours. Why are you changing now?" Aidan hoped his brusqueness would startle the young man into answering.

"I'm going to the white man's world, and I want

to blend in with as little suspicion as possible," Shadow Hawk stated, with an upward and defiant tilt of his chin.

Laurie's footsteps in the hall filtered through the doorway. She entered with her ivory-handled mirror. As she nervously started to hand the mirror to Shadow Hawk, she almost dropped it, causing Shad to grab her wrist to steady her. She winced in pain. Shadow Hawk glimpsed the discoloration on Laurie's arm he had inflicted earlier. Shame turned his face red with regret.

Aidan noticed Shadow Hawk's darkening face as he took the mirror from his daughter.

"If you think you're red-faced now, wait until you view the looking glass," Aidan said expectantly.

SHADOW HAWK SLOWLY lifted the mirror to his face and looked at himself with trepidation. It was worse than he imagined. His hair was sticking out in one place where waves had once been, causing short, stunted curls to appear. Next to that, the straight wisps were hanging over the top of the curls, making his hair look like bumpy prairie dog mounds.

The other side of his hair was still long with waves running through the strands.

He did look like a mountain goat that was shedding its winter coat. Shadow Hawk set the mirror on the table and exhaled a slight groan.

Laurie gently laid her hand on his shoulder and comfortingly said, "I cut Papa's hair all the time, and he has a lot of waves in his, too. I think I can fix this."

Aidan's eyes twinkled even more as he saw the dull expression on Shadow Hawk's face. "Yes, Laurie does a fine job at cropping my bristly mane. I'm just sorry she didn't get to you first. But, take heart, Shad. It'll grow back. Give it a few months, and you won't even know you've cut it. However, I don't think I'll stay and watch the rest of the festivities." Aidan turned to Laurie, kissed her forehead goodnight, and headed toward the stairs. As soon as her father disappeared, Shadow Hawk cleared his throat.

"Let's get this over with," he said crisply. Laurie took the shears in her hand and began the laborious task of trying to straighten out Mrs. Gates' mess. Tears almost welled up in her eyes as his long, wavy strands fell to the floor.

Shadow Hawk could feel the hesitation as she sliced away at his dark, thick waves. Occasionally, he could hear a sniffle when she paused while trying to hold back tears. He remained stoic and revealed no emotion, but his heart raced as it ran like the deer before a summer storm. Each touch of her hand or gentle brush of her clothing was sweet torture.

Finally, Laurie whispered shakily, "I'm finished."

She laid down the scissors and reached for the looking glass. Shadow Hawk's hand touched hers as she handed him the mirror. Breaking the contact, he lifted the looking glass to his face and his eyes took on an expression of disbelief. He appeared older, and his features were more defined. His father's face now stared back at him. Seeing the unexpected man he had come to despise so made him frown.

SHAD'S EXTENDED PAUSE made Laurie more anxious than she already was. The change in his expression told her much of what he must not want to say. Having not eaten since breakfast made her more sensitive and nervous than she might have been otherwise, and she concluded he didn't like the finished product.

Her eyes began to tear up. It was when she sniffled that he turned to her.

"What's the matter, Angel?" Shad questioned her softly with a true look of concern in his dark eyes.

"You don't like your haircut, do you? I did the best I could." She began to cry again, wondering what was wrong with her. How come she couldn't stop being so emotional? Why did he have this effect on her?

Shadow Hawk jumped to his feet and, without considering whether he should, he placed his hands on her shoulders, whispering to her in Cheyenne, "Angel, I don't care about my hair. I care about you. I love you, and anything you do to me is okay. Sweet Angel, please don't cry."

He took a deep breath and whispered again in English, "My Angel, please don't cry. My hair is fine. You repaired Mrs. Gates' attempts, and it's fine." With that, he slowly released his grasp from her shoulders.

SHADOW HAWK FELT a dam break inside, as if he had finally admitted something to Laurie he'd wanted to say for days. He stared at her as if he was trying to tell her something with his eyes, holding her gaze for several seconds, hoping she would speak to him, to tell him his feelings were reciprocated. When she made no response, except to watch him with a mystified expression, he finally bit his lower lip and looked away.

Then, slowly, Shadow Hawk turned and disappeared into the great room, leaving a dumbstruck Laurie surrounded by his strewn, dark locks.

LAURIE REACHED DOWN with damp pools swimming in her eyes to gather the treasured remnants of Shad's glorious hair to take to her room. At least she would have this, even if there was nothing else left for her.

— 18 —

LAURIE WAS UP early the next morning. She had cut a length of her own long hair and braided it. She tied both ends with satin turquoise ribbons and went silently down the stairs to the great room. Shadow Hawk was already up and at the stables. Laurie quietly placed the braid in the buffalo hide satchel he carried. She stealthily slipped from the room and headed to the kitchen.

"Shad will have some reminder of me, regardless of how he may try to forget," she murmured, comforting herself.

Mrs. Gates eyed Laurie, smiled her morning greeting, and commented, "Ya' are up early this mornin', too. I met Shad at the back door with your papa. As I was comin' in, they was goin' out. Said they'd both be back for breakfast in 'bout an hour or so." She continued cracking the eggs as she finished with, "I saw Shad's 'ead this mornin', an' it looks a whole lot better than I could 'ave done. 'E's one of those men whose 'air looks good long or short. It's just a shame 'e's leavin' today. I was just gettin' used to havin' 'im around."

The housekeeper cut Laurie a sideways glance, and the young woman felt her stomach tighten at the mention of Shad leaving. Yesterday, her papa had sat in her room and talked with her about several things concerning their visitor. It had helped her understand why he was going, even though it didn't soften the ache in her heart. The one thing her papa never mentioned was Shad's engagement, and she didn't bring it up. Now she wondered why both her papa and Shad were up so early. What could they be doing?

"Mrs. Gates, did they say what they were after?" Laurie queried the housekeeper.

"Your papa said 'e was goin' to give Shad a 'orse or two," came the reply. "Your papa and 'e 'ave already made arrangements for Shad to return them at a later date, accordin' to the way they was talkin'."

Laurie sat down at the comfortable kitchen table. Her heart leaped. Had Mrs. Gates said he was going to return them? That meant he would be coming back sometime soon. Her somber mood lifted at the prospect of being able to see Shad again. She wondered which horse or horses he would take. They had several to choose from, but none were the ones he had told her he enjoyed riding the most. Laurie knew which horse Shad said he preferred. Her Shadow!

She didn't want to entertain the thought of parting with the beloved mare, yet her heart was already broken at the notion of never seeing Shad again. Surely, he would know how much he meant to her if she loaned him her Shadow. He knew how much she loved her horse. He also knew she had been willing to risk her father's wrath and even her life for the adored beast.

Without saying a word to Mrs. Gates, Laurie headed out the door for the barn stable. As she approached the large building, the door swung open with her father leading out the most spirited of the stallions, Desperado. Shad followed, closing the double doors behind them.

"Well, what are you doing out here so early this cool, windy morning? Making sure that Shad didn't choose your Shadow as a going-away present?" Her father grinned at her as he handed over the reins to Shad, who was managing to keep his distance from Laurie with an unemotional expression that told of his strength and determination to be gone from the ranch today.

"That's why I came out." Laurie paused for a moment before continuing. "I want Shad to take my horse," she said quickly and with force. She wanted both of them to know she was serious.

This time it was her papa whose jaw dropped in astonishment. "What did you just say?" He chuckled with the unexpected words he had heard his daughter utter. "Would you repeat that again, this time a little more slowly?" With a humorous tone to his words, he pushed his daughter, "I don't think my ears heard you correctly, and I want to be sure I got it right."

A flustered, warm-faced Laurie replied, "You heard me the first time, Papa. Shad told me he likes my horse the best of all. He likes her because she's part mustang. Isn't that right, Shad?"

Now it was Shad's turn to turn red-faced. He glanced at Aidan and took a breath before he answered. "Yes, I do like her pony. She's built like the horses of my people. They have more stamina than most horses. They're fast, and they can survive on less food and water."

Laurie showed a gratified smile to her father, feeling she had won an argument.

But Shad went on to say, "However, where I'm headed, they will expect a different horse than an Indian pony. The towns I plan to visit will be more accepting of a horse like this." He patted Desperado's dark, sorrel mane.

Laurie's was crestfallen. He wouldn't be taking her mare, which meant he wouldn't be bringing her back. Maybe he wouldn't return at all.

SHADOW HAWK SAW Laurie's demoralized expression, and he was unable to take his eyes from her. He couldn't stand the disappointment written on her face. He spoke in his soft, deep voice, "But I do like riding your horse better than any of the others here. If I were riding home, I would definitely borrow yours."

Aidan laughed, getting Shad's attention. "I've got a solution. I told you to take two horses in case you needed to pack anything. Why don't you go ahead and take the little mare? She won't give you any trouble, and you know how much she likes you. She won't be the same after you leave. Little Shadow was already hollering for you when you were leaving the barn with Desperado. I think she's jealous."

Shad looked at Laurie to be sure that was what she wanted. The hope in her misty blue-green eyes told him everything.

"Well, Angel, if you're sure that's what you want, I'd be pleased to ride your Shadow until I reach town."

He had given up trying to call her Laurie. Since Angel was her Christian name, no one had seemed to mind. He could see her delighted expression light up her whole face. That was what he wanted, to please her, now and forever. The satisfaction he felt pleasing his angel was worth any additional stress it might cause him.

Aidan glanced from one of the young people to the other, taking in the contented expressions on both of their faces, and he smiled at the suggestion. "It will be strange to not have Shad around, but it will be even stranger not having my daughter's horse around, either. I don't know what Laurie has in mind, offering her horse so willingly. Everyone on the ranch loves the little mare. I can't think of a single person who would be glad to see her gone, except maybe Arthur. He never has seemed to like the little beast, and from the way Little Shadow acts around him, the feeling is mutual."

"Thank you, Papa." Laurie beamed.

"Well, son, if we can't change your mind, at least come in and get some provisions before you go." Aidan spoke gruffly, covering his emotions.

Shadow Hawk heard the word "son"' and the word "we." He felt very comforted by the casual way Aidan addressed him. The man was certainly making it hard for him to leave. He had begun to feel like he belonged. That was a new sensation for him. He hadn't felt like he belonged anywhere in a very long time. Since they had left their trapper's cabin all those years ago, he'd always felt he had to prove himself. But here it was different; he had been accepted without any expectations.

He would truly miss Aidan and their quiet conversations. His wisdom had already helped him see things in his own life that he needed to alter and improve. And his faith, that was another thing Shadow Hawk respected. Aidan never took credit for anything. He always gave the tribute to God. Shadow Hawk could only wish he had such a deep understanding of the God that Aidan seem to know so intimately.

But he had also heard "we" when Aidan spoke of him leaving. Angel had never said anything about him not going. Thinking about her wanting him to stay changed his outlook entirely. His angel hadn't requested him to stay. He knew in his heart she never would. He could understand the reason with her being betrothed to Arthur, but it crushed him as a stone falling from the highest cliff, despite his knowledge.

What puzzled him was why she wanted him to take one of her most valuable possessions, her horse. He understood the attachment she had to her animal, and that filled him with questions. How would this benefit her? What could she gain by letting him have her horse? It didn't add up. Before he could work out the situation, Mrs. Gates rang the breakfast bell, and his questions had to wait. Instead, all he could do was think about them as they walked to the house in silence.

Upon entering, they were greeted with the smells of fresh bacon and eggs. Mrs. Gates had already put the food on the dining table and was getting the coffee cups filled. After Aidan asked the blessing, they began eating without the usual chatter of conversation. Everyone seemed in a solemn mood.

"Well, I can tell by the quietness that Shad must be leavin'. None of ya' could think of a reason for 'im to stay even a wee bit longer?" the housekeeper asked, as she looked pointedly at both Aidan and Laurie.

"I tried my best. He knows he's leaving me shorthanded." Aidan defended himself to Mrs. Gates as he continued, "But he promised he'd return as soon as he's finished his business. So, at least we have that hope."

"I said I would return the horses. I never promised anything more," came Shad's firm retort.

Laurie remained strangely silent, only picking at her food. Mrs. Gates stood beside the table, her arms crossed, and she inquired, "Which of the horses will ya' be a'takin'?"

"Desperado and Little Shadow," answered Shad.

"What? Ya' are takin' my dearie's Shadow?" Mrs. Gates shot back her question in surprise. "No wonder the little girl's sad. Everyone knows 'ow she loves that beast."

Laurie glanced up from her plate and smiled gratefully at the housekeeper's remarks.

"It was her idea, not mine," Shadow Hawk replied quickly. He had begun to wish he hadn't agreed to take the animal if it made him the cause of Laurie's discomfort.

"Dearie, do ya' want Shad to take your 'orse? Are ya' sure?" the housekeeper insisted.

"Yes, I want him to take my horse," Laurie whispered. With that, she pushed her plate away, only taking time to drink a little of her milk.

Mrs. Gates looked thoughtful for a moment then replied, "Well, at least I guess ya' made one man 'appy. My husband said that Arthur of yours could 'ardly stand your Little Shadow. 'E said 'e was always trying to get ya' to ride some other horse when 'e was here to go a'ridin' with ya'. 'E'll be pleased that she's gone."

Shadow Hawk looked darkly at Laurie. He understood, now. She was getting married and didn't want her horse to be a problem. It would be easier for her if the little mare wasn't here when Arthur came back to claim her as his bride. It wasn't because she cared about his feelings; it was all about making Arthur happy. He should have known.

Shadow Hawk felt the urge to leave and to leave now. When he pushed his chair back, the legs scraped on the floor, causing everyone to glance in his direction. He tried to speak, though his voice was choked with emotion.

"I think it best if I go now. Aidan, I am much obliged for your kindness and generosity. I don't know when I'll be returning with your horses, but I give you my word that I will bring them back."

Aidan stood up slowly, shook the young brave's hand, and said, "I trust you, Shad, as a man of integrity. I won't be worried about the return of my horses. However, I'd like to have a word of prayer before you set off."

Aidan asked God to bless Shad on his journey and to help him find the answers his heart was searching for. He also prayed for God's Divine protection and peace, and for Shad to be returned safely to them.

Shadow Hawk was deeply moved by the way Aidan cared for him. He almost wanted to stay despite Laurie, despite everything, but he had other things driving him. The part of his heart that had been filled with resentment for his father was still too strong for him to dismiss so lightly. It was with great heaviness that he lifted the weighty buffalo hide satchel, laden down by the goodies Mrs. Gates had packed before he returned to the house for breakfast.

The housekeeper gave him a hug. Aidan handed Shad five gold pieces, despite the youth exclaiming that he didn't need the money. Aidan said he wouldn't loan him a horse if he didn't take the coins, insisting, "Just in case."

Shad swore he'd return the gold pieces when he returned the horses.

Laurie was the last one to see him off, and it wasn't until he was on her horse that she came up to him and spoke. What she said astonished and pleased him equally. In Cheyenne, she spoke a traditional parting statement, "You are in my heart."

"Where did you learn that?" he questioned her with a smile, while drinking in every part of her. He knew he might not ever see her again. He wanted to remember every detail of Angel, his angel. Her hair and deep turquoise eyes burned themselves into his memory.

"I have my ways," was all she would say, though her smile showed she was thrilled that he was pleased with her for speaking Cheyenne.

Shadow Hawk stared down at her with moisture-blurred eyes. This angel with her long, auburn tresses had changed his heart and almost his world. Yet, she wasn't his to love, not as he wanted. He would need to tell her good-bye forever. That wasn't how he had wanted it to end. He wanted to say other things, too, but his wisdom told him the longer he prolonged his parting, the harder it would be.

"I love you, my sweet angel, and my heart is yours, forever." His words were spoken in Cheyenne, revealing his heart, although his angel wouldn't know them as such. His farewell remark was in English, to ensure that she understood. "You are in my heart, also."

He lifted the reins, touched his heels lightly to the animal's flanks, and with a jerk, rode off on the young mare. There was a crispness in the morning air, and with steam snorting from the horse's nostrils, she moved forward. The stallion Shadow Hawk planned to ride when among the white man followed him.

WITHOUT LOOKING BACK, he never saw what he was leaving, a tearful Laurie staring at the only man she had ever really loved.

— 19 —

IT WAS TWO days since Shad had left, and Laurie's heart was still breaking.

She got up and dressed through her tears every morning and in a fog of incomprehension went out for her ride on Thunder, a massive beast with a regal air that was admired by all on the ranch. Most of the hands would be honored to ride the elegant creature. Not Laurie. Thunder wasn't the same as her Little Shadow. The horse couldn't read her intentions like her own did.

She also didn't care for the jerky movements Thunder made when trotting across the meadow, though even during her grief, she admitted that was an unfair assessment. Little Shadow had an exceptionally smooth gait. Even so, her eyes would fill with moisture, and her heart would wrench itself with the loneliness inside. At her deepest misery, it was as if Thunder was showing off, and Laurie would return more frustrated than when she began her ride.

Afterward, never one to punish an animal for her own foibles, she would take him back to the stables and let one of the hands put him out for the day. Returning to the house, she would help Mrs. Gates with breakfast. It kept her busy, and she needed to stay occupied, or she would burst into tears.

The housekeeper admitted she appreciated the additional help in the kitchen, showing Laurie small moments of warm affection. One morning, when the girl's eyes were especially damp, Mrs. Gates set her pie-making duties aside and wrapped her arms around her young protégé. For a full five minutes, her caring arms supported the flame-haired nymph while her sobs wracked her slender body. When the scene drew to a close, the older woman looked Laurie in the face, brushed the tears away, and told her that with spring coming on, there would be garden vegetables to can and jellies and jams to make, along with fruit to dry for next winter. She would be happy to have the extra assistance to make things go quicker.

LAURIE FOUND BREAKFAST gave her time to think. Mrs. Gates was busy in the kitchen, the housekeeper's husband was having breakfast with the hands, and Laurie's papa liked his early morning meal to suit his schedule, not the other way around.

When they could, they enjoyed the meal together, but ranching was her papa's life, and situations didn't always follow the tick of the clock. Numerous times, Laurie had breakfasted alone. It was a peaceful respite from her nights of turmoil and deep-seated despair at the losses that had overtaken her life.

This morning her papa had yet to come down, and Laurie was certain the smell of pork sausages, eggs scrambled in drippings, and steaming biscuits would draw him in soon. The sun outside the window was just lighting the mountains in the distance, and she let her mind wander to the next few months. She had always helped in picking the garden and the orchards, but for the past four years, Rose, a young neighboring rancher's wife, had come and helped out in trade for Mrs. Gates assisting her can her garden as well. She would stay for three days straight while most of the canning was done. Then her husband would come along with their two young sons, and they would make the eight-hour journey back home with Mrs. Gates in tow. Four days later, Daniel would go after his wife and bring her back to the ranch.

This year Rose was expecting their third child sometime in mid-summer around the latter part of June, or perhaps the first of July, so she wouldn't be helping out. Just as always, though, Mrs. Gates would go and assist the family with their canning and stay to help with the midwifery duties.

Rose and her husband, Diego Rivera, were from Texas. They had moved to this part of the continent after their Spanish land grant was no longer honored by the United States. Greedy settlers had come to the San Antonio area and were taking land deeded to old, established Spanish families. Even though his family had fought for their land, most of it was lost, leaving only a small parcel of the once-vast holdings the Riveras had owned.

Rose's family had been of the white settlers who had moved to Texas after it had become an independent country. She had met Diego at the mission school they attended on his family's ranch, and they had fallen in love. Five years ago, they married and moved to the Colorado territory with the hope of raising cattle and building a new life for themselves. They now held a small ranch and a few head of cattle.

Although life could be hard, they seemed to be content. They visited the Kerrigan's about three times a year, staying for two or three days. The last visit was Thanksgiving when they had announced the news of their impending child. They were hoping for a girl. Laurie enjoyed their company and their two small, lively sons. One was four in February, and the other would be two in September.

Laurie was still thinking about the Rivera family when her father sat down at breakfast.

"Papa, do you think I should go over and help Mrs. Gates when Rose Rivera's garden comes in?" She also suggested the housekeeper might need her assistance with the children, though the real reason was needing to see walls that wouldn't remind her of

Shad.

Aidan smiled. "Well, I reckon we need to give it some consideration. How's our patch doing after the freeze?"

Before she could answer, an approaching horse sounded outside. Mrs. Gates commented from the kitchen, "I can see out the window well as anyone, and 'ere comes your beau, Arthur. Finish up, Laurie, so's you can get out and meet him."

Laurie dropped her spoon in midair and squelched a muffled scream. "Oh, Papa! I don't feel I can face him today. Tell him I don't feel well. Tell him I can't see him. Please, Papa," she begged. Laurie slipped her chair out, crumpled her napkin and left it at the side of her plate, and dashed for the stairs and the sanctuary of her room.

ARTHUR RODE UP on a horse he had won in a poker game a couple of years before. It had been a beautiful, spirited steed when it first came into his possession, but he had broken it. Now the horse barely showed signs of life beyond a gallop. Arthur was quite pleased with the job he had done. This was the same general idea he had for Laurie once she became his. However, for now, he had to be very careful how he manipulated the situation. He still intended to get rid of the half-breed. He had already talked to the local Indian agent about a supposed Indian attack threatened against the Kerrigans. He wanted to make sure just enough suspicion was aroused if it was needed.

He stepped to the front door and knocked. He enjoyed knowing Mrs. Gates was in the kitchen and would need to walk through the entire bottom floor of the house to reach the door. He liked forcing subordinates to work. It made him feel powerful and reminded them of their place. He was surprised when Aidan opened the door and greeted him.

The rancher stepped onto the large veranda and carefully closed the door behind him, leaving no opportunity for Arthur to know any business inside the house.

"Morning, Arthur. What brings you to our neck of the woods?" Aidan smiled amiably as he spoke.

Slightly aggravated, Arthur returned the greeting, "I thought perhaps I would catch Miss Laurie before her ride, and we could stroll together for a time. I didn't notice her as I arrived, so I assume she's still out riding, maybe in the upper meadow, perhaps?" He had hoped Aidan would already be out on some cattle venture, as he so often was, but obviously not. He would be forced to deal with him today.

"No, she's not in the upper meadow to my knowledge." Aidan looked amused as he glanced past Arthur, as though searching for his daughter.

"Well, her horse isn't in the stockade. Has she not gotten her from the stables?" Arthur queried.

"I don't reckon her horse is in the barn, either." Aidan spoke slowly, seeming to enjoy the mounting frustration in the young man.

"Humph." Arthur cleared his throat with distinct emphasis, picking up on the vague answers, and wondering what was afoot. "If Laurie's not out riding, and her horse isn't in the barn, where is she?" His eyes narrowed, and he could feel his anger mounting.

"Who? Laurie or the horse?" Aidan grinned.

Arthur's irritation was almost to the point of exploding. Who did Kerrigan think he was, trying to unsettle him? The man knew exactly who he wanted. Despite what he would like to say, Arthur calmed himself and chose his words carefully.

"I would like to speak with Miss Laurie if she's available." Arthur meted out the sounds in a forced and measured manner, so as not to let his extreme irritation through.

"She's not available right now, but I'll be happy to tell her when I see her that you spoke after her," Aidan finished and put his hand on the door.

"Wait," Arthur requested in an anxious tone. "You mean I rode all the way out here and wasted my time for no reason?"

"You enjoyed the ride and the sunrise, didn't you? That's a gift from God in itself. Seeing a new day is never a waste."

"What about the stranger? How is he faring?" Arthur wanted to know just what was going on behind the door of the Kerrigan house. He was confident that the half-breed was taking full advantage of anything he could get his hands on.

"I guess that's something you'll have to ask him

yourself. I don't answer for other men, only for myself and what's mine." Aidan bid Arthur a good day and opened the door to step back inside, leaving the man standing befuddled on the front veranda.

Arthur was determined to get some answers, so he headed to the stables and the corral. He mounted his horse and rode away from the ranch a half hour later even more confused. The stableman informed him the half-breed had left a few days before and taken Laurie's horse with him. That was extremely odd to Arthur, considering how much she loved and admired the beast. But, it was fitting to know that both half-breeds no longer occupied the Kerrigan domain.

Despite that kernel of satisfaction, it still left a sour note in him that all this had happened without his knowledge. Also, why wasn't he allowed inside the house, if no one was there? And where was Laurie? He had been assured she was home, just not feeling well, according to Mr. Gates. This was strange, especially considering the way Mr. Kerrigan had behaved when questioned about her. Why was he keeping his daughter from him?

THE NEXT FEW weeks passed without incident. Arthur returned and once again wasn't given the opportunity to talk with Laurie. He left exasperated and more determined to see her the next time. He knew there were ways to get access to the girl.

He finally planned on creating a diversion to get Aidan away from the ranch. Then he could talk with

Laurie and convince her to marry him. Afterwards, he could continue his plan of mining and power. He was more resolved than ever to claim the Kerrigan holdings as his own. The rumors of gold in Colorado had been circulating since the California gold rush almost ten years earlier. When Arthur heard that the trapper they had killed had gold, his dead body was searched, but he had been carrying very little, only a few nuggets. He was convinced the man knew where there was more, but he had died with his secret and taken it to his grave.

That half-breed who looked like the trapper certainly didn't have any gold on him. Nor did he appear to have access to any, judging by his dress and belongings. Even so, Arthur was confident there was gold somewhere close by, and he intended to claim it first.

— 20 —

THE WARM, EARLY June weather had brought out the wildflowers, and they were in full bloom. Laurie was enjoying the view of the meadow on her morning ride when she saw a buckboard in the distance. Who would be riding up on their place this early in the day? She pulled on the reins and stopped her steed, studying the advancing party. Her heart pounding, she turned the big animal, and with a touch of her heels, she headed back to the ranch in a full gallop to inform her father about the approaching visitor. As soon as Aidan heard the news, he opened a door in his massive, carved oak desk and pulled out his spyglass. He stepped onto the porch and lifted it to his eye to see if he could recognize the driver. He came back shortly and announced that it was Diego Rivera.

Laurie was surprised. She and Mrs. Gates had planned on leaving at the end of the month to help with the Rivera's canning and the birth of their new child. Something must be wrong for Diego to be coming all this way.

As his buckboard approached, wailing cries could be heard by Laurie and her father. He drove up to where Aidan and Laurie were standing, sending dust flying under the feet of the panting horses. In the back of the wagon among crowded boxes and supplies were his two sons and two tiny infants. They were wrapped and lying on quilts to cushion the ride.

There was no sign of Rose.

"Mr. Kerrigan, I have terrible news." Diego's eyes began to water, and his voice shook with emotion. "My wife was expecting twins, and they came early. It was only she and I. She barely delivered the last one before she . . ." He couldn't bring himself to say the word. He silently mouthed "died" as tears began to flow down his cheeks.

Laurie's face went cold with grief. How could this happen to such a happy couple? In an instant, her thoughts were stopped with the man's announcement of even more serious matters.

Diego continued, "The little ones need constant attention. I cannot take care of them and run my ranch."

"A housekeeper, Diego? I'm certain Mrs. Gates could help until someone could be hired." Aidan glanced at his daughter, and Laurie nodded her agreement. She could manage the kitchen until the housekeeper returned.

"It's more than that, my friend." Diego wiped his eyes with his sleeves, leaving dusty streaks across his cheeks. "Even with help, it would be impossible for me to live there without my Rose. I have no choice but to go back to Texas where I have family. I must think of my sons. I cannot raise them alone. The twins are only six days old and will never survive the trip." His voice choked up, and it was a minute before he could continue. "I wasn't sure they would survive after my wife's . . . death."

"How can we help?" Laurie asked, her heart breaking, this time for someone who'd faced a harder difficulty than even she.

Tears continued to drip slowly down Diego's tanned cheeks. "I would like to request a very big favor of you and your daughter." Diego held his breath a moment then looked at Aidan with desperate eyes and asked, "Do you think you and your daughter could take care of my twins? I don't know who else to turn to. I know my wife enjoyed being around your family. It kept her from being so homesick. Please, Señor Kerrigan," he murmured in a barely-heard whisper.

AIDAN GLANCED TO where his daughter was already taking charge. She had reached into the buckboard and picked up one of the wailing infants. At her soft voice and gentle touch, the little one gradually quit crying. Aidan grieved at the horrible predicament his neighbor was in. He couldn't imagine having to give up his precious daughter, but he could easily imagine the consequences of not taking these infants. Even though this was very abrupt, he accepted that life in this wilderness he called home often took sudden departures from the paths people intended to travel. It could be harsh, also, as evidenced by Diego's request.

He said a silent prayer and then replied, "Diego, we're so sorry for your loss. Rose was like a daughter to me, and she was a wonderful wife to you. Of course, we will take care of the twins for you."

"Thank you, Señor Kerrigan." Diego's eyes began to flow again, in an unabashed display of relief and gratitude.

Mr. Kerrigan put his arm on Diego's shoulder and spoke in a low voice, "I know what it's like to lose the love of my life. My wife has been gone almost ten years now. I still miss her. Every day I'm thankful for my Laurie. She's been a real blessing to me."

Diego smiled at Aidan's comforting words. "The boy is named Artemio Shiloh Rivera after both our fathers, and the girl is named Angelina Rose Rivera after our mothers. Please tell them that I love them, but I had to do what was best."

"Of course. They will understand." Aidan consoled the man with a soothing tone.

Diego handed Aidan an envelope. "I'm leaving a letter that gives you the deed to my homestead. Please take my cattle as payment for the kindness you are doing for my family. There is also a note that tells my children about their family and where we live in Texas. I'm headed that way, and I think I can get there before winter if I start now. You're welcome to the cabin and anything you want. My dream is to return someday, but I don't know if that will ever be possible. I only took what I had to have to make the trip. Our garden is still there, too. I picked a few vegetables, but here was no use in taking them only to have them spoil."

Aidan was moved by the young rancher's dire condition. He told him to wait while he went into the house. He brought out 10 gold pieces and said, "I'm buying your cattle and saving the ranch as an inheritance for your children."

Diego was touched by Aidan's generosity. He thanked him profusely and finished by giving each one of his tiny infants a kiss. Aidan held Artemio in his arms while he said a short prayer, and then he waved as Diego climbed aboard the buckboard, lifted the reins, and with a call to the horses, headed southeast.

LAURIE FELT OVERWHELMED at the prospect of raising two babies. After their devotions the first evening, her father assured her he was confident she could do it—with Mrs. Gates' help, of course. The first few nights the infants slept in Laurie's bed while one of the upstairs guest rooms was being converted into a nursery. Aidan made the long journey to the Rivera's cabin and retrieved a cradle and a few other items needed for the babies. Once back at the ranch, he retrieved Laurie's hand-carved cradle from storage, as well. Both were set up in the freshly prepared nursery to welcome their new charges.

Within two weeks, the tiny babies had settled into the household and were loved by all. Because of their premature birth, their arms and legs were little more than sticks. Laurie questioned their tiny size, wondering at how they managed to survive each day, and Mrs. Gates observed that it would be many weeks before they took on the appearance of the fat, overfed newborns most parents normally welcomed into their lives.

Their presence in the Kerrigan household kept Laurie's mind busy. Thankfully, she didn't have time to think about Shad and her beloved Little Shadow. She was occupied from morning until night with feeding, changing, and entertaining the tiny, fragile things. Though her eyes still misted at unexpected times, her hands remained busy with the new arrivals.

ON THE THIRD week of the new additions to the ranch, Arthur made another trip out. He was determined to see Laurie. He hadn't spoken with her since April, and it was now the first week of July. He had formulated a plan to get Mr. Kerrigan out of the house, and as he rode up to the building, he let his eyes rove the various parts of the compound, noting the ranch hands busy in the corrals, and one man just walking into the barn. He would announce he had seen cattle on the loose, and they appeared to have the Kerrigan brand. The hands would be occupied, forcing Aidan to head a party to search for the wayward herd. He felt confident his plan would work, and with a cocky step, he strode briskly to the kitchen door and knocked. The housekeeper yelled, "Come on in."

As he opened the door, he was startled to see Laurie sitting at the kitchen table with a small baby in her arms, and Mrs. Gates holding another one. Before he could say anything, Mrs. Gates said, "Hand me Angel, and I'll change 'er and Shiloh. Then I'll bring your babies back to ya'."

Laurie planted a kiss on the dark-haired little girl and then handed her into the housekeeper's waiting arms.

Arthur stood frozen in absolute revulsion. How could these babies be Laurie's? Who could be the father of these two infants? He stared as the housekeeper carried them out of the room.

Laurie smiled at Arthur, and she asked, "They're beautiful, aren't they?"

Still stunned, he only nodded, and then he found the nearest chair and sat down. He felt the life and energy draining out of his body. How had he let this happen? He'd been told that she wasn't feeling well, but never did he suspect this. Mr. Kerrigan must have been hiding her from him because he didn't want Arthur to see Laurie in a family way. Then, if these were her children, where was her husband? As importantly, who was her husband?

Laurie interrupted his thoughts with, "I never thought I'd be called into motherhood so young. But apparently God thinks I can handle it. Raising babies is a huge responsibility."

Arthur made no comment, just looked at her in dumbfounded dismay.

Laurie stood, lifting a cloth to wipe her hands. "I hope you don't think me rude, Arthur, but I truly don't have time for your visits, anymore. Mrs. Gates will be returning the twins to me shortly, and I'll have to take them upstairs for a nap."

Arthur questioned, "When did they arrive?" He was still dazed by the whole scenario.

"They came early. Mrs. Gates and I weren't expecting them until about now. It was quite a shock to us all."

The back screen opened, and in came Aidan Kerrigan for the midday meal. "I noted your horse outside, Arthur. It's a beautiful day for a ride, isn't it?"

Arthur nodded, still dumbstruck. His world had just been knocked out from under him. He had plans for the Kerrigan ranch, big plans, and now they were ruined because of this stupid girl. How could she destroy his life like this?

While Arthur was still in his almost stupor-like state, the housekeeper returned with the infant twins. Arthur stared at them and for the first time noticed their dark hair and richly hued complexions. Their coloring didn't match Laurie's. Who would be close enough to woo her?

Suddenly, it hit him like a bolt of lightning. The half-breed! They had to be his! Thoughts ricocheted through Arthur's brain. But how? They only found him a couple of months back. Or at least that's what Laurie had wanted him to believe. But what was it her father had said? He had known him before he was introduced to Arthur. How long before? He needed some answers.

"Where's the father? I'd like to congratulate him," Arthur queried suspiciously, still staring at the tiny babies. Laurie took one from the housekeeper and held it lovingly in her arms. Now, maybe he would get an honest reply.

"Headed somewhere south, I reckon," came Aidan's careless response. "We haven't seen him in some time."

Arthur hardened his expression, feeling disgust and dismay sweep over him. Mr. Kerrigan didn't seem to be the least upset by his daughter giving birth, and he seemed equally unfazed by the children's father abandoning his newborn twins.

Laurie kissed the infant she held on the forehead, and she called without looking at Arthur, "Thank you, Arthur, for coming to see me, but I must keep the little ones on a schedule. Otherwise, they won't sleep well tonight. I must carry them to the nursery for their nap." She and Mrs. Gates headed for the staircase, each carrying a baby.

Arthur no longer had any reason to linger. He had been blindsided by this new development. He would need to return to town and think, perhaps at Slim's Saloon, where the liquor flowed like water and people made sense. He must come up with a new scheme. His friends at Slim's would surely have advice for him, although he must be careful not to reveal too much of what he knew about the ranch and where the gold might be found. He couldn't let all his well-laid plans evaporate because of two useless little brats. No, he had worked too hard and deliberated too long to be ousted by that half-breed.

Arthur stood to his feet, and he smoothed his hair back before speaking. In the most neutral tone he could muster, he offered words that he was sure would ease the moment and hide his fury. "I'm sure congratulations are in order. I, of course, had no idea. But, since this seems to be a decision you are totally in favor of, Mr. Kerrigan, that means you are pleased with the arrival of the twins, I presume?"

Arthur hoped to read some disappointment or despair on the older gentleman's face. However, he was gravely mistaken. What he saw and heard troubled him more than the first revelation.

"Not only am I pleased with it, I encouraged it. There's nothing like young children to make a house a home. I think Laurie is turning out to be a wonderful mother."

Arthur couldn't believe the man's attitude. Aidan had encouraged his daughter to have children with that half-breed scoundrel. Did they even bother to get married? Arthur made a half-hearted attempt to sound nonchalant as he probed the situation further.

"How long has Laurie been married, if I may ask?"

"She's not." Aidan grinned as he answered.

In those flippant words, Arthur saw the situation as it must be, and it painted the Kerrigan household as different than he had imagined. Kerrigan had encouraged his daughter to produce offspring with a vagabond, while at the same time insinuating she was too good for Arthur or anybody else. His pious Christian attitude was wasted on that low-life, good-for-nothing scam artist.

Arthur's churning thoughts were halted by Aidan's strong, determined voice.

"God works in mysterious ways to bring his will into our lives, Arthur. What we must do is not judge others but try to love them and give them an opportunity to know Christ for themselves." Aidan went on to say, "If I were to try to judge you, I'd say that you were a gambler with something to hide, maybe something to do with the young man who was here, or perhaps his father. My mind goes back a few years. There was a gang of ruffians and outlaws around these parts about ten years ago. It seems a lot of bad things happened around then. But, with the California gold rush, most of the bad hombres went away, though not soon enough for me. Some innocent people suffered and died unnecessarily before they hightailed it out of Colorado and her bounty."

Aidan stopped and stared at Arthur. His eyes seemed to bore through him. Arthur felt himself break out in a sweat, and he began to shake ever so slightly. He licked his lips and started absently popping his knuckles. Aidan must know something, but exactly what, he wasn't sure. All Arthur wanted to do was get out alive. He had to escape before he was exposed as the thief and accomplice to murder that he was. But how could he do it without giving himself away?

With his heart pounding, Arthur spoke in his most unctuous voice, "I'm glad you're not judging me, because you would have judged wrongly. I can see I've wasted enough of your valuable time, so I'll take my leave. Give my best regards to your daughter and her babies. There's no need to escort me; I'll see myself out."

As Arthur blurted out his parting statement, he was already to the door and headed to his horse. He had a foot in the stirrup and his leg over the saddle in one motion, and yanking the reins from the hitching post, he kicked the animal in the flanks, sending it into a frantic gallop away from the house.

NEVER HAD AIDAN seen a man so set on getting away from somewhere. With a snort of derision, he turned to see Mrs. Gates with a grin on her face. Suddenly, he laughed at what she must be thinking. Aidan knew Mrs. Gates had never liked the man much, and he also knew there would be no love lost if he never returned. However, as he reached for the remnants of the bread that had been cooked the day before, he realized he had a lot to mull over. He added a slice of meat to his bread to make a sandwich for dinner, and he took a bite to settle the thoughts running through his mind.

— 21 —

IT WAS LATE August, the end of summer would arrive soon, and Shadow Hawk was headed back to his mother's people. By mid-September, the morning air would be crisp, and long shadows would dapple the forest floor. He needed to be back in time to help his mother move to the winter camp.

He had found none of the answers he was searching for, but he had found a measure of serenity. No one had seen or heard about his father since his disappearance, yet everyone told him the same story. He had been a good trapper and seemed to love his family.

As his wavy hair lengthened over the summer, many people commented on the resemblance to his father. Some seemed genuinely pleased to make his acquaintance. Slowly, the anger he had harbored for years turned to futility, and the revenge changed to remorse. Only Aidan's words seemed to bring him comfort and peace. Something about the man made him feel better about his father and about himself.

And, of course, there was always his angel. He had only been on the trail two days when he discovered the braided lock of dark auburn hair pushed to the very bottom of his satchel. He knew his angel had put it there to remind him of her. Even if she hadn't done so, how could he forget the most wonderful creature in the world? He was consumed with thoughts of her. He knew he would never forget her, no matter what else happened in his life.

He had only a few days' ride left to reach his tribe. It would be different going back, and he had mixed emotions about returning. He wasn't the same warrior who had left in the early spring. Just in the short time he was away, he had matured and accepted himself for who he was, the son of Jeremiah Hawke. But he was also the son of Laughing River and a Wolf Soldier of the Southern Cheyenne tribe.

With no answers about the man who had been married to his mother, he began to reconcile his father's disappearance. It was as if he had died, and Shadow Hawk found himself grieving for him and wishing he was there. He thought of questions he wished he could ask his father. Even though he had spent most of his years with the Cheyenne, no one in the tribe had spoken of his father even once.

The only man who had ever seemed to understand and fill that void was another white man, Aidan. His easy-going manner and reassuring voice reminded him of the man he had loved for the first years of his life. Although Shadow Hawk had known the man only for a few weeks, he had become a father figure to him and had made a lasting impact on his life.

However, he knew from his broken heart that he couldn't return to live or work at the Kerrigan ranch. He could never trust himself around Angel. She might be married by now. He would only go there to return the horses, and then he would leave. He wouldn't spend a single night. He would never stay there again.

Having resigned his heart to a life of loneliness and solitude, Shadow Hawk made his way toward the summer camping grounds. He hadn't yet reached his destination when a group of warrior-clad Wolf Soldiers appeared on bare-backed ponies out of a stand of trees. They confronted him in a very aggressive and threatening manner, surrounding his mount and secondary animal, and penning him in. The leader held up a weapon, and his companions did the same, and they moved in, yelling, as if he were a white man who had no right to be on their land. This surprised Shadow Hawk, because his tribe was usually peaceful with the local people, including the white man. It was only after he had yelled to them in Cheyenne that they recognized him.

As they approached him, they brought upsetting news. Gold had been discovered, and white men, miners and settlers, would soon be rushing onto their land, trying to claim it as their own. They were leaving early for the winter camping grounds, maybe never to return. The Indian agent had already been there and said he couldn't hold back the people if they came in force and in large numbers. He had also told them the Indians had no rights and weren't allowed to own the land themselves. None of the land they lived on could be claimed as their own.

The agent had come to them in July, as soon as he had heard the news about the first claim being signed, telling them he was trying to prepare them for the worst. He felt bad for the tribe; he had been their advocate and friend for many years. However, he knew the signs and wanted to give this Cheyenne band at least an opportunity to escape before they were killed or forced to leave.

Shadow Hawk was disturbed. His tribe would have difficulty relocating. They already had to defend their space from the Arapaho, who were constantly trying to hunt on their land and steal their horses. The white men in this area had always been accepting, for the most part, and in turn, the Southern Cheyenne had been accepting of them, too.

As he drew near, he could see the tribe breaking down the camp they had called home for the past several months. They usually didn't leave until the first snowfall. That wouldn't be for another four to six weeks.

Shadow Hawk realized the seriousness of the

news as he searched for his mother. He spotted her as she was bringing dried venison into her lodge. She didn't recognize him for about three breaths, and then she shouted, "My son who was lost has now returned. He has found his way home to his mother's heart." Tears of joy ran down her face as she hugged him. Soon, yells of greetings could be heard as other warriors shouted out their welcome as well.

It was nice to see his mother again. For the first time in weeks, his heart felt a twinge of gladness. He hadn't realized how much he missed her. He had so much to tell her, but first he knew he had to apologize.

"Mother, I'm here to say I'm sorry for not believing you. My father must be dead. I have failed you as a son and want to ask for your forgiveness. I will always be a devoted son to you and will try my best never to let your heart be disappointed in me again."

Shadow Hawk finished with his head bowed in submission to his mother.

LAUGHING RIVER HAD tears in her eyes. She could tell that in the brief time her son was gone, he had truly matured. Shadow Hawk had always said his father abandoned them, and she had sensed deep down in her son the hope of his father returning. It was now clear he had reconciled to his father's death. His acceptance of his death let her know he understood his father would never return.

But something else was different about him.

Shadow Hawk was even more reserved than she remembered. She noticed the large stallion and the smaller horse her son rode. She asked him where he had gotten the horses. All he said was, "I borrowed them from a friend." He told her he would be returning them before they left for the winter camp.

"You must hurry," Laughing River encouraged. "Our people plan to leave before the next full moon."

That would be in less than a week.

SHADOW HAWK HADN'T planned on that happening so soon. He wasn't prepared to face his angel, but it didn't seem he had a choice.

He stayed up late telling his mother about the adventures he had, but there was one part he couldn't bring himself to share. He intentionally left out his angel. His mother might sense something more had happened than he was telling, but she remained silent. He would reveal all to her when he was ready.

The next day he spent catching up with the other Wolf Soldiers. They were glad for his safe return, even if his shortened hair did make him look much like a white man. It had grown back quickly, however, and now almost touched his shoulders. His mother told him how much he favored his father with his hair cut in the same style he wore.

Laughing River had also noticed a certain auburn braid partially exposed in his leather satchel, reaching out to touch it one evening when Shadow Hawk opened his satchel. However, she said nothing and just watched him. He kissed the braided lock before returning it to the satchel. Laughing River remarked that Shadow Hawk was truly a man now, if someone had his heart.

The next morning, he rose early and told his mother that on the following day he was returning the horses he had borrowed. When questioned how long he would be away, he answered, "I'm riding to the Kerrigan ranch. I shouldn't be gone over one day, though my return might be dawn the following morning."

His mother smiled in pleasant surprise. "I remember going there with your father. They were very nice. The wife was very friendly, even though I didn't speak good English at the time."

It was Shadow Hawk who was surprised, now. "You knew Mrs. Kerrigan? Angel . . . I mean . . . Laurie told me she died when she was a young girl."

His mother's expression saddened as she remembered the news. "The man was a good friend of your father's. I'm glad you made his acquaintance. Your father went to visit him two or three times a year and took you there a time or two when you were a little boy." Laughing River smiled at the fond memories of their past life. "So, you are leaving one day, and then returning the next? I will plan for two days."

"No," Shadow Hawk quickly answered, "only one day. It's a long ride, but I need to return their horses and also help you get ready for the move to our winter camp."

While he was finishing, there was a commotion outside, and the Indian agent for the local tribe rode up, his horse's feet sending dust flying. Many men stopped what they were doing and began to gather, for it was surprising to see him so early in the morning. The agent noticed and remarked on the difference in Shadow Hawk's appearance, and he smiled as he spoke, "You look more like your pa every day. He was a good man. However, the news I'm bringing isn't good." His smile had faded, and he now wore a grim face.

"What does the white man wish to do that will further harm us? It must surely be so." Several warriors who had gathered at the agent's appearance jostled each other in agreement.

"Three more claims are being filed on this land. There's no guarantee you will even be able to keep your winter home further south. The talk is relocation entirely. I'll fight it for as long as I can, but I suspect it will happen sooner or later. This is the beginning of the end, I'm afraid."

Shadow Hawk was sobered. He couldn't imagine living anywhere else. His people had been here for multiple generations, and this was their home.

This was a lot to think about before he left to return the horses. Together with the other Wolf warriors, he gathered to thank the agent for his honesty. The man would stay a couple of days and then go on to other tribes under his jurisdiction. That would at least give Shadow Hawk enough time to get back before the move.

LAUGHING RIVER HAD listened to the Indian agent as well, and it tore at her. She knew the feeling of hopelessness that her tribe would soon experience. She had felt it when her husband hadn't returned. Without options, she had returned to her tribe, leaving her once-tranquil life behind. Now, here she was faced with leaving the only other life she had ever known. At least she was with her people, no matter what happened.

She approached Shadow Hawk. "Why don't you leave today? You can return tomorrow morning, and that will give us time to break down everything and pack. With the news we've just heard, we may have no choice but to leave sooner than the tribe planned." She paused for a moment and sadly commented, "I'm sorry they found your father's gold."

Shadow Hawk looked at her in disbelief. "What do you mean?"

"Your father and Mr. Kerrigan found gold many years ago. It was in the mountains on their ranch. They made a vow to never tell because of all the greediness that was caused by the California gold rush. Someone found out your father had gold, and that's why I believe he was killed. He was worried about leaving for the fort; however, he needed to trade his furs for building supplies. He was ready to start building our new house. He had formulated a design similar to the Kerrigan property, as I had told him how much I enjoyed visiting their ranch. I believe Mr. Kerrigan intended to help in the construction."

THAT WAS MORE startling news for Shadow Hawk. His father had been planning to be a rancher like Aidan. That would have been nice. He and Laurie would have grown up as neighbors, and perhaps their friendship would have developed into something more. He might have been her suitor instead of Arthur.

Nonetheless, all that was taken from him by his father's untimely death. However, this did explain the gold his mother had kept hidden all these years. She had been wise not to reveal it to anyone. It could have caused problems with their tribe, or possibly she might have been killed for it. Shadow Hawk shuddered to think about what might have happened.

He went into their lodge to get his satchel and a few provisions for the ride. His mother followed him in and spoke in low hushed tones

"I wish you to take these saddlebags to the Kerrigan's ranch. They trusted you with their horses. Our gold will be safe there. I'm afraid for our lives if we carry these bags with us much longer. Someone might try to search our things." She showed him the bags under the buffalo hides in the corner.

Shadow Hawk nodded his head yes, and he headed out to get the horses ready for travel. He picked a painted mustang named Concho from their five mounts. The animal was high spirited and fast. Shadow Hawk would ride Concho and bring the other two in tow behind. Little Shadow would follow without question, but the gold-filled saddlebags were heavy, and the other animal was filled with a feistiness that could defy Shadow Hawk's easy control. Anyone observing them would know something was amiss, and he couldn't afford to be waylaid on the journey. Laughing River understood his dilemma and offered to help.

"I could ride alongside, and then you would only need to tow one. The horses without riders could carry the bags covered by a deerskin. You could put the few furs you have on top. It would appear as though you were loaded for trading."

Shadow Hawk saw the sensibility in the suggestion. It would be easier than trying to do this alone. But did his mother really want to go at a time like this? With everything so unpredictable, did she think it was wise to leave the camp?

He asked her, "It would require making camp on the trail. Do you want to be gone an extra day? The tribe is moving soon."

Laughing River assured him that she wanted to come. So, they quietly packed a few things out of the view of prying eyes and headed towards the Kerrigan ranch. Shadow Hawk was mounted on Little Shadow, Laughing River was astride Concho, with Desperado, Keecha, and the gold in tow.

— 22 —

LAUGHING RIVER AND Shadow Hawk had ridden well over halfway toward the Kerrigan ranch when they heard an approaching horse. They quickly sought cover to see who might be coming their direction. After waiting only a few minutes, it was a shock to see Arthur riding rapidly toward the Southern Cheyenne camp. What business could he possibly have there?

Laughing River could tell by her son's troubled expression that he recognized the white man. She had never seen the stranger before. Shadow Hawk offered no explanation while they waited to get back on the trail again, but his brooding was a familiar scene to his mother. He was so much like his father, letting his emotions show through.

When he finally did speak, it was with a hurt tone.

He told his mother briefly what he knew about the man and how he didn't trust him based on what Aidan had told him. He finished in a rancid voice, "I wish this trip was finished. I want to get this over."

His words were spoken very differently than in his earlier tone that had teetered on excitement at seeing Mr. Kerrigan, whom he had addressed as Aidan. Laughing River questioned Shadow Hawk, "Do you not wish to see Aidan again? I thought he was your friend."

BEFORE HE ANSWERED, Shadow Hawk glanced at his mother riding calmly on Concho. He wished he could tell her about his angel. He wanted to, but it would be pointless to do so. He knew she wasn't his angel, but Arthur's. What would be the purpose of talking about someone who didn't care about him as he cared about her?

If only Angel hadn't been so sweet and kind to him. If only her father hadn't been so friendly and understanding. If only he had met her before she met Arthur. That was where he stopped thinking about "if only." They were like the dreams he once had of his father returning, only to be awakened by the harsh truth of lonely abandonment.

"My son, are you not speaking to your mother?" Laughing River looked at her son with a raised eyebrow.

Shadow Hawk ducked his head and replied, "No, Mother. Aidan and I are friends. I shall be happy to see him again. There are other complications that made my words speak harshly."

His mother smiled at him. "I think this might have to do with the long strand of braided auburn hair I saw you push down in your satchel. This is the main reason I wished to come with you. I want to see who could change my son's heart so completely, whether it is Aidan's influence, or perhaps his daughter's."

"You must not embarrass me, Mother." Shadow Hawk now wished he'd kept the braid of hair hidden.

"How old is the daughter of Mr. Kerrigan? You spoke her name. I think you said it was Angel. Is that true?"

Shadow Hawk was aggravated with the questions about Angel, but he knew he had to say something. He could not refuse his mother this information.

"Her name is Laurie, and she's seventeen, almost eighteen. But her name is also Angel and Lover of Horses. She truly does love her horse. She was willing to risk her life for it. I'm riding it now. This is Little Shadow."

His mother smothered a laugh. "Shadow on Little Shadow. Lari is her name, like what your father called me?"

"Yes," came a steely reply, as Shadow Hawk tried to hide his emotions about Laurie. "But her true name is Lareowyn. In her family's old language, the Eowyn means Lover of Horses."

"You seem to know quite a bit about this Lari. I'm pleased you found someone nice on your journey.

Is she the only friend you found? The braid must be hers, surely."

"Yes," he barked, exasperated by the incessant questions. His mother's interest didn't irritate him, but the memory of his disappointment in his angel's marriage commitment to another man did. As his horse plodded along, he let his thoughts meander over all that he had learned and wished for at the Kerrigan ranch. As the hooves of the horse struck the ground, small tufts of dust surrounded the prints left in the dirt, and sometimes the air would stir and carry them away. For the next few hours, they traveled in silence, at times in a dusty confluence of their own making.

As darkness began to swallow the sky, the two travelers settled into a small cave under a rocky ledge. Shadow Hawk tethered the horses, and Laughing River spread blankets in the gathering gloom. They would spend the night and return to the trail at dawn.

IT HAD BEEN hours since Laughing River's son had offered conversation, and his brooding manner told her she would have no company this night. When her head rested against the cave floor, the day's travels took her to sleep in moments.

Shadow Hawk had no such recompense. His agitated tossing awakened his mother on more than one occasion. The next morning, Laughing River looked at her son, and his tired eyes revealed the restless night he had endured. As she turned to fold the blankets, she smiled inwardly, hoping her own anxious emotions were hidden from her son. She knew the look she read in his actions. This boy of hers, this youth who, over the summer, had turned into a man, was wrestling with love for this girl who had given him a lock of her hair. As they mounted their ponies and continued their journey, she felt her spirits lift. Maybe God had answered her prayers after all. At the end of this day, she would know.

Laughing River closely guarded her own hopes and dreams as they crossed the river that led up to the Kerrigan ranch. Would this beautiful place she remembered so fondly still hold its treasured place in her imagination? She held her breath as she and her son crossed the final ridge into the valley; it was as beautiful as she remembered. Mountains framed the background with deep green meadows surrounded by tall pines and aspens.

"God truly smiled when he created this beautiful place," she whispered softly to him as they saw the ranch house looming in the far distance.

They had only traveled a few hundred feet more when the sound of hooves echoed around them. They waited cautiously to see who it would be. Aidan Kerrigan came riding up on Midnight, grinning from ear to ear.

"I saw you coming and thought I would ride out to meet you. Get off that horse, son, and give me a proper greeting."

Shadow Hawk was off his horse in a matter of seconds, and before he could draw a proper breath, he was wrapped in a bear hug from Aidan. Laughing River was touched to see visible tears in the older man's eyes. Shadow Hawk appeared emotionally moved by Mr. Kerrigan, too, telling that he had missed Aidan about as much.

"I've prayed for your safe return every day since you left," Aidan exclaimed, as he clapped the young man on both shoulders. "I'm glad the good Lord has heard and answered my prayers."

IT WAS ONLY after the greeting that Aidan seemed to recognize Shadow Hawk's mother. She was sitting quietly with her long dark hair gently swaying in the breeze. Even Shadow Hawk admitted she had his eyes, the sort he had been told could melt a person all the way into his or her soul.

"Oh, I see you brought your mother with you." Aidan took off his hat and greeted her with, "Pleased to see you, ma'am. You've got one fine son. We've grown real attached to him here."

Shadow Hawk could see a little embarrassment on the part of his mother. She said nothing, only smiled. Her English was probably rustier than her son's, so Shadow Hawk spoke up quickly.

"Aidan, my mother hasn't spoken English in a very long time. However, she wanted to come with me to return the horses. She wanted to also ask a favor of you. We can discuss it when we get to the house, if that's acceptable to you."

Laughing River held up her hand to indicate she

wished to talk. Aidan laughed, remarking that she didn't seem to have any trouble understanding the white man's words, even if she'd not spoken them in years.

"I want to thank you for helping my son find his way," enunciated Shadow Hawk's mother, in a melodious, contralto voice, in slow but perfect English, in the same soft tones Shadow Hawk used.

Shadow Hawk was surprised by his mother's excellent command of the English language.

"He helped us as well, so the feeling is mutual," Aidan remarked, as he mounted his horse and headed back toward the ranch house. Then he yelled over his shoulder, "I'll tell Mrs. Gates there will be two additional guests for supper."

AS SOON AS Aidan reached the house, he went straight to the kitchen. The housekeeper looked up, her puzzled expression revealing that she could tell immediately something was afoot.

"Set the table for two more this evening. Shad's back, and he brought his mother," was all Aidan said, as he headed to go wash up. Mrs. Gates just smiled as he exited, calling out that her Laurie would be happy that her true love was returning.

LAURIE HEARD HER father rustling around in his room. It wasn't uncommon for him to come up before supper, but usually he stepped in and spoke to her first or checked on the twins. They were just lying down from their last feeding, and Laurie was exhausted. She couldn't wait to eat dinner herself and go to bed.

Her days were long and busy with the babies starting to grow. They were almost three months old and were finally starting to look like something other than newborns. She splashed some water on her face and ran her fingers through unruly locks that had slipped out of the braid she kept them in.

She was just about to step out of her room when she heard her father's voice in the hall. As she caught his initial exclamation, she realized they were having company for dinner. She quietly and firmly shut her door in the middle of his excited remarks and leaned her head against the rough wooden wall, refusing to listen to his directions to Mrs. Gates, as she moaned to herself in despair.

It couldn't be Arthur, not after the last time he was here. How could he have the nerve to show up at the house, and for a meal? She had made it clear she had no desire to ever talk or visit with him again.

— 23 —

LAURIE ASSUMED ARTHUR must still be trying to exercise persistence in his quest for courtship and probable marriage, and the idea disgusted her. She considered avoiding the meal altogether but dismissed the idea. She refused to remain sequestered in her room, a prisoner of that odious man, when this was her house and not his. She determined she would let the iron in her backbone be her stamina; she would be pleasant; and when the evening was done, she would see him off as a stranger.

She also refused to dress for the occasion. Arthur deserved none of her best. She would dine in her daily clothing, with her hair in the morning's braid, and he would see she had no time for him or finery.

When she arrived at the table and saw her father

wearing his best work clothes, she queried, "Did you say Arthur was coming to supper?"

"No, I said we were having guests. Shad and his mother are on the way. He's also riding your Little Shadow."

Laurie's heart leaped to her throat, and her pulse quickened. She let out a small scream in delight. Then she remembered how she looked.

"Oh, Papa! Why didn't you tell me? I can't face him like this, and he's bringing his mother? I'll be back in just a minute. I must at least comb my hair."

She made a dead run for the staircase and her room to freshen herself. Gone were the tired feelings and desire for rest. Shad was coming. She hurriedly removed the older housedress she was wearing and slipped into her new, deep turquoise Sunday dress. Nervously, she began to attach all the pearl buttons.

It was too good to be true. Her Shad was returning. She couldn't get dressed fast enough. She began combing out her long, thick hair. She had been wearing it pulled back and braided into one long braid to stay out of the twins' reach, but not tonight. She would let it cascade down her back. It had grown so long, it almost reached the bend in her knees.

She was just finishing up when she heard the first indication of a flaw in her plans. A high-pitched whimper emanated from the nursery. No, not now, she thought, but it was clearly one of the twins. She rushed into the adjoining room and found Artemio wide awake. Laurie picked him up to keep him from disturbing his sister.

"Shush, little Art. You'll have to come with me." She lovingly carried him down the stairs as they heard the arrival of horses outside.

The boy was fussy in her arms and wanted down. Laurie placed his blanket on the floor of the great room and laid him on it. She was nervous and anxious to see Shadow Hawk, and she was certain the little boy could feel her excitement. He certainly acted so.

Artemio began to cry just as she heard the knocking on the door. Laurie had no choice but to grab the baby and carry him with her to greet their visitors. She swung open the big door, and there stood her rugged Shad with his wavy brown hair almost touching his shoulders. A beautiful Indian woman was with him. Shad's mother was breathtaking with his same dark eyes. Suddenly, Laurie felt shy to the point of speechlessness.

Fortunately, her father was right behind her and bellowed, "Come on in."

SHADOW HAWK FROZE in stunned silence. There stood his angel, lovelier than ever, and she held a baby in her arms. He was rooted in place until his mother gently nudged him through the doorway.

He entered with one of the heavy saddlebags and a few furs in hand. While he returned to the horses to get the other saddlebags, Laughing River met him at the door.

"I see the color of the young woman's hair. She is

the one from your satchel, correct?" She glanced around and smiled at Aidan, then softly said, "Your home is as beautiful as I remembered."

Shadow Hawk was at the door, half inside and half outside, watching as Aidan looked around at the rooms he had called home for several weeks. He'd learned in his time with the Kerrigans that Aidan's father had built it, but to him, it was home, and he rarely thought of it in aesthetic terms. Aidan thanked Laughing River for the compliment, commenting that he was pleased it seemed new and fresh to her.

Shadow Hawk said nothing as he entered with the final saddlebags but just stared at the tiny infant in Laurie's arms. He hadn't anticipated this. Not this soon, anyway. She had to have been with child before he left.

He glanced up to find Aidan's eyes on him, and they both turned see his mother watching Laurie holding the child.

"Excuse my manners," Aidan announced. "This is one of the newest additions to our family. This is little Art. His twin sister Angel is upstairs napping."

He offered to give Shadow Hawk's mother a quick tour of the place before dinner. Laughing River graciously accepted. With that, Aidan took Lari's elbow and escorted her to the stairwell to show her the nursery.

Shadow Hawk immediately caught the connection of the twins' names. Art would simply be a shortened form of Arthur. And of course, they named the little girl Angel after his angel. This was proof that not only was Laurie not his angel, but she had never really cared for him. Indeed, she had been carrying Arthur's children the entire time they were together. No wonder she had felt ill the past few days he had been here, and that was the reason she had avoided him.

Shadow Hawk never spoke a word; he just stared at Laurie with his burning eyes, attempting to hide his emotional anguish.

LAURIE COULDN'T GET out a sound, either. Her mouth was dry in the presence of the man she had missed and dreamed about daily.

Shad's disillusionment showed on his face as he looked from the baby to Laurie. The silence was deafening. Even Artemio was quiet while he rested the next few minutes peacefully in her arms. Finally, Laurie opened her mouth, but before she could explain, Aidan's voice brought took the evening another direction.

"Supper is ready. Shad, I've given your mother a brief tour, but I believe our meal is about ready. Laurie, go see if Art will lie back down, and we'll meet you in the dining room."

Laurie made her way to the stairs, and unsure what she would say when she returned, she held the baby tightly as the stair treads took her farther and farther from the man she loved.

WITH HIS INVITATION, the big rancher escorted

Lari and a bewildered Shadow Hawk to supper. Aidan could see the expression on Shad's face, and it made him grin ever so slightly. The poor boy is in torment, he thought. He really should be told. Before he could reveal the identity of the little ones, however, Mrs. Gates came bursting into the room with a platter of food.

"There's my favorite young man. Shad, come give your ol' 'ousekeeper a hug."

SHADOW HAWK WAS truly happy to see the Kerrigan's jovial housekeeper again. He hugged her while she wiped her misty eyes. Despite his dismay over the baby, he had missed everyone and was happy to be back.

It was when he held his arms around Mrs. Gates that the cold reality hit him like a splash of water from a deep mountain pool. He felt at home here. Yes, he had been happy to see his mother at the Cheyenne camp, but it hadn't felt like home. It never had. The last place he'd ever felt at home was in the trapper's cabin with his parents.

Now that he was here again, he felt like he belonged. Despite everything, with his heart torn from his chest, it still felt like home. That made him more miserable, because he knew it could never be, not with Laurie married to another man. No matter how much he wanted to stay, he couldn't.

Laurie was back downstairs, and her father seated her next to him. Of all places, Aidan had put her next to Shadow Hawk. He saw Laurie's hesitation at sitting next to him. Of course, she didn't want to sit beside him now that she was married and had children, but it didn't seem to matter to Aidan one bit. All he did was smile and continue to talk to Laughing River.

That surprised Shadow Hawk, too. His mother seemed to enjoy speaking English. She blushed every now and then when she couldn't say something correctly, but Aidan didn't seem to mind. Then the rancher stood and offered a prayer of thanksgiving for the safe return of his "son," Jeremiah, Shadow of the Hawk, as he asked God's blessing on the food. Shadow Hawk smiled afterward knowing that Aidan had said his full name and still called him by the moniker "son." Shadow Hawk also enjoyed the casual way that everyone in the household addressed him as Shad.

WHILE APPROACHING THE house, Shadow Hawk's mouth had watered for Mrs. Gates' cooking. Now, sitting at the table next to Laurie, and after everything that just transpired, his appetite drained away, even though the steak and potatoes, along with squash from the garden, fresh light bread, and a cherry pie smelled delicious. The idea of eating made his stomach knot up, and he was certain he'd be sick if he tried to force anything down.

He tried to admire the food as if it tempted him, and he smiled half-heartedly at Mrs. Gates when she stepped in to see how he liked the meal, but he couldn't concentrate on anything except the turquoise dress sitting next to him. He noticed Laurie seemed to have lost her appetite as well.

Aidan looked down the table at them with a knowing grin on his face. Shadow Hawk was aware of his attention, and he knew he should eat to show gratitude for Aidan's generosity, but neither he nor Laure ate or spoke to anyone else at the table. Aidan calmly took a few more bites of his food while still conversing with Lari. Then he glanced at them again, as if he'd decided something had been enough torture enough for too long.

"Well, Shad, what do you think of our new arrivals? They don't favor Laurie much, do they?" He winked at Laughing River.

"Papa!" Laurie blushed a deep crimson red. "Of course, they don't favor me. They . . ."

Her father interrupted her, asking his daughter a very pointed question, "They favor their daddy, don't they, Laurie?"

Shadow Hawk felt anger building, bubbling inside like a hot spring. He was being taunted. He wanted to explode. Why was this man who had said he was a friend baiting him? He thought Aidan liked him. He had even called him son. Now he was getting a morbid thrill out of knowing that he cared about Angel and couldn't have her. Shadow Hawk's eyes narrowed, and the room was much too warm, as his breathing quickened in his fury.

Then Shadow Hawk heard his mother speak. "We

never judge a horse by its color, my son. Looks can be deceiving."

Shadow Hawk refused to listen. He was almost shaking with fury at the thought of everyone being so happy for Laurie and Arthur and their children while his heart continued to shatter even more. He started to rise, but one look in Mr. Kerrigan's direction told him otherwise.

"Stay seated," was all it took to still Shadow Hawk's action.

He sat with gritted teeth, trying to ignore everything and everyone, especially the person sitting beside him. Why did he have to love her? His emotions rippled across his face, and he could hardly control his shifting expressions.

Then Aidan began to explain, "Laurie isn't the mother of these precious babies God gave us."

Shadow Hawk wasn't sure he had heard correctly. He looked at Aidan for confirmation.

"But He has entrusted their care and keeping into our hands," Aidan continued.

All Shad's thoughts were on one thing. Angel wasn't their mother! A sense of relief and embarrassment simultaneously filled Shadow Hawk's heart, while Aidan recounted the sad story of Diego and Rose Rivera.

Laurie became upset when she realized Shad had thought she was a mother of two, and she broke down in tears, exclaiming that Shad should have known she was a Christian and wouldn't behave otherwise.

Didn't he remember their days together? All the time he was here, hadn't he been able to read her morals? She didn't love Arthur, and that should have been obvious to anyone who knew her.

LAUGHING RIVER COULD see the confused expression on Laurie's face as she stared at her son. Aidan had revealed the twins' parentage while in the nursery checking on little Angel. Despite the confusion, or perhaps because of it, Laughing River could see that this beautiful girl was desperately in love with Shadow Hawk.

He showed all the signs of feeling the same way.

She had seen the way he treated her lock of hair as though it was something sacred. Despite that, there was something hindering their relationship. Neither of them seemed to see the love the other one felt. They needed some time to work this out. It was unfortunate she and her son were returning tomorrow and then leaving the area for the winter, or perhaps even forever.

Aidan complimented the housekeeper on such a fine meal. Then he said he needed to check on the stock and make sure the cowboys were treating Shad's horse okay. He asked if Shad wanted to accompany him.

Laughing River observed that she would like to go and needed to talk with Aidan privately, anyway. She instructed her son in Cheyenne to be nice to the girl and help her. Shadow Hawk spoke back to his mother in the same language and told her this girl didn't need his help.

Then, his mother looked at him and smiled. Shadow Hawk bristled, turned red, and he got up and left the table, muttering that he would show no respect for any woman who would do nothing except offer him insults.

AS LAURIE, WITH her eyes burning, prepared the babies' evening meal, Mrs. Gates brought the two infants down for their final feeding before she got ready to leave for the evening. She had already changed them, and they were in their little nightgowns. The wear and tear of the day had taken its toll on Laurie. She decided to sit in the great room and feed them. She was surprised to find Shadow Hawk sulking in a chair before the fire.

"Oh, I didn't know you were still here. Would you rather I fed them somewhere else?" Laurie asked softly.

"It is your house. You may do as you want," Shad retorted with a gruff tone. "I'll be the one to leave."

He rose and started for the door. Laurie was appalled that things were taking the same turn as before. She was trying to make a connection with this man, and everything she did irritated him. She didn't know what to do.

However, Mrs. Gates, carrying Angel, pressed Shad into service. "Shad, come over 'ere and 'elp me with little Angel. I need to get some things done in the kitchen fer tomorrow, seein' it's Sunday and all. Ya' know I don't like to work on the Lord's Day."

SHADOW HAWK COULD see the housekeeper was in earnest about asking for his help, or at least he thought so. He knew she would like to be home soon, herself. With great reluctance, he sat on the sofa at the opposite end as Laurie and let Mrs. Gates place little Angel in his arms.

The baby was so small and fragile. She opened her sleepy eyes and took the bottle. He could see she was darker than his angel, with skin almost the same color as his. She. Her hair was straight and very nearly black. She was more like a Cheyenne baby than a white child.

He glanced to Laurie to see her cut him a sideways glance, yet she didn't say a word. At least he was sitting in the same room with her, and no one was making a scene. Why did it have to be this way between the two of them? Why did he have to love her, when she didn't love him? She looked down at Artemio as though thinking, At least you love me.

Shadow Hawk continued to watch the care his angel was giving the little one in her arms. If only they were together, this could be their baby. Why did she love Arthur? What did she see in him? It was obvious Aidan didn't care for the man. The rancher had made that plain even to Shadow Hawk.

Shadow Hawk noticed Laurie sigh a deep, weary breath. She had already removed her shoes and was putting her feet up on the sofa. She stretched them out a bit. He could tell by her actions she was exhausted. They sat in silence for a few quiet minutes while the babies finished their bottles. Shadow Hawk glanced at his angel again.

"Why do you not take them up to bed?" He made his suggestion softly so as not to disturb the baby on his chest.

"Are you asking me to leave?"

"No," came his quick response. "I see how tired you are."

"I'd rather stay down here with you if that's acceptable. I haven't seen you in a long time, and I missed you. I think maybe this would be a good time to talk." Laurie whispered her words in one big shaky breath.

Shadow Hawk smiled just thinking how quickly she said it. He could see the anxiousness in her eyes and knew she wanted to be here. But why would she want to stay down here if she was in love with someone else?

When he didn't respond to her entreaty, she shifted position with the baby, as if to stand.

"I thought you wanted to stay here with me," he grumbled.

"I do. You seem to not really care," she replied, with her voice starting to quiver.

"Angel, I never said that. I just don't want you to be too tired." He kept his voice low and soft to avoid disturbing the babies.

Laurie started to sniffle, and after a futile attempt to control it, she began to cry. Warm, soft tears dripped down her cheeks onto the small blanket holding Artemio.

Shadow Hawk was appalled at what he was seeing. Not tears again. His angel's tears were what he couldn't stand. He hadn't even been around her but a few hours, and he was melting like snow in late spring. He had promised himself he would be strong, and when he thought the twins were hers, he felt he had his feelings under control. Then, when relief washed over him as he found out the truth about the babies, it triggered his old thoughts of longing again.

Shad was up and over to her in two quick strides, although he was especially careful to not wake the little angel in his arms. He touched Laurie's hand and gently spoke his truest emotions to her.

"Oh, Angel. I've missed you. My heart has been lost without you. I love you. I cannot help myself. I thought I would get over you, but all my thoughts lead back to you. I hold your lock of hair every night before I go to bed and ask your God to bring me back to you. Nothing or no one can take your place. Please tell me you love me, too. Please, Angel. Just say it once, that's all I ask. Just tell me somewhere in your heart you have a place that loves me. That's all I need to hear, and I'll never leave you again, Angel. I promise."

Laurie stared at him with tear-filled eyes. "Why do you always speak in Cheyenne when I truly want to talk to you? Why won't you converse with me in English?"

At a sound behind them, Laurie turned to see her father and Laughing River standing and looking at them both. They had come in the back door just as the tears had started, and just as Shadow Hawk was telling Laurie how much he loved her.

"How long have you been here?" Shadow Hawk asked his mother in Cheyenne.

"Long enough." The reply came from Aidan, but it was in Cheyenne. Shadow Hawk didn't know Aidan could speak Cheyenne. How was that? He was a white man, but then again so was his father, and he had spoken it fluently. It made sense that Aidan would know a little of it, too. How much did he overhear? The older man's face revealed nothing.

Laurie looked at her father, "Is everyone going to speak Cheyenne but me? I only know a few phrases."

Laughing River smiled at her and said, "Maybe someday I can teach you."

Laurie smiled back through red-stained eyes. "I would like that very much."

Aidan sat down in the large chair and gave Laurie a somber look. "Laurie Angel, we need to talk. There might be trouble coming our way, I'm afraid. Go put the babies in bed and come back here, so we can all discuss this together."

Lari offered to help, so she and Laurie carried the babies up to the nursery. After the women left the room, Aidan looked over at Shadow Hawk.

"Your mother told me about the gold and the claims being filed on the land. But what I want to know is who you saw on the way here. I didn't really get a clear picture of what your mother was trying to tell me. She said the word husband and then Angel, referring to Laurie, I suppose. I couldn't make the connection. The only man my daughter wants to marry is sitting right here on this sofa."

"What?" Shadow Hawk blurted out in a shocked tone.

"You heard me. Do I need to tell you in Cheyenne for you to understand?" Aidan looked seriously at Shadow Hawk. "My daughter has been sick, depressed, lonely and just plain 'onery since you left her. Is there a reason you don't want her for a wife or to be my son-in-law?" Aidan asked his question pointedly and in a very sincere manner.

"Arthur, what is he to your daughter?" Shadow Hawk wasted no time responding to the question.

"Arthur is no more than a pompous young man that would like to marry Laurie, not for Laurie's sake, but for the Kerrigan wealth and power. But Laurie has never been interested in him the way she is in you."

"But I thought she was betrothed to him . . ." Shadow Hawk blurted lamely, thinking of all the time he had wasted, if it truly was just a misunderstanding. Now that Shadow Hawk and Aidan had cleared the mix-up in the language barrier, there was no longer a reason for any confusion.

"Never," Aidan replied with a laugh.

Shadow Hawk was stunned into shocked silence, feeling all the wind had been knocked out of him. No wonder his angel was so confused by his behavior. He had misunderstood all along. She thought he didn't care about her. Angel was hurting because he had misunderstood one little word. He felt very foolish and wanted desperately to speak to Laurie as soon as possible.

Aidan leaned forward to catch Shad's full attention. "I'd have to be dead, and so would all my ranch hands before Laurie ever ended up with that pretentious ruffian. Only Arthur thought he had any rights to Laurie. A few days ago, she set him straight on that. He'll probably never bother her again. If he ever takes it in his mind to, I'm ready." Aidan finished on a more serious note, "Now, who was it you saw on your way here?"

The gray world of despair had been blasted from around Shadow Hawk. All he could think of was his angel and how mistaken they had been about each other. He was startled to feel the touch of Aidan's hand on his knee.

"Are you listening to me? Am I invisible?"

"Oh, I'm very sorry, Aidan. It was Arthur. He was heading toward the Cheyenne camp."

AIDAN'S EYES GREW wide. That wasn't news he wanted to hear.

— 24 —

AIDAN FELT UNSETTLED and concerned. Why would Arthur be riding to the Cheyenne camp except to stir up trouble? Shad told him he had never seen him there before, and that meant there was no good reason for him to be headed that way now. Arthur had to be up to something that would benefit him and no one else.

Aidan still considered the notion of Arthur being tangled up somehow with Jeremiah or Shadow Hawk very possible. When Laurie and Laughing River entered the room, Aidan let a somber expression settle on his face.

"Let's sit on the sofa and discuss your plans," he suggested.

Laughing River made her way to the sofa and positioned herself by her son, while Laurie sat a few feet away, having dried her teary eyes. She also had a smile playing across her lips. Her conversation with Shad's mother had improved her countenance, and her whole attitude seemed changed.

Aidan began with prayer, asking for Divine guidance in their situation. Then he said, "We've got to come up with an idea to keep you here through the winter, to see if the gold booms into a California gold rush or just a few miners. That will help determine the fate of the Southern Cheyenne Tribe in these parts."

Laughing River looked firmly at each of the people sitting in the room. "There is nothing to discuss. We must leave tomorrow to be able to make it to the winter camp. The Indian agent made it very clear that Indians cannot own land, no matter how long they have hunted or lived there. We are treated as strangers and outcasts in our own territory." Her voice carried the sound of sorrow as each soft but precisely clipped word punctuated the space.

Aidan could tell by her expression that she didn't want to leave. Nor did he want them to. He had grown especially fond of her son, not to mention Laurie's feelings for Shad. It would break his daughter's heart, and she might not ever get over it if Shad were to leave permanently. It would be a catastrophe to have the young man banished to some other part of the country and not to be able to see him again. Aidan recalled instances of that happening before, and it would most likely continue to happen to the neighboring tribes. With gold being prospected, no one was safe, especially not the Indians. If only Jeremiah were here, this wouldn't be happening to his family, Aidan had no doubt.

They all sat in silence for a moment, and then Aidan looked up with a dawning realization, caught Shad's eye, and smiled.

"Your father was Jeremiah Hawke. He was a white man and a landowner. You have as much right to own land as any other son of a white man." Aidan looked to each person for approval to continue. "I don't know where your father filed the deed to your land, but your pa would have never decided to build unless he had full ownership to your property. As his son, you have every right to live and build a homestead here in these mountains, that is, if you want to stay and not go with the tribe."

This time Aidan looked directly at Laughing River, not at Shad. The young man had his eyes fixed on Laurie, and Aidan was confident the youth would never leave again, if Laurie revealed the depths of her love for him. Aidan had made it clear to him that Laurie didn't care for any other man. By his mannerisms, the young man felt he had only a little chance of the love he felt for his daughter being returned, but if he did, he would be hers forever.

Laughing River spoke softly to her son in Cheyenne. He turned to her and nodded, but before he could comment, Aidan answered, "Go get the title and return with your things here as quickly as possible."

Laughing River spoke boldly in her native Cheyenne, "This is all happening too quickly. I do not know if we should leave our people. We've had to make the journey earlier than usual just to be accepted in our winter camp. If we were to stay, we would have to depend on you for help. I could not live in your home forever. My son and I would have to wait until spring to build even if we were to stay. Even then it might take another year to construct a lodge for us. I think that would be too long to impose on you, and who knows what will happen because of the gold."

Shadow Hawk translated for his mother. The air seemed to go out of the discussion, and even Aidan had to admit Laughing River's reasoning was flawless.

Laurie got her father's attention, asking, "Papa, could they use the Rivera's cabin until they built their own?"

Aidan smiled and silently thanked God for such a brilliant daughter. This was the best idea yet. He could keep Shad and the young man's mother close by.

"Why, of course they could. Not only that, the Rivera's land is pretty nigh to Jeremiah's trapper cabin. Only a map will tell, but their property might even butt up against each other. What do you think about that?" Aidan asked his question both in English and

Cheyenne.

LAUGHING RIVER GLANCED at her son and then at Laurie. She knew that no matter where her son was, his heart would be with the beautiful, auburn-haired girl. Now, after talking with her upstairs, she decided her heart would be with him, too.

Laughing River had lived away from her people before and been content. That was because of Jeremiah, though. She looked at her son again, and for a second saw her late husband in him. She knew if he was with his woman, he would be satisfied.

Aidan broke the silence, "At least consider it and pray about it before you say no."

Laughing River shyly glanced in Aidan's direction. "I believe that God brought us here today to help us. We will be content to stay among the white man's people if my son so desires."

SHAD CONSIDERED THAT only a few hours ago, his answer might have been very different. But now, having the hope of being with his angel forever, he could think of no other reply.

"Aidan, thank you for your offer, and we will accept. We will leave in the morning to gather our things and our horses. We will return with the deed to my father's, I mean, our land."

Shadow Hawk shook Aidan's hand, and in that firm grip, the young brave knew he had made the wise decision.

LAURIE LOOKED ON, smiling, knowing that her Shad would be moving closer to her permanently. There might still be some hope of him someday feeling the way she did for him.

His mother seemed to think that he cared about her. At least he was being nice to her now, and that was a start. With that settled, Laurie decided it was time to get the sleeping arrangements completed. She was about to speak when Laughing River made a grim expression, looked at her son, and began speaking to him in soft and low Cheyenne.

"We must talk; you cannot keep hurting this sweet girl. I won't let you treat her like you have been."

Aidan intervened, speaking slowly in Cheyenne, "I think we've worked it out."

Laurie looked between them, confused and frustrated at the conversation she couldn't follow. Before she could make up her mind to intervene, the conversation shifted into action once more.

"Are you defending my son against your own daughter?" asked Laughing River, again in her native tongue. Her expression softened, and this time she seemed pleased that Shadow Hawk was so fondly regarded by this family.

Laurie, however, was starting to blink back tears that were trying to form in the corners of her eyes. "Why is everybody speaking in Cheyenne? I don't understand what's going on. Papa, why won't you tell me what everyone is saying?"

Laurie was fully aware she was letting her emotions override her good manners. She had been through a very long day, and now nothing was making sense to her. Soft tears started down her face again.

Shadow Hawk moved down the sofa next to Laurie. He very gently took her hand in his. This time he spoke his heart in English. "Angel, don't cry. It's all fine. Everything's good, now. I think I misunderstood your father, and now I want to know the truth."

His soft, deep voice soothed her immediately. Just having Shad speaking nicely to her enhanced her mood tremendously. She smiled through her watery eyes, waiting on him to say more.

"Hmm." Aidan cleared his throat. "I think I'll get a cup of coffee. Would you like one, too?" he asked Laughing River.

"That would be nice," she said, as she followed Aidan out of the great room.

Now alone, Laurie trembled as Shadow Hawk moved closer to her on the sofa. He put his large, tanned hand over her small, soft, creamy one, squeezing it ever so gently. His dark orbs stared into the deepest recesses of her being. He said nothing for a full minute, and then he finally spoke.

"I want to know," he began huskily, his words breaking clumsily at the end, and then he started over again with a clearer voice, "I want to know how you feel about me."

He continued to hold her hand, sending Laurie's

heart into her throat. Her ears buzzed at his question. Now he was asking how she felt about him. What kind of game was he playing with her emotions? He had to know she loved him. She had given him her most treasured possession, her horse. Why was he even questioning her? He said there had been a misunderstanding between him and her papa. What did that have to do with her feelings for Shad? She was a little baffled by it all but thrilled to be with him. For now, just his closeness and amiable manner made her content.

"What kind of misunderstanding did you and my father have?" Laurie questioned him, enjoying the touch of his hand around hers.

Shadow Hawk pulled his hand away from hers and held her face. He peered deeply into her eyes, seeming to soak up every bit of her.

"I thought you had promised your heart to another. Tell me, is that true? Do you belong to another man? Do you love another man?" His voice had a rough edge to it that mirrored the roughness of his tortured expression.

"No," Laurie whispered without hesitation.

Shadow Hawk let out a long breath. "Then say it, Angel. Say that you love me. Please, sweet Angel. Say it!"

AS THE FINAL words left Shadow Hawk's lips, he stopped, aghast. He had spoken in English. He hadn't meant to. He intended to speak in Cheyenne, like always. He had been so anxious and desperate that he didn't even think about it.

Now his angel knew his heart, and it was exposed.

What if she didn't feel the same way? What if he had made a mistake, and she didn't love him? He paused, waiting, holding his breath, fearing what she might say.

Very slowly and carefully, Laurie said the words Laughing River had taught her to say in Cheyenne only a short time ago when they were in the nursery. "I lo-ve you. My heart is yours."

He stared at her. He couldn't believe it. He grabbed her hand, gripping it firmly in hers. "Say it again, Angel. Say it again, please, sweet Angel."

Laurie repeated the phrase again with more confidence. Shadow Hawk just looked at her tenderly.

"Did I say it wrong?" Laurie asked him.

"No, sweet angel. You said it perfectly." Shad squeezed her hand, now confident he could be happy the rest of his life. Those were the sweetest words he had ever heard. His heart was light, and he felt like he was walking on air. The God of his father had heard his prayer and answered it. He had no doubt, now. Shadow Hawk knew there was a God in Heaven who loved him.

THE SILENCE GAVE time for Laurie to wonder about Shad's feelings. She had seen his reaction to her words, but he hadn't yet told her how he felt. She had prayed for strength to be able to accept whatever answer he gave her. With careful determination, she searched Shad's smiling face and questioned him.

"What are your feelings toward me? I've told you the truth, and now it's your turn to be honest with me." She spoke very softly, hoping her nervousness wouldn't be too obvious.

Shad simply pulled her closer to him and said the same thing she had told him in Cheyenne. Then, he repeated it in English, and he added, "I've told you this every time I spoke to you in Cheyenne. I've loved you from the moment I saw you in the cave and I knew you were my guardian angel. I was devastated when I thought you loved Arthur and not me. I was hurt when I thought you gave me Little Shadow to ride because you didn't want your horse to come between you and Arthur. Then, when your father explained it to me, I was relieved. I couldn't wait to find out if it was true or not."

At a sound from across the room, the young couple looked up to see Aidan and Laughing River coming into the room. "Well, have we got things worked out?" questioned Laurie's father.

Laurie jumped up and hugged Laughing River. Then she reached to hug her father in an excited whirl. "Oh, yes, Papa! He loves me! Did you know it? He loves me! He said so, didn't you, Shad?"

Shadow Hawk stood up from the sofa, smiling and red-faced, and Aidan questioned him, "Is there anything you'd like to ask me, son, or do I have to beg you to be my son-in-law? This is the white man's custom. You ask the father for the daughter's hand in marriage and then give him all the horses you own." There was a twinkle in Aidan's eye when he finished.

Shadow Hawk grinned, as though it didn't matter what the rancher said, if Laurie could be his.

"Papa! Don't tease him. Shad, you don't have to give my Papa anything!" Laurie looked at Shad and then her father.

Her father just smiled and said, "It was worth a try."

Laughing River quietly slipped off the wide gold band she wore on her first finger and handed it to Shadow Hawk.

"This is the ring your father gave me when I became his woman. Please know it is full of love and happiness. I want you to give it to your Angel. Your father also gave my father many furs and three horses for me. Your father told me it was the best trade he ever made." Laughing River smiled at the memory.

Shadow Hawk stepped up to Aidan and spoke very clearly without hesitation or nervousness. "Aidan Kerrigan, I would like to be the husband for your daughter. I will take care of her and be a good man to her, as long as I live. I give you this promise as a man and as a warrior of the Southern Cheyenne Tribe."

Aidan hugged the brave young man. "Welcome to the family, son. 'My lodge is your lodge; my hunt is your hunt. We beat with one heart from this time on.' "

THE TRADITIONAL CHEYENNE vow brought tears to both Shadow Hawk's and his mother's eyes. He was a man now, with permission to have a woman, his Angel.

Shadow Hawk reached for Laurie's hand and placed the ring on her finger as he asked her with tear-filled eyes, while standing in front of their parents, "Will you be my woman forever, and be content to stay with me in my lodge?"

He started to speak again but was interrupted by the loud crack of a rifle. The startling sound was unexpected, but gunfire was a well-known signal to take caution, and Aidan reacted accordingly.

"Get down and get out of the light!" yelled Aidan.

More gunfire punctuated the air. They were under attack, but by whom?

— 25 —

WHOEVER WAS FIRING on them didn't take them by complete surprise. Normally they would have been in bed an hour or so before, but with all the excitement of the arrival of Shad and his mother, everything had been delayed. Aidan was grateful they were still awake.

As he went for the rifles, he glanced around to be sure everyone was safe and was unable to find Shad. Then a hand reached for the kerosene lantern, and he was relieved to see it was the young man. Turning the light down, the room grew dark so that only the shadows of the people crouched there could be seen.

The babies started to cry upstairs at the sound of the gunfire. Laurie started to crawl across the floor when a hand reached out and startled her. Shad motioned for her to stay still, and he disappeared up the stairs, returning shortly with one infant tucked safely under each arm.

Despite the continued gunfire, the infants were calm as he whispered softly to them in Cheyenne. His magic with the horses seemed to extend to the small humans, also. He placed them on the floor and told Laurie to stay down with them. He took the rifle Aidan handed him and slowly crept into the shadows.

A few moments later, the sharp, repeated ruckus outdoors stopped. Arthur's recognizable voice shouted at the house, and he sounded drunk. What was he trying to do now?

"Aidan Kerrigan, I need to talk to you. Come on out here where I can see you. Your house and bunkhouse are surrounded. You do anything funny, and your pretty little girl will pay the price. Everyone will think it's an Indian uprising, come to reclaim their rightful land." Loud, raucous laughter punctuated the night.

Aidan started for the door, but Shad's hand stopped him. He whispered that he wanted to confront the man. Aidan shook his head no, but the young warrior stood firm, making it clear that fighting was what Shadow Hawk knew. He hissed in an insistent tone that he was a Wolf Soldier and acquainted with to-the-death competition. No one was coming in and hurting his family, Indian or white man. Arthur had threatened his Angel, which meant an all-out war.

"What are you waiting on? I want to talk to you

now, do you hear me?" The surly shout was louder than before. By the sound of his voice, Shadow Hawk explained to Aidan, he could tell Arthur's location and the direction he was facing. He nodded to Aidan to go ahead out the front door and to trust him to take care of the raucous intruder. Aidan opened the door and stepped out into the moonlight-filled night. Scattered, wispy clouds drifted by, occasionally dimming the reflection from the distant orb. He stood against one of the large pine pillars on the veranda, trusting in it for at least some protection.

"How can I help you?" Aidan drawled slowly, his senses keenly aware of any sound or movement. A voice came from behind one of the large granite boulders a short distance from the house.

"Why, I'm gonna marry your daughter, and you're going to sign the marriage license. Then you're gonna disappear, just like that trapper did all those years ago. I know that you're on to me. I was just a kid when we killed him. I was scared, then. He didn't even have hardly any gold on him, and all we wanted was for him to tell us where he was finding it. We tried to get him to fess up. But he never said a word.

"Then when you brought that half-breed into your house, I knew my time was up. Then I got to figuring he might be the son of that trapper, and he might know where the gold was. But by the time I reached the Cheyenne camp, he was long gone. I did rummage through his lodge and found me a land title. I brought it with me. So, I'll be mining on his place, too.

"Me and Laurie will own the ranch and all the gold on it. If she behaves herself, she might get to live to enjoy it. If not, another terrible accident could always happen."

Arthur's voice was starting to shake. Aidan knew the sound. Fear. It was a long way from town, and he was likely coming down from his drunken high. He listened for others that might be hidden in the darkness of the shadows. If he could stall Arthur long enough, the fool's nerves would begin to affect his stamina. The man needed to get this over with, and in a hurry, and that was likely causing him to rush his timing. Aidan knew that could blow the man's plans, and he pressed him with a challenge.

"Why another accident, Arthur? We can come to an understanding on this. Be reasonable."

"Nah, just send Laurie out to get the papers, and then you can sign them and give them back to her. If you do anything peculiar, I'll kill her or you, or whoever I find in my sights first, do you understand?"

"Perfectly," was all Aidan uttered, and he stepped back into the house. He prayed for strength as he moved through the door. Now he knew the truth about Jeremiah's death. It had been the outlaw gang that had gone on to California. Thank God they had all cleared out, well, except for Arthur, who was still convinced there was gold in these Rocky Mountains.

The man was right, too. There was gold, lots of it

right here on the property, enough that he and Jeremiah never would have needed to worry about a thing. Now this crazed killer wanted his daughter. He would never let that happen. He turned to share his concerns with Laughing River and Laurie.

As Aidan started to speak, Laughing River tugged at his sleeve. "Give me one of your daughter's dresses. I will go in her place. I will not let the only woman my son has ever loved die like my husband. Yes, I heard what he said. He was talking about my Jeremiah. If you don't help me, I will go out there now. I want to see the face of the snake who would kill a man such as mine."

Aidan knew there was no use arguing with her. Like her son, when her mind was made up, it wasn't easily changed. He motioned to his daughter to do as Laughing River asked, and Laurie slipped into the stairwell and changed dresses with Shad's mom. Lari headed toward the door and whispered to Aidan, "Pray for me that my husband's God will protect me."

LAUGHING RIVER OPENED the door into the partially cloudy, moonlit night. Wispy clouds drifted over the moon, and she became no more than a woman with long flowing hair on the veranda.

"Well, Laurie. At last our dreams will come true. You'll finally be mine along with the ranch and the gold. Nothing will stop us now. Come on over here and sign the marriage license and tell your father to do the same. Then return it to me, and we'll be on our way. The half-breed will find his twins along with most of the workers strangely gone. No one will ever know what happened to them, just like the half-breed's father."

Before Laughing River could move forward or speak, the man speaking to her let out a wet oomph, and she knew her son had found him.

ARTHUR FELT PAIN rivet his shoulders, as his arms were yanked up behind him and his gun clattered to the rocks. "Ughh," he moaned, as he turned his head to see the shadow of a man standing behind him with a gun aimed at him. He looked carefully and realized it was the half-breed.

"I wish you to die a quick death, not like the one you gave my father." Shadow Hawk began twisting crude rope tightly around Arthur's wrists. "However, I am a man of honor, not of twisted cruelty."

Before Arthur could get a word out, a woman appeared at the Indian's side. She spat her words at him, "You killed my man, and my son's father. You wanted to kill his woman's father and maybe her. But you will never kill again. A snake does not deserve to live."

"What are you going to do with me?" Arthur let out a yelp, as Shadow Hawk yanked him roughly to his feet.

"Tie you in the barn where you cannot get away. Perhaps Aidan will treat you more kindly than me, but I think not."

Together, with the two Indians controlling Arthur's stumbling walk, they directed him in the darkness towards the barn, where they roughly strapped his hands to a sturdy beam and left him quivering in the darkness, alone and filthy, until he could be dealt with by Aidan securely and permanently.

IN THE HOUSE Laurie couldn't hear what had happened. When the door opened, and Shad and his mother came through, she forgot what he had said about staying on the floor. She was so relieved to see him and his mother that she jumped up and flew to his arms.

Shad held her close as he looked over at Aidan and said, "It's finished. Arthur's tied up and in the barn. If you wish, you can deal with him in the morning, or I can take him to my people, and they can have their way. He killed my father because of greed."

"He can't escape?" Aidan narrowed his eyes at the youth.

"He can't even move." Laughing River smiled. "I am able to tie a knot no white man can undo."

Shadow Hawk whispered into Laurie's ear, "He made me live a life without dreams until I met you. Then he threatened to take you from me, too. I can't let that happen."

"Son," Aidan interrupted, "about Arthur's accomplices—"

Shad laughed sourly, "I had to incapacitate two sentries before I reached him. I don't know how many more men are out there, but I saw signs of at least four more. This isn't over. They are perhaps waiting for some kind of signal or sign before they start firing again. I had to see that my Laurie was safe. Now, I must finish what I started."

Aidan said, "We'll draw them out." He crawled to the back door and checked to be sure it was clear. Then he reached for the bell and let it ring. As soon as it did, he faded back into the house. "That will bring the ranch hands out. Now we'll have some armed backup."

Suddenly, there was gunfire in every direction, much of it coming from the direction of the bunk-house. It was starting again, but this time Aidan and Shad were prepared. They tumbled through the doors into the darkness outside, with their guns firmly ready, and determination in their limbs. Without direction, the outlaws would soon disappear. They had been driven by one man with a goal, and that man now lay captured and bound up in the barn.

By a little after midnight, the ranch began to settle back down. Laurie comforted the infants, remarking that the outlaws must have found the two guards by now and realized their dreams of getting rich were destroyed. When there were no more shots for a time, she carried the sleeping children to the nursery, before heading back downstairs.

ONCE SILENCE REIGNED again over the compound, Aiden and Shadow Hawk made their way back into the darkened ranch house. Aiden told his companions he wished to check on the bunkhouse. Just then, there was a knock at the back door. The voice on the other side was Daniel Gates coming up to the house to check on them.

Aidan reassured them everyone in the ranch house was fine, including the twins who had been taken back to their cribs.

"Everybody's alive down our way. A couple of cowboys got some glass in 'em, but it's nothin' they can't live with. Mrs. Gates is a bit more upset, though. They shot 'er favorite bowl that was sittin' on the table."

Aidan told him about the gold being discovered and about all the things Arthur had said. Daniel replied he and some of the cowboys would take care of the mess, and that someone would stand guard over Arthur until Aidan could resolve the situation in the morning. Things were still, now, and he didn't figure there'd be any more trouble before the sun came up. Daniel said he was headed back to the bunkhouse to check on things, and then he was off to his place.

Aidan looked over at Shad and told him how much he appreciated his help.

"I'm glad you were on our side," Aidan chuckled, as he directed his pride at Shadow Hawk.

"I AM A soldier. It's what I do. I protect my people," Shadow Hawk said solemnly, as he squeezed his angel's hand and then smiled.

Shad felt the love of the Kerrigan family pour over him. He knew their God had sent him here to heal his fractured heart. He finally felt at peace, and he knew this was where he belonged.

Laurie looked at the ring on her finger and said, "I'd like to answer the question you asked me before all this started. I would love to be your woman and share your lodge. Now, when can we get married?"

"Not soon enough for me!" Shad exclaimed and pulled her close.

AIDAN AND LAUGHING RIVER smiled at the happy couple. What was wrong had been made right, and although there was no secure promise for the future, not in the vast reaches known as Colorado, they were certain that if anyone could make a life of happiness, these two could.

Did you like this book?

There's more!

Discover all three books in the much-loved
Reunion Series by DeLora Conley-Walls.

Trusting Heart Reunion

Can a betrayal ever be fully forgiven?

Timeless Heart Reunion

Can love spark anew after a lifetime of loss?

True Heart Reunion

A true love comes along but once in a lifetime.

Find these and more at:

◆◆◆ THREE SKILLET

www.ThreeSkilletPublishing.com

and

Amazon

www.ingramcontent.com/pod-product-compliance
Lightning Source LLC
Chambersburg PA
CBHW060849250626
47159CB00008B/2667